"You can fight me all you like, lady, but you will kiss me."

"Why, you arrogant, conceited—"

The words were lost as his mouth closed over hers. Elgiva struggled but there was no chance of escape and he took the kiss in his own good time.

"Let go of me! How dare you treat me like this?"

"I shall not let you go. As to what I dare…."

Elgiva's cheeks turned a deeper shade of pink at the warmth and the nearness of the man, the faint scent of leather and musk.

He kissed her again, the pressure of his mouth forcing hers open. Thereafter the kiss grew gentle and lingering. Elgiva shivered but her hands ceased to push him away. The thought returned: no man had ever kissed her like this.

* * *

The Viking's Defiant Bride
Harlequin® Historical #934—February 2009

Author Note

The idea for *The Viking's Defiant Bride* came to me in a gift shop on the green below Bamburgh Castle in Northumberland, England. That was where I found a copy of Roy Anderson's wonderful little book, *The Violent Kingdom,* easily the best purchase of the whole trip. One paragraph and I was completely hooked.

Amongst other fascinating details, there was an account of the great Viking invasion of 865 AD. As soon as I read it, I knew what my story was going to be about. With such a turbulent history, Northumberland is powerfully atmospheric on many levels, truly a historian's delight, so it was no hardship at all to explore the area and do the necessary research. Some happy hours were then spent collating the material in The Anchor at Seahouses. It's just possible that there may be better lobster bisque in England, but I seriously doubt it.

the VIKING'S
DEFIANT BRIDE

JOANNA FULFORD

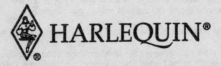

HARLEQUIN®

TORONTO • NEW YORK • LONDON
AMSTERDAM • PARIS • SYDNEY • HAMBURG
STOCKHOLM • ATHENS • TOKYO • MILAN • MADRID
PRAGUE • WARSAW • BUDAPEST • AUCKLAND

Recycling programs
for this product may
not exist in your area.

ISBN-13: 978-0-373-29534-0
ISBN-10:   0-373-29534-0

THE VIKING'S DEFIANT BRIDE

Copyright © 2009 by Joanna Fulford

www.eHarlequin.com

Printed in U.S.A.

For my parents and for Brian who, between them,
have supported me in every way possible.

Prologue

Denmark—865 A.D.

The only sound in the great hall was the crackle of flames in the hearth. Flickering light from the torches cast a ruddy hue over the assembled warriors who sat stony faced before the implications of the news they had just received. In every heart was burgeoning sorrow and disbelief. All eyes turned to the three brothers at the high table. The sons of Ragnar Lodbrok surveyed the messenger quietly enough, but their eyes spoke of incredulity, of grief and rage.

'Ragnar dead?' Halfdan's voice was grim, his fist clenched on the arm of his chair. 'You are certain of this?'

'Quite certain, my lord.'

Beside Halfdan, at his right hand, Earl Wulfrum was very still, his face expressionless save for the blue eyes, now two chips of ice. Involuntarily, his own hand tightened round the hilt of a wicked-looking dagger in a gesture that mirrored his sword brother's, even as his mind struggled against the knowledge of Ragnar's death. Ragnar the warrior, the war leader, fearless, powerful, respected, a prince among his people; Ragnar the Terrible, whose ships, once sighted, struck terror into the hearts of his enemies; Ragnar, who had been as a father to him, who had found him that day when, a ten-year-old boy, he had stood alone in the smouldering ashes of his home, the bodies of his slain kin all around; Ragnar, whose rough and careless kindness had taken in the son of his oldest friend and raised him as his own, who had given him his first sword, taught him all he knew, and raised him to the warrior caste in turn. And now he was gone, his fire quenched for all time.

Wulfrum revealed nothing of these thoughts, hiding his pain as he had all those years ago. What ill fate was it that he was always spared when those he loved were slain? Too much care and love made a man vulnerable. It was a lesson he had learned early in life, a lesson harshly reinforced now. If you did not love, there could be no hurt. Was it thus, then, that a man must protect himself? His jaw tightened. There would be a reckoning here. The blood feud that killed his kin had had a far bloodier resolution when the boy grew to manhood. How much more then the slaying of Ragnar?

He was drawn from his thoughts by Halfdan, voicing the question that was in his own mind.

'How?'

'As we neared the Northumbrian coast, a fearful storm arose and many of our ships were wrecked. Those of us who reached the shore were attacked by King Ella's soldiers. We were heavily outnumbered and many were slain. Lord Ragnar was taken prisoner. The king ordered his immediate death.' He paused for a moment and took a deep breath. 'He had him thrown alive into a pit of poisonous snakes.'

A collective gasp followed his words as the magnitude and horror of it sank in.

'And how did you come to survive, Sven?' Invarr's voice was cold and his eyes raked the messenger from head to toe, but the man met his gaze and held it.

'We fought our way back to the ship and put to sea. After

nightfall we turned back and at first light Bjorn went ashore. He speaks the Saxon tongue and he learned the truth from some in the market place. 'Twas said that before he died Ragnar sang a death song in which he prophesied that his furious sons would avenge him, and then he laughed. They said he died laughing.'

As they listened it seemed to each man there that he could hear the echo of that laughter, and their hearts swelled. Ragnar's courage was legendary. He would make a brave death. That it should not be in battle was a dire misfortune indeed, for he would not win his place in Valhalla and feast in Odin's hall.

'You did not seek to avenge Ragnar?' demanded Hubba.

'To what end? We were a handful against hundreds.'

Hubba's hand went to the axe by his side, but Halfdan shook his head.

'Sven is right. To try to attack Ella under such circumstances would have been madness. Worse, it would have been stupid. Now he will fight another day.'

Hubba glared at him. 'Are you saying that Ragnar died for nothing?'

Wulfrum, silent and intent, waited for the reply, feeling all around him the same curbed rage.

'No. Ragnar shall be avenged and by an army greater than any yet seen.' All eyes were upon Halfdan as he rose to face the assembled throng. 'We shall send a fleet of ships four hundred strong.'

Wulfrum regarded his sword brother with admiration. What he was proposing would be the greatest Viking raid ever known. Almost instantly he corrected himself: not a raid, an invasion.

'Let every man who can wield an axe or sword prepare,' Halfdan continued. 'We shall sweep through Northumbria like flame through tinder. We shall beard Ella in his castle and he shall know the taste of fear. His death shall not be swift, but he will long for it before the end. This I swear by my own blood and by the sacred blood of Odin.'

He drew the blade of his knife across his palm, his gaze meeting those of his brothers. Immediately they followed suit and mingled their blood with his. Then his gaze moved past them and rested on Wulfrum. In it was an invitation, an ac-knowledgement of friendship and brotherhood. Wulfrum's eyes never left Halfdan's as he unsheathed his dagger and drew the bright blood forth before mingling it with theirs. Bound by the blood oath, their honour was now his honour, their purpose his purpose. Halfdan nodded in approbation, then turned back to the silent watching crowd.

'Who will sail with us to avenge Ragnar Lodbrok?'

A roar of approval shook the rafters and every hand was raised. He looked round the hall, gratified to see resolution in each face. Then he raised his hand for quiet.

'Make ready. Three moons from now the sea dragons sail for England.'

Another roar greeted this.

'A fitting revenge for Ragnar,' Wulfrum observed.

'We shall have more than revenge, brother,' replied Halfdan. 'There will be rich rewards too for those who serve well—land and slaves to work it. And women.'

Wulfrum grinned, knowing whither the conversation tended. 'And the Saxon women are reputed fair, are they not?'

'Aye, they are, and it's high time you took a wife. A man must get sons.'

'True. And when I find a woman who pleases me enough, I shall wed and breed sons aplenty.'

'Your standards are high, but even you might lose your heart to a Saxon beauty.'

'I have never lost my heart to a woman yet. They satisfy a need like food and drink, but they have no power to hold us long.'

'You say so for you have never been in love.'

'No. Nor am I like to be. It is not necessary to fall in love to get sons.' Wulfrum laughed. 'My heart is my own, brother, and I guard it well.'

Chapter One

Northumbria—867 A.D.

Elgiva sat on the goatskin rug before the fire, her arms clasped about her knees and her gaze on the flames. It was said that some had the skill to read the future there. Just then she would have given much for such a glimpse to help resolve the chaos of her thoughts. The present dilemma was desperate, but what to do for the best?

She glanced once at her companion, grateful for that comforting presence. To Elgiva, Osgifu had been both mother and confidante. The older woman had entered the service of Lord Egbert as a nursemaid when her husband died. At forty she was comely still, a tall elegant figure, for all that there were lines on her face and white strands in her dark hair. Her grey eyes saw more than other people, for she was known to have the second sight, to see those things hidden from ordinary mortal view. Her skill lay with the runes, not the fire, but the accuracy of her words was sufficient for people to regard her with awe, even fear. Elgiva had never been afraid, only curious. Osgifu's mother had been a Dane, a trader's daughter, who married a

Saxon husband. From her she had inherited the gift of the sight and a wealth of stories besides.

When Elgiva was a child, Osgifu had entertained her with tales of the Norse gods: of Thor, who wielded the thunderbolts; of Loki the trickster of Odin; and Fenrir the wolf. Elgiva had listened, enthralled by stories of Jotenheim, the realm of the frost giants, and of the dragon, Nidhoggr, who constantly gnawed at the roots of Yggdrasil, the mighty ash tree connecting earth and heaven. Osgifu had taught her the Danish tongue too, albeit in secret, for she knew Lord Egbert would not have approved. When they were alone, the two of them spoke their secret language and knew their words would be safe from other ears. She alone knew the secrets of Elgiva's heart and it was to her Elgiva turned in times of trouble.

The younger woman sighed and, turning her gaze from the glowing flames in the hearth, looked full at her mentor.

'I don't know what to do, Gifu. Ever since my father's death Ravenswood has slid further and further into chaos. My brother did nothing.' She paused. 'Now he is dead too, and his sons are but babes. The place needs a capable hand.'

She did not add, *a man's hand*, but Osgifu heard the thought. She also acknowledged the truth of it. Lord Osric, concerned only with skill at arms and with hawking and hunting, had taken little interest in the running of his late father's estate, preferring to leave it to his steward, Wilfred. A good man at heart, Wilfred had performed his duties well enough under Lord Egbert's exacting rule, but after, with no master's eye on him, he began to neglect small things, putting off until the morrow what should have been done today. The serfs under his control took their example from him, and Elgiva, on her daily rides, had begun to notice the results. Ravenswood, which had hitherto always looked prosperous, began to take on an air of neglect. Fences were not mended, repairs botched. Weeds grew among the crops and the livestock were not properly tended.

The roofs of the barns and storehouses leaked, and she felt sure that the stored grain and fodder within were not as strictly accounted for as they had been. When she had mentioned these things to Osric, he had brushed her aside. The problem grew worse. She had spoken to him again and received short shrift.

'A woman's place is in the house, not meddling in matters that do not concern her.'

'Ravenswood is my concern,' she'd replied, 'as it should be yours.'

'You take too much upon you, Elgiva.' He had eyed her coolly. 'If you had a husband and children of your own, you would have no time to interfere in the affairs of men. You should have been married long since.'

Her brother was right about that and Elgiva knew it. Had Lord Egbert lived, he would have found a bridegroom for her. There had been no shortage of suitors. She had loved her father dearly and he had made no secret of the fact that she was the child of his heart. Her company had been congenial to him for she knew how to make him laugh. A fearless rider, she had often accompanied him on the chase. His death three years earlier had changed everything, and for the worse. Osric, careless, feckless, had become the Thane of Ravenswood. Elgiva, well tutored in domestic matters, saw to it that the household ran smoothly, but she could do nothing about the wider problem. However, their conversation had put Osric in mind of his responsibilities towards his sister.

'I shall find you a husband. These are troubled times and a woman should not be without a protector, even if there is truth in only half the tales we hear of the Viking raids.'

That too was beyond dispute, but she had assumed that he would forget the matter as he did with everything not immediately concerned with his own interests. She had been quite wrong. One day, about a month after the former conversation, he announced that Lord Aylwin had asked for her hand. At first she had not known whether to laugh or cry. A wealthy and respected Saxon lord, wise governor of rich lands, Aylwin was a near neighbour. He had been the friend of her father and, his own wife having died some years earlier, he sought a new bride. At forty he was old enough to be her father and his sons were grown men, but he was still strong and vigorous. Elgiva had baulked. Although she had nothing to say against Aylwin as a man, she knew she could not feel for him what a woman should feel for a husband. In truth, she had never felt it for any man of her acquaintance. However, women of her rank did not marry for love. If both partners respected each other, it was enough. But not for her, she thought, not for her. Osric had not understood.

'Do you know anything against Aylwin?'

'No.'

'You know he is wealthy and of good reputation? A man to be respected?'

'Yes.'

'Then why should you refuse him?'

As Elgiva sought for the words to explain, Osric had pressed his advantage.

'You know Lord Aylwin sought your hand long since.'

'And I said then I did not love his lordship.'

'Love? What has love to do with it? This is an advantageous match.'

'I do not deny it. He is also old enough to be my father.'

'He is in his prime and will make you an attentive husband.'

'I will not consent to such attentions.'

With that she had marched out of the room and there the matter had rested. Osric, for all his faults, still had a certain fondness for his sister and would not force her to a marriage that was distasteful to her. Life had gone on much as before until, a month ago, Osric's horse put its foot in a hole while they were out hunting. Horse and rider fell with force—the former breaking its foreleg and the rider his neck.

The shock had been great and the sorrow also. At a stroke Elgiva found herself alone with all the care of a large estate and two young children. Osric's wife, Cynewise, had died in child-bed at the age of twenty. It was a common enough occurrence and, for women, one of the hazards of marriage, but for Elgiva it had been an added shock. She knew that Osric would have married again, in time, for a man might well have several wives in his lifetime. For a woman alone the future looked bleak. When she had told Osgifu that she didn't know what to do, it had been prevarication and they both knew it. She must marry and soon. But Aylwin?

'What do the runes say, Gifu?'

Elgiva knew already what they would say, but she needed to have it confirmed. The runes never lied. Carved out of ash, a tree sacred to Odin, and indelibly marked with ancient eso-teric symbols, they would point the way as they had done before. Osgifu regarded her with a steady gaze.

'Ask your question.'

Elgiva drew in a deep breath. 'Shall I marry Aylwin?'

She waited, hands locked together, as Osgifu scanned the rune cast. The silence lengthened and her grey eyes narrowed, a sharp line creasing her brow.

'Well? Shall I marry?'

'Aye, you will be married, but not to Aylwin.'

'Not Aylwin?' Elgiva was puzzled. 'Then who?'

'I do not know the man.'

'What does he look like?'

'I cannot tell. The upper part of his face is hidden behind the plates of his helmet. He wears a shirt of fine mail and in his hand he carries a mighty sword, as sharp as a dragon's tooth.'

'A warrior? A Saxon lord, then. Shall I meet him soon?'

'You will see him soon enough.'

Thereafter she became strangely reticent and all of Elgiva's questions could draw nothing more from her.

* * *

The mystery stayed with her but, as the days passed, she knew she could not wait indefinitely for some stranger to ride by and rescue her from all her problems. A woman alone was vulnerable. A woman with wealth and land was doubly so once it became known she had no protector. It was not unknown for such to be married under duress to an ambitious and ruthless lord with a strong retinue and no aversion to the use of force. She shivered. Better to wed a respected man who would treat her well and restore Ravenswood to its former self. It came to her that she must wed Aylwin and soon. Love was all very well in stories of high romance: real life wasn't like that. Her brother had been right. It was an advantageous match. Perhaps, with time, she might come to love Aylwin. Certainly she would make him a dutiful wife and bear his children. Her mind glossed over the details, unwilling to dwell on the matter. Should she be so nice when, every day, girls of thirteen or fourteen were married off to men thrice their age? The question now was how to bring this about. She had refused Aylwin's suit. Could she now go a-begging?

In the event the matter was solved for her when, a few days later, the servants announced the arrival of Lord Aylwin accompanied by a small group of armed men. She received him in the great hall and, having bid him welcome, offered his men refreshment and allowed him to take her to one side. She wished that she had had more warning—she was suddenly aware of her sober-hued gown and her hair braided simply down her back without ribbon or ornament. It was hardly the dress of a woman receiving a suitor. However, Aylwin seemed to find nothing amiss and smiled at her. Of average height, he was stocky and powerfully made for all that the brown hair and beard were grizzled with grey. The expression on the rugged face was both sympathetic and kind, but the eyes spoke of admiration.

For a while they spoke of Osric and he said all that was proper, but it did not take him long to come to the real purpose of his visit.

'Your brother's death leaves you alone and in a most difficult situation, my lady. In these times a woman must have a protector.'

Elgiva heard in his words the echo of her brother's and felt a *frisson* along her spine. Heart beating much faster, she knew what was coming and waited for it.

'I would like to be that man.' He paused, eyeing her with an unwonted awkwardness. 'I am no longer in the first flush of youth, but I am still in good health and well able to protect you. I can also swear my undying loyalty and devotion.'

Elgiva felt her face grow warmer and for a moment her amber eyes were veiled. Aylwin, mistaking the reason, drew in a deep breath.

'Let me protect you, Elgiva. I do not ask you to love me now, but perhaps in time that may come. Meanwhile, be assured that you will be loved, my lady.'

Hearing an unmistakeable note of sincerity, she looked up swiftly, meeting his gaze.

'Does it surprise you to hear that?'

'I had not thought…that is—' She broke off, floundering.

'Have you any idea how beautiful you are?' he went on. 'From the first day I saw you I wanted you for my wife. My Gundred has been dead these five years and a man grows lonely. I think you are lonely too. May not two such comfort each other?'

Elgiva nodded. 'I think that perhaps they may, my lord.'

For a moment he did not move, the dark eyes intent on her face. 'Then you will marry me?'

'There would be certain conditions.'

'Name them.'

'That the rights of my nephews are protected and that you act as overlord of Ravenswood until they can act for themselves.'

'Agreed. If you wed me, they shall be reared as my own sons.'

'I would also ask for a decent interval of mourning for my brother.'

'It shall be as you ask.'

'Then on midsummer's day I will become your wife.' Elgiva's voice was perfectly level as she gave him the commitment he sought.

Taking her hand, he pressed it to his lips. 'It is an honour I scarce hoped to have.'

'I will try to make you a good wife,' she replied.

The proposed date was three months hence, but if Aylwin had hoped for an earlier wedding, he said nothing. Having got what he wanted he was prepared to give a little ground, knowing it would do his cause no harm.

'Will you pledge your hand to me openly, Elgiva?' he asked then. 'I do not ask for a huge feast—I know it must be repugnant to you in the circumstances—but perhaps a small gathering?'

Elgiva was not surprised by the request. What it meant was a public declaration of intent. It also made clear to all concerned that Elgiva and thus Ravenswood were spoken for, that both lay under the protection of a rich and powerful lord. From the moment their betrothal was announced she was as good as his and no man would touch her. It also meant a respite, time to grow used to the idea of the bargain she had just struck.

'It shall be as you wish, my lord.'

He smiled. 'I am content.'

She had wondered if he would try to kiss her, but to her relief he made no further attempt to touch her. He took his leave not long after that and Elgiva watched him ride away with his men. Then she went in search of Osgifu.

The older woman listened in silence, her face impassive as she took in the news.

'Do you think it was wrong to accept him?' Elgiva asked at length.

'You did what you thought you had to do, child, both for yourself and for Ravenswood.'

'Aylwin will be a good husband and he will restore these lands to their former glory. I cannot bear to see things thus.'

'I know.' Osgifu hesitated. 'But, can you be a wife to him?'

'I must, Gifu. There is no choice now. Surely you see that?'

'Yes.' She put her arms round the girl's shoulders. 'I think you have nothing to fear. It is my view that he will be a doting and most indulgent husband.'

Elgiva nodded and tried to think positive thoughts. Neither of them mentioned the rune cast.

The betrothal feast went as planned, a small and select gathering of neighbours and friends who came together to see the couple pledge to each other. It was in every way a most suitable match and no one thought anything of the discrepancy in the ages of the pair who were soon to marry. It was widely held that Aylwin was a clever and knowing man for at a stroke he doubled his holdings and gained a most beautiful wife into the bargain. Elgiva in her blue gown, embroidered at neck and sleeve, her golden hair braided with matching ribbons, looked very fetching indeed. It was noticed that her prospective groom could hardly keep his eyes off her and was most assiduous in plying her with food and wine, carving choice cuts of meat and serving her with his own hands.

In truth, Elgiva had little appetite but did her best to hide it. Her heart was unwontedly heavy but, unwilling to disappoint her guests with a glum face, she smiled graciously and tried to look as though she were enjoying herself. As she noticed the gaze Aylwin bent upon her, the reality of the situation hit her with force—in three months' time they would be married and he would take her to his bed. She must give herself to him whenever he wished and, eventually, she would bear his children. He had fine sons already, but, if the look in his eye was aught to judge by, he intended to sire more. Elgiva took another sip of wine to steady herself. She had wanted this, had agreed to it of her own free will. Now she must live with the consequences. If he was to be her husband she must get to know him, to learn his likes and dislikes, to discover what would please him. She had no doubt of her ability to run his household efficiently for she had been schooled in domestic duties from childhood. The rules of the bedroom were unknown territory, though familiar to him. She reminded herself sharply that it was not necessary to love for a marriage to work. As long as there was respect. Please, God, she prayed silently, let it be all right.

The feasting done and the hour growing late, the women retired, leaving the hall to the men. Elgiva knew the hard drinking was about to begin and had given orders to the servants to keep the guests plied with ale and mead as long as they wanted it. She was not sorry to make her excuses and bid her future husband a goodnight. He kissed her hand and pressed it warmly. From his flushed face and the hot glow in his eyes it was clear he had had a lot to drink, but his speech was unslurred and his balance still unimpaired.

'Goodnight, Elgiva, and sleep well. Would this were our wedding night that I might share that bed with you.'

She managed a smile. 'In good time, my lord.'

Then she was gone, leaving the hall behind and seeking the sanctuary of the women's bower.

In spite of the late night, Elgiva woke early and for several moments lay still beneath the fur coverlet, enjoying the comfortable warmth of the bed. Though the first grey light of the spring dawn was filtering through the shutters, she could hear no sound of birdsong and the cock had yet to crow. Only Osgifu's gentle snores broke the heavy stillness of the new day. The nurse would not stir for a while yet. Elgiva rose and dressed quickly for the air was chill, pulling the gown over her linen kirtle and sliding her feet into leather shoes. Then, throwing a mantle about her shoulders, she moved to the doorway, pausing once to glance back. Osgifu slept on. For a moment Elgiva watched, her feelings a strange fusion of love and disappointment. She had trusted her. Even now she could hear her words: *The runes never lie.* But the runes had lied, and Osgifu had been wrong. Immediately Elgiva upbraided herself. Why should she be surprised to discover human fallibility? She wasn't a child, for heaven's sake. It was time to face facts and shoulder the responsibilities that fell to her.

Elgiva left the women's bower and made her way through the hall. It was not her most direct route out, but she was hungry and knew there would be a fair chance of finding something to eat without summoning a servant. All about her, men lay snoring on the rushes among the scraps of food, or sprawled on benches and tables among the debris of the feast. After the copious quantities of mead and ale they had drunk she had no fear of waking the sleepers and guessed there would be a few sore heads this morning. She retrieved part of a loaf from the table and broke a piece off. It was growing stale, but it would do for now. Chewing on the bread, she made her way silently among the sleeping forms, wrinkling her nose at air thick with the reek of smoke and spilled ale and male sweat, skirting the hearth where the remaining embers of the fire smouldered in mounds of grey ash. Hearing her approach, two wolfhounds looked up from their slumber, but the low rumbling growl died in their throats as they recognised her. One got to his feet, wagging his tail, shoving his nose into Elgiva's hand. She stroked his wiry head absently and then moved on towards the door, eager to be gone for the confines of the hall were stifling and a sharp reminder of things she wished to forget.

The side door was ajar, a clear indication that she was not the first abroad. Through the gap she could see a man relieving himself in the midden across the way. He had his back to her, but from his dress she guessed him to be one of Lord

Aylwin's men. Elgiva seized the moment to slip out and round
the end of the hall. From this vantage point she could observe
without being seen. Presently, after having answered the call
of nature, the man returned whence he came and Elgiva was
able to make her way to the stables unnoticed.

Here too, all was quiet, for even the serfs were not stirring
yet. They had taken their fill of Ravenswood's bounty the previous evening and there was none to mark her passage along
the row of stalls to the one where Mara was tethered. Hearing
her approach, the bay mare turned her head and whinnied
gently. Elgiva reached for the bridle hanging on the peg and
slipped into the stall. Minutes later she was leading the horse
out. Once in the open air, she vaulted astride and headed for
the gate. The watchman roused himself and, responding to her
greeting, swung the portal open. Elgiva held Mara to a walk as
they passed the houses in the hamlet. Here were signs of life:
a spiral of smoke from a roof, a dog scratching itself before an
open door. She suspected it would be much later before those
in the hall roused themselves. Glad to have escaped for a time,
Elgiva breathed the cool morning air gratefully, though it could
not dispel her sombre mood or the memories that occasioned
it. Later she would return and play her part before them all.

Pride and a sense of family honour had led her to spare no
expense in the celebration of the betrothal feast. It was, after
all, a cause for celebration, an excellent and judicious match.
The union would not only unite two great Saxon houses, but
would bring advantage to both sides. She had entered into the
arrangement of her own volition. Her future husband was a man
she could respect. Why, then, in the face of such good fortune,
did her heart feel so heavy?

Elgiva was startled out of these sombre thoughts when her
horse shied. She tightened her hold on the reins, looking about
her, but could see only shadows beneath the trees and curls of
mist in the hollows. The wood was locked beneath an eerie si-

lence. The mare snorted uneasily and Elgiva frowned, her gaze taking in the details of the surrounding woodland. The silence stretched out around her, unbroken by any breath of wind, or birdsong or sound of any living thing. Then she discerned movement ahead through the trees where a lone horseman was approaching, bent low over the saddle. Elgiva hesitated, wondering whether the safest course was to flee, but something about the rider's posture gave her pause. He was swaying and for a second she wondered if he were drunk. Just as quickly, she rejected the idea, for as he drew closer she could see he had come far. The horse was lathered, its chest and flanks darkened with sweat, its legs and belly all bespattered with mud. Pulling up, she let the rider approach. Mara whinnied and sidled, but Elgiva kept a firm hold on the rein. The oncoming rider was a man of middle years and, like his horse, all muddied. His face was grey and lined with pain and she could see the side of his tunic was stiff with dried blood. He stared at her as if she had been an apparition and then she recognised him.

'Gunter!'

Her uncle's steward—he must have ridden far. It was a two-day journey and from the look of him he had ridden fast. His horse was all but spent, and he too. Every word cost him effort.

'I bring urgent news for Ravenswood, my lady.'

'We are not far from home. Come, let me take you there.'

He nodded and together they retraced Elgiva's path. As soon as they were within the gates, she summoned help. Grooms came running to take the horses and another helped Gunter into the hall. Men were stirring now and looked up in surprise at their entrance. Elgiva saw Aylwin there with several of his men. He hastened over to her.

'Gunter, my uncle's steward,' she explained. 'He is wounded. I don't know how badly.'

Aylwin took one look at the dark stiffening patch on the man's tunic. 'He has lost much blood. His hurts must be tended.'

Elgiva dispatched a servant for her box of medicines. Another brought a goblet of water and helped raise the injured man a fraction so she could hold it to his lips. He drank greedily, but Elgiva would only allow him a little to begin with. Then she and Osgifu set about dealing with the wound. It was a sword thrust, deep but clean. As far as she could tell it had not pierced any internal organs, though it had bled copiously. Between them they stanched the bleeding and cleansed the wound, before fastening a clean pad over it with long strips of linen cloth. Gunter bore these ministrations in silence, though his face was very pale. Then she allowed him a little more to drink.

'You must rest now and try to recover your strength.'

'Lady, I must speak. My news will wait no longer.'

'Say on then, Gunter. Does it concern my uncle?'

'Aye, my lady, and ill news it is.'

'What of my uncle? Is he sick?'

'Nay, my lady. He is dead with all his kin and his hall is burned. A great Viking war host marches north.'

A deathly silence followed as those present tried to grasp the enormity of the news.

'The rumours are true,' murmured Aylwin.

'Aye, lord. We had little warning of their coming, but even if we had, it would have made no difference for the sheer weight of their numbers. Those Saxons who were not slain were enslaved. I was wounded and left for dead. When I came to, the hall was a blackened ruin and my lord was dead. I found a stray horse and got away under cover of darkness.'

'It was as well you did,' said Elgiva. She glanced at Osgifu, who looked as shaken as the rest.

'You are right, child. We should have had no warning else. As it is, we must prepare to defend ourselves as best we may.'

'Truly spoken,' said Gunter, 'for the sons of Ragnar Lodbrok seek a terrible revenge for their father's death.'

'We had heard of this,' replied Aylwin. 'There were tales of a great Viking war fleet a year or so ago, but we had thought the raiders much further south.'

'That is so, lord,' Gunter continued, 'though not by design. It seems they set sail for Northumbria, but their ships were blown off course and brought them instead to the Anglian coast. Since then they have swept through that kingdom with fire and sword. We heard that they looted the abbeys at Ely and Crowland and Peterborough. 'Tis said that at Peterborough Hubba killed eighty monks himself.'

Startled exclamations greeted this and men looked at each other in mounting horror.

Gunter drew in a ragged breath. 'They have taken Mercia too. Now that York has fallen, all of Northumbria is threatened.'

Aylwin's hand went automatically to the hilt of his sword. 'What of King Ella?'

'They captured him and acted out their revenge. His ribs were torn apart and folded backwards to resemble a spread eagle. Then they threw salt in the wound and left him to die.'

Elgiva felt her stomach churn. She had heard many times of the brutality of the Norsemen, but never anything so barbaric. Beside her Osgifu paled, and she heard several sharp intakes of breath from those around.

'You must prepare to defend yourselves,' said Gunter. 'The Viking host wintered at York, but the spring thaw draws them forth again. It is only a matter of time before they come.'

'But surely if Ella is dead they have what they want now,' replied Osgifu. 'They will leave with their plunder as they always do.'

'This time they want more than plunder. Halfdan has let it be known they want land and they plan to take it.'

'Land? Do the pirates mean to stay?'

'It would seem our shores are more fertile than their northern fastness.'

'They will find the price dear.' Aylwin's face was grim. 'My sword is ready, and those of my kin.'

Elgiva could see the determination on the faces all around her and knew a moment of shame that he was ready to fight on her behalf when she had earlier had misgivings about her betrothal to him, putting thoughts of her happiness before Ravenswood. As she looked up he caught her eye and smiled.

'I swear, no harm shall come to you while I live, lady.'

Elgiva began to feel distinctly guilty. 'I thank you, my lord. If it comes to a fight, my family will be much in your debt.'

'They are soon to be my family too,' he replied. 'It is fitting my sword be ready to use in their defence, and in yours.'

Elgiva smiled a little in return, liking him more in that moment than ever before. However, her thoughts were soon distracted for Aylwin had turned away and was already organising the deployment of the men.

'Every man and boy able to hold a weapon must prepare. There can be no knowing how soon the Viking host may march. We shall double our guard and watchers shall be placed at the boundaries to give word of any approaching force. If the Norsemen come, we shall be ready for them.'

He gave his orders and men departed to do his bidding. Elgiva turned to check on Gunter, but he was asleep and Osgifu was with him.

'I will watch over him the while,' she said.

'Will he survive, do you think?'

'He has lost much blood, 'tis true. But he is a strong man and, God willing, he will come through this. What he needs is rest and quiet.'

'I pray God that he may have it.'

'Amen to that, child.'

Elgiva left her and went outside, making her way to the steps leading to the rampart that ran along the inside of the palisade. From there she had an excellent view of the preparations taking place as everywhere men hastened to ready themselves for the defence of Ravenswood. Beyond the hall with its attendant stables and storehouses and the high wooden pale, the countryside lay still. An area of open ground surrounded the pale, and beyond it was pasture and woodland. Usually Elgiva thought of it as a place of peace and solitude, but now those quiet glades held menace. Her eyes scanned the trees, seeking for any sign of movement that might reveal a hidden enemy, but there was nothing to be seen save a few serfs driving their swine to feed. In the little hamlet people went about their business, though looking fearfully about all the while. The knowledge that Lord Aylwin had posted sentinels through the estate offered partial reassurance; at least there would be no surprise attack. Perhaps it was as Osgifu had said: now they had exacted their vengeance on King Ella they would adventure no further. It was a slender hope for the greed of the pirates was legendary. Their periodic raids were a fact of life for the unfortunate coastal dwellers, and the Norsemen had regularly carried off women and livestock along with any other loot that seized their fancy. Then they had sailed for their northern lands taking their booty with them.

Elgiva shivered to think of the poor souls taken off to a life of slavery in a strange country, of the women who must become unwilling wives or concubines to their new masters. It would be better to fight to the death than submit to such a fate as that. As she glanced away from the distant trees, her gaze fell on the roof of the bower. Within her chamber was the chest where she kept her gowns. Underneath them was the sword her father had given her some years before. He had taught her to use it too, holding that a woman should be schooled in self-defence as well as a man. Elgiva was resolved. If need be, she too, would fight and kill to defend her home.

Chapter Two

The Viking attack came within days; the sentinels on Ravenswood's boundaries returned in haste to report the sighting of a marching host hundreds strong. Elgiva had been sewing in the women's bower with Osgifu when the peace was shattered by the wild ringing of the church bell. Her hands paused at their task and for a moment or two she listened before the implications sank in.

'The alarm.'

'Dear Lord, it cannot be.' Osgifu threw down her sewing and hastened to the door, but her companion was before her. Both of them halted in dismay on the threshold; outside was a scene of urgent haste with men running to their posts, buckling on swords as they went. They stopped a man-at-arms who was hurrying to the palisade with a large sheaf of arrows.

'What is it? What's happening?'

'The sentries have reported sighting a large enemy force, my lady,' he replied. 'It is advancing on Ravenswood.'

Osgifu paled, looking in alarm at the armed men running towards the ramparts. 'An enemy force?'

'Aye, the Vikings approach.' He inclined his head to Elgiva.

'Your pardon, lady, but I dare not stay longer. I must to my post.' With that he was gone.

The two women ran to the hall where Aylwin was barking orders to his men. As they hastened to obey, he turned to Elgiva.

'Go bar yourself in the upper chamber, my lady. It will be far safer. Take Osgifu and the children too.'

Before she had a chance to reply one of Aylwin's men spoke out, throwing a dark glance at Osgifu.

'I've been told that this woman is of Danish blood, my lord. How do we know she can be trusted?'

Elgiva surveyed him with anger. 'Osgifu has served my family faithfully and well for many years. Her loyalty is not in question nor ever has been.'

The man reddened. 'I beg pardon, my lady.'

Aylwin glared at him, then nodded towards the door. The other took the hint and beat a hasty retreat.

'I'm sorry, Elgiva.' Aylwin laid a soothing hand on her arm. 'Such times make men cautious.'

'So it seems.'

With an effort Elgiva forced down her indignation. It would not aid their cause to quarrel among themselves. She turned to Osgifu.

'Fetch Hilda and the children and the women servants. Then go with them to the upper floor.'

If Osgifu had been in any way discomforted by the conversation, it was not evident. Returning Elgiva's gaze, she asked, 'What about you, child?'

'I will come presently, but there is something I must fetch first.'

'Make haste then, my lady,' said Aylwin. With one last warm smile he hurried off to join his men outside.

Elgiva raced back to the bower and, throwing open the chest in the corner, retrieved the sword from the bottom. The familiar weight of the weapon was comforting. At least they should not be completely defenceless if the worst came to the worst. Closing her hand round the scabbard, she slammed the chest shut and went to join the others, barring the stout door behind her as Aylwin had instructed. Then she took up a station by the far window. The shutters were pulled to, but through a broken slat she could see much of the hustle and activity below as men ran to their posts. Aylwin had his plan ready days earlier and each one of his retainers knew where he was supposed to be. Within a short time they were ready, armed to the teeth, and grimly determined to defend their homes and their lives.

The clanging bell had brought the peasants from the fields and the wood to seek the relative safety of the pale. No sooner were they gathered within than the men on the wall called out a warning as the forward ranks of the Viking host appeared. Like an army of sinister wraiths, silent and intent, they emerged from among the trees into the pasture beyond. One of their archers loosed an arrow, killing a Saxon guard where he stood. Then, as though at a signal, a great shout went up from the invaders, splitting the stillness, and they surged forwards as one.

'Merciful heavens,' murmured Aylwin. 'Surely this can be no ordinary raiding party. There are hundreds of them.' By his private reckoning his men would be outnumbered five to one.

Beside him, his armed companion had made a similar calculation. 'This is revenge indeed for their dead chieftain.'

What Aylwin might have said next was lost in a hissing rain of arrows. It covered the advance of the Viking vanguard that carried ladders to raise against the walls. Swiftly the defenders loosed their own arrows in reply, but each time one of the attackers fell he was immediately replaced and the assault renewed. The Saxons maintained a deadly fire from above, but to right and left the invaders swarmed up the ladders and over the walls. The first were cut down without mercy, but their comrades followed hard on their heels and soon fierce battle was enjoined, filling the air with shouts and the clash of arms.

Peering through the gap in the shutters, Elgiva stared in horror at the scene of carnage below and murmured a prayer. Everywhere she looked the Viking marauders were pouring in over the walls.

'God in heaven, can there be so many?'

Giants they seemed, these fierce warriors, cruel with battle thirst, each face alight with lust for blood and conquest. With sword and axe they cut down all who stood in their way, crying out the name of their war god.

'Odin!'

The cry was repeated from four hundred throats as the Norsemen drove forwards, fearless into the ranks of their foes. The defenders fought bravely but the sheer weight of numbers pushed them back, step by step, the enemy advancing over the bodies of the slain, remorseless, hacking their way on. As the defenders fell back, Elgiva could see another group of the enemy without the palisade, dragging a huge battering ram into position. It was the trunk of a tree, fresh hewn and drawn on a wheeled timber cradle. Under cover of ox-hide shields the marauders rolled the supporting cradle back and forth, building momentum until the end of the trunk crashed against the gate. The stout timbers creaked, but held. Elgiva stared in horrified fascination as with each swing the gate shook. Alive to the danger the nearest Saxon defenders rallied to the gate and swarmed to the rampart inside the palisade, raining arrows and rocks on to the men beneath.

For a little while it seemed that they had met with success; several of the Vikings fell and the momentum of the great ram was lost. It was a brief respite—in moments reinforcements arrived and other warriors stepped up to take the places of their fallen comrades. The assault on the gate began anew. The timbers shuddered and splintered. Amid the clash of arms and shouts of men a thunderous crack announced the breach, followed by a roar of triumph from the invading horde who poured through the gap like a tide beneath their black-raven banner.

Helpless, Elgiva could only watch as the Saxon defence crumbled and her retainers were beaten back towards the great hall. Beside them Aylwin and his men fought on, shoulder to shoulder, returning the enemy blow for blow. Half a dozen more men fell under Aylwin's sword while all around him the group of defenders grew smaller and more desperate, redoubling their efforts, hacking and thrusting and parrying, each man determined to sell his life dear. Tireless they seemed, yet one by one they fell. Aylwin fought on, laying about him with a will, his sword smoking and bloody as it rose and fell, slashing and cutting until the bodies were piled before him. And then its edge struck the blade of a huge war axe. The sword shivered and Aylwin was left undefended. He hurled the sundered hilt at the foe in a last act of defiance before the enemy blade cut him down.

Elgiva's hand flew to her lips, stifling her cry, and she closed her eyes a moment, forcing back tears. Weakness would not help Aylwin now, or any of the survivors who would depend on her. Striving to regain some measure of self-control she turned from the window, sombrely regarding the other occupants of the room. Seeing that stony expression, Hilda let out a terrified sob as she cowered, clutching the baby, Pybba, to her breast. The nursemaid was but six and ten years old and plainly terrified. Osgifu stood beside her, pale but silent, her arm about the three-year-old Ulric, who clutched her skirt and bit a trembling lip. Around them the women servants sobbed.

In the hall below were gathered a handful of men left for their defence. Violent banging on the barred outer doors announced the invaders' intent and the great timbers shuddered. Elgiva knew it could only be a matter of time before they broke through for above the din she heard the sinister thunk of axes against timber. A woman screamed. Minutes later the door gave way amid a roar of voices and the clash of weapons as the defenders tried to stem the tide of invaders. Shouts and shrieks filled the hall. More invaders poured in through the shattered doorway. Several made for the stairway in pursuit of plunder. Elgiva heard the heavy footfalls and men's voices. Someone tried the chamber door and found it barred. Then she heard a man's voice.

'Break it down!'

There followed the fearsome sound of axes in wood. Hilda let out a stifled sob of terror. The baby began to cry and in desperation she tried to quiet it, while little Ulric looked on, wide-eyed with fright. Elgiva looked from them to the door, which shook under the assault. In another minute the first blades were visible through a hole in the timber, a hole that grew larger with each blow. A few more moments and they would be through. With beating heart she backed away to the far side of the room, watching the splintering wood in helpless horror, struggling to control her growing fear. With her back to the wall, she closed her hand round the hilt of the sword and, taking a deep breath, drew the blade from the sheath.

As she did so the door burst asunder and the first three men fell into the room, followed by half a dozen more. Their greedy gaze fell immediately on the cowering group in front of them and they strode forwards, seizing upon the women servants. One man grabbed hold of Hilda, who clutched the baby in one arm and the terrified Ulric in the other. Osgifu strove to come between, but a heavy blow sent her reeling back into the wall. She hit her head and fell, stunned. Hilda shrieked, struggling wildly against the hands that held her, her screams mingling with those of the baby.

Outraged to see such treatment meted out to the weak and helpless, Elgiva stepped forwards.

'Leave them alone! Let them go!'

It proved a futile protest, but the words drew attention from a different quarter and Elgiva found herself confronting another armed man. Tall and well made, fair of hair and beard, he might have been handsome save for the thin cruel lips drawn back in an indulgent sneer.

'Well now, what have we here?'

Her face blazed with loathing and contempt and her hand tightened round the hilt of the sword.

'Viking scum! You would make war on women and helpless infants! Come, try your luck here! I'll slit your belly and spill your yellow guts for you!'

All eyes turned towards Elgiva, registering surprise, and then, on seeing the sword, amusement.

'Have a care, Sweyn,' called one of his companions in mocking tones. 'That one is a regular fire eater.'

Sweyn bared his teeth in a smile, his cold grey gaze speculative. 'A warrior maid, no less. One of Odin's daughters, perhaps, and fluent in our tongue. That will be convenient when I give her instructions in bed.'

Appreciative grins greeted the words and the speaker turned away for a moment to share the joke with his companions. Elgiva darted in for the attack. From the corner of his eye he saw the flashing blade aimed at him and leapt aside. The thrust that should have pierced his heart merely gashed his arm. Incredulous, he clapped his free hand to the wound, staring at the dripping blood, amid roars of laughter from the rest. Undeterred, Elgiva laid on with a will and for several moments Sweyn was forced to defend himself most dexterously before the onslaught, being driven back several paces. However, very soon greater strength and skill began to tell and then it was Elgiva who was forced back step by step until she came up hard against the far wall. A heavy blow beneath the hilt numbed her hand and wrist and with a gasp of pain she dropped the sword, only to find the Viking's blade at her throat.

'Beg for mercy, vixen!'

Elgiva spat at him. She knew he would kill her now, but she would not give him the satisfaction of seeing her fear, of hearing her plead. Lifting her chin, she let her gaze travel the length of the bloody sword until it met that of the man who held it. The tip of the sword pierced the skin and she felt the warm trickle of blood. With pounding heart she waited for the final thrust. For a long moment there was silence. Then the blade was lowered a fraction and for a fleeting second there was something like admiration in his eyes.

'No,' he said softly, 'I will not kill you. What a waste that would be.'

'You speak true, Sweyn!' called a voice from the assembled group behind. 'Take her to your bed. I wager you'll never have a livelier piece.'

Another shout of laughter went up. Elgiva felt her cheeks flame as she heard Sweyn laugh, saw his hot gaze strip her.

'I'd rather be dead.'

'You're not going to die,' he replied. 'Not yet.'

He sheathed the sword and, stepping close, seized her by the waist, bringing his mouth down hard on hers amid shouts of encouragement from the watching men.

Elgiva struggled in furious revulsion, but to no avail. In desperation she bit down on his lip. With a cry of pain and outrage, he released her abruptly, his hand moving to his mouth where the blood welled. Giving him no time to recover, Elgiva brought her knee up hard. Instinct made him move, though he still caught a glancing blow. She heard a grunt of pain and he reeled backwards while his companions redoubled their mirth. Elgiva didn't wait to see how badly she had hurt him, but turned and fled across the room. Hilda was still struggling in the arms of the young man who had first seized her, but, hampered by the baby, could do little. The crying Ulric was standing beside the still figure of Osgifu. Elgiva reached him and flung her arms around him.

Across the room Sweyn staggered to his feet. Seeing the movement, Elgiva looked up and, as her gaze met his, she saw the murderous rage in his eyes. He crossed the intervening space and with a crash flung open the shutters. The room flooded with light. Then he tore Ulric from her arms and raised him aloft. Realising his intent, Elgiva screamed.

'No!'

Sweyn's lips twisted in a chilling smile.

Then a much louder voice sounded above all. 'Hold!' There was no mistaking the tone of cold command. 'Enough! Put the child down, Sweyn.'

Elgiva, very pale, tore her gaze from the man by the window and risked a glance at the speaker. She had a brief impression of a tall, dark-haired warrior in a mail shirt. His face was concealed behind the plates of his helmet, but it was clear that all the intruders knew him and that he had authority with them for the room fell silent. His blue gaze locked with that of the other man. Frantic, she looked back across the room at Sweyn. For one hideous moment it seemed as though he would follow his intent, but then, to her unspeakable relief, he slowly lowered Ulric to the floor. Bewildered, the little boy ran to Elgiva, who held him close. Ignoring them, Sweyn confronted the other man.

'Did we not swear to avenge Ragnar with fire and sword?'

'Aye, man to man. Do men make war on babes?'

'A mewling Saxon brat. What does it signify?'

At this casual dismissal of helpless innocence Elgiva, sickened, thought her heart might burst with rage. She missed the casual glance that the dark warrior threw her way before his gaze locked again with Sweyn's.

'Slaves are valuable, no matter what their age, and we have need of them. There will be no more killing here this day.' The tone was calm, but no one missed the inflexion of iron beneath.

Sweyn shrugged. 'Whatever you say, Wulfrum.' He turned back to Elgiva. 'Even so, I have a reckoning to settle with this one.'

Elgiva struggled to her feet and, thrusting Ulric towards

one of the serving women, backed away. Sweyn came on. She turned and fled for the door.

She never reached it for in her blind flight she hurtled head-long into the warrior who had spoken before, stumbling against him, her hands slamming into chain mail as she tried frantically to push him aside. He stood like a rock. Strong hands closed round her arms, bringing her flight to a dead stop.

'Not so fast.'

The voice was low and even, the tone amused. Elgiva's gaze, currently level with a broad chest, travelled upwards, took in a powerful jaw and strong sensual mouth, parted now in a smile. She twisted in his hold, but her efforts made no impression except that, if anything, his smile widened.

'I'll take the wench, Wulfrum.' Elgiva's pursuer halted a few feet away. 'I'll teach the Saxon bitch to mend her ways and that right soon.'

He took another step forwards and Elgiva spun round, shrinking back involuntarily against Wulfrum for the expression in the other's eyes was terrifying.

'By Odin's blood, it looked to me as if she was teaching you a thing or two, Sweyn,' said a warrior, who stepped forwards to stand beside Wulfrum.

Amid the mirth and jests that greeted the remark Elgiva looked round and then froze. The speaker was a fearsome fig-ure, a giant of a man all bedaubed with blood, and a good head taller than any present. Grey mingled with the brown of his hair and beard, and his weathered face was seamed with lines, but his dark eyes were cool and shrewd. In one fist he held a great bloodstained axe.

'Ironfist is right!' called another. 'She's too hot for you, Sweyn!'

Sweyn glared. 'We'll see.'

'You are careless with your captives,' said Wulfrum. 'You let the wench escape. I caught her. She is mine now.'

Elgiva looked up in alarm, but Wulfrum's gaze was fixed on Sweyn. One hand rested on the hilt of his sword, the other on her shoulder.

'True enough,' said Olaf Ironfist. 'We all saw it.'

Murmurs of agreement greeted his words.

'Nay, Wulfrum. I say she is mine.'

'Not so. You let her get away.'

'Wulfrum speaks true,' said another.

A chorus of agreement greeted this. Sweyn darted angry looks to left and right, but could find no support. Elgiva held her breath, praying that he would not prevail, quailing to think of the revenge he would take. It was in her mind to run but, as if he read her thoughts, Wulfrum tightened his hold a fraction.

'Take the bitch, then,' replied Sweyn. ''Tis but a wench after all.'

'Aye, and there are plenty more,' said a voice from the doorway.

All heads turned in the direction of the speaker and the men fell silent, parting to let Lord Halfdan enter. Although only of average height, he was powerfully made and, like Wulfrum, carried with him an aura of authority. When he reached the group around his sword brother, he took in the scene at a glance.

'There are women and slaves aplenty in England and land enough for all.' His voice carried without effort across the room. 'Therefore there is no reason to quarrel.' He bent his gaze upon Elgiva, scrutinising her. 'A comely wench, Wulfrum. She will fetch a good price in the slave market, unless of course you plan to keep her.'

'I do intend to, my lord.'

'Well then, keep her close.'

'I shall, my lord.'

'Put the matter beyond dispute.' He glanced across the room at Sweyn. 'It seems to me she would make a fine Viking bride.'

'Never in a thousand years!'

The words were out before she could stop them and Elgiva felt her throat dry as both men turned their attention towards her. Wulfrum laughed and his arm closed about her, ignoring the resistance it encountered.

'A spirited piece,' said Halfdan, 'and impudent too. She must learn who her master is.'

'I will never acknowledge any Viking as my master!'

'Oh, I think you will—eventually.' He smiled down at her. Elgiva's stomach churned.

'She will learn,' said Wulfrum.

'From you?' Her tone was blatant disdain. 'I think not.'

'Aye, from me.' He took another look at the face turned up to his and all former reservations about marriage evaporated like mist in the sun as he made his decision. 'For, by all the gods, I will have you to wife.'

'I will never agree to that.'

'You have no choice, my beauty. You belong to me now.'

'No!'

'Oh, yes. Unless you would prefer to go with Sweyn?'

She swallowed hard, every fibre of her being wanting to spurn him, but when she looked upon the alternative, her heart was filled with loathing and contempt.

'Well?'

'I will not go with a coward and a child slayer!'

Wulfrum looked from Elgiva to Sweyn. 'The girl has chosen.'

'Then I wish you joy of her,' replied the other. The cool tone was at variance with the expression in his eyes.

It had no effect on Wulfrum. 'I shall find joy enough, I have no doubt.'

'Then it is settled.' Halfdan turned back to Wulfrum. 'You have done good service under the black-raven banner. From henceforth this hall and these lands shall be yours. The slaves too, to do with as you will.'

'You are generous, lord.'

'Aye, to those who serve me well.' He glanced at Elgiva. 'As for the girl, take her—she is a worthy prize.'

'Indeed she is.'

Elgiva glared at them. The Viking chief threw her a mocking smile.

'Your fate is clear, wench, and you had best submit.' He turned to the assembled warriors. 'Go down to the hall. Summon the others. I would speak to all.'

The men turned and began to troop out of the chamber, one carrying the screaming Hilda under his arm.

'No!' Elgiva fought the hold on her. 'Take your filthy hands off her!'

On the floor Osgifu began to stir. Wanting to go to her, Elgiva strove harder.

'Come,' said Wulfrum.

'I will not. Let *go* of me, you pirate scum.'

For answer she was thrown over a broad shoulder and, regardless of violent struggle and loud protest, was carried from the room. Only when they reached the hall did he set her down, but a strong arm about her waist prevented any chance of escape. Breathless and furious, Elgiva threw him a venomous glance and wished in vain for a sword to disembowel him with. Undismayed, Wulfrum grinned. Then his gaze moved on from her across the hall and she became aware that Halfdan was speaking.

'Tonight we shall feast in celebration of our victory. We shall rest here long enough to bury the dead and tend our wounded. Then we push on until all Northumbria is ours.'

A rousing cheer tore from the throats of the assembled men. He held up his fist for silence.

'Before we leave we shall witness the joining of Earl Wulfrum and this fair Saxon maid in marriage. She will bear him fine sons who shall inherit this land after him. Let it be known that the Norsemen are here to stay.'

Another cheer shook the rafters. Elgiva closed her eyes and

took a deep breath, trying to steady herself, determined to stifle the wail of terror rising in her throat. When she opened them again, it was to see Wulfrum watching her. Under that cool gaze her resolve stiffened.

'If I am to take a wife, I would have a name to lay to her,' he said.

For a moment she was tempted to refuse, but then common sense came to the fore. If she did not tell him, he might well beat it out of her.

'I am Elgiva, daughter of Egbert, and sister to Osric, late the thane of this manor.'

'Elgiva. The name is pleasing—as pleasing as the outward form.'

She felt herself grow warm beneath that keen scrutiny. Wulfrum smiled and removed his helmet. The face beneath might have been chiselled from rock, so strong were the planes of cheek and brow and jaw, the latter accentuated by a beard close trimmed and dark as the hair that fell over his shoulders. The eyes regarding her now were the startling blue of a summer sky. She saw their expression change and he reached out a hand, lightly touching the cut on her neck.

'You are hurt?'

'No. 'Tis merely a legacy of your brave friend, Sweyn.'

He ignored the gibe. 'How is it that you speak our tongue so well, Elgiva?'

'I was tutored in it by my nurse. Her mother was a Dane.'

'It is an advantage I had not thought to find.'

'An advantage indeed, for now I can call you the loathsome reptile you are and have you understand.'

Wulfrum was not so easily goaded. If anything, his enjoyment grew.

'You could say it in your own language if you wished.'

Hearing him speak the words in fluent Saxon, she was temporarily at a loss.

'I have learned much in my travels,' he explained.

Letting his hand drop a little, he brushed the top of her gown. Elgiva instinctively took a step back. The smile widened.

'Soon you will beg me to touch you, lady.'

'That I never will.'

'You say so now—you have yet to share my bed. May I say I look forward to it?'

Hot colour flooded her face and neck, but before she could reply Ironfist appeared beside them. He glanced down at her for a moment and then took her chin in one huge hand, turning her face to his.

'By all the gods, not bad.' He let his hand slide to her arm, encircling it easily. Then he looked at Wulfrum and grinned. 'She's a little slender for my taste, but to each his own.'

Elgiva glowered. Did these Viking clods think her a prize horse to be mauled thus?

'I'm glad you approve,' replied Wulfrum.

'Thor's beard, 'tis high time you took a wife. A man must breed sons.'

'I intend to.'

'I'll cut out your liver first!'

Both men looked down at her in silence for perhaps the length of two heartbeats. Then they laughed out loud.

'I do believe she'd try,' said Ironfist. 'You'll have trouble with this one, believe me. Are you equal to the challenge?'

'Trust me,' replied Wulfrum. He turned her to face him. 'Come, Elgiva. Let us seal our betrothal.'

Before she could anticipate him she found herself being forcibly kissed, drawn hard against him, held in strong arms and kept there at his pleasure in an embrace that left her breathless. No man had ever kissed her like that, a kiss that was both knowing and disturbingly assured. When he released her, the warmth of his mouth lingered on her lips. Her eyes blazed as she hit him, the crack ringing loud. There was a sharp intake of breath from others nearby and heads turned to watch the developments with keen interest. Not a man there but expected to see the mutinous wench laid at Wulfrum's feet with one blow of his fist. To their surprise he merely grinned.

'I suppose I deserved that.'

'You said it,' replied Ironfist.

Elgiva launched a second blow, but Wulfrum caught her wrist and held it. 'Now that's no way to behave towards your future husband.'

'I will never take you as my husband.'

'You will, Elgiva, believe me, and that soon enough.'

Before she could reply Lord Halfdan drew near.

'Come, that's enough romantic dalliance, Wulfrum. You can deal with the wench later. There is work to be done.'

'As you say, my lord.'

'Take her back to the upper chamber and put a guard on the door. Then join me outside.'

Wulfrum nodded and turned to Elgiva, ignoring her attempts to pull free.

'Don't you dare touch me!'

He raised an eyebrow and threw Olaf a speaking look. The hand round her wrist tightened and he strode to the stairs, drawing her after. Resistance was futile for his grip was like a vice. When they reached the upper chamber, he pushed her inside.

'Until later, Elgiva.'

Then he left her, pausing only to issue instructions to the guards outside the door. Breathless and shaking, she watched him go.

When she was satisfied that he really had gone, she turned and looked fearfully at the scene before her. The two children were still there, apparently unharmed and being comforted by frightened servants. With enormous relief Elgiva saw one of the latter help Osgifu to her feet. The older woman was still dazed. Her lip was cut and a dark bruise was already showing down her cheek. Hastening forwards Elgiva guided her to a chair before pouring a little water into a basin and gently bathing the cut lip. Osgifu sat very still throughout, though her hands trembled slightly in her lap. As she had no access to her medicine chest, there was relatively little that Elgiva could do for she had no arnica or salve to hand. The best she could manage was a cool compress on the bruised area of the face.

For some time neither woman spoke, each trying to come to terms with the terrible events that had shattered the peaceful course of their lives and changed it for ever. Eventually it was Osgifu who spoke first.

'Are you all right, child? They did not hurt you?'

'No, I am quite well.'

'Thank God for it. And the children?'

'Both well too.' Elgiva cast a glance at the open window and shuddered. If Sweyn had had his will, both her nephews would be dead, impaled on the spears of the horde beneath. It had been prevented. Remembering Wulfrum's ringing command, she could only be thankful he had appeared on the scene when he did. Seemingly he had no taste for the slaughter of babes, either. He had kept her out of Sweyn's clutches too. She knew that if he had not, the other would have exacted a terrible revenge for she had bested him and caused him to lose face before his comrades. It was not a thing he was likely to forgive. There could be no forgetting the expression in the cruel grey eyes.

Unable to read her mind, Osgifu guessed accurately enough the thoughts passing through it. She had been stunned for a short time, then disorientated, lying still until she could be sure of her bearings. None of the invaders had paid any further attention to her and she had heard much of the conversation in the room, listening with mounting concern for Elgiva. The girl turned to her now.

'Did you hear?'

'Aye, enough.'

Before they could speak further, Ulric broke free of the woman who had been holding him and came to them. Elgiva scooped him up and sat him on her knee, holding him close, speaking words of reassurance. The tears that had risen in her eyes unbidden were swiftly quelled. A show of weakness would not help anyone, least of all herself. If she hoped to survive the ordeals that lay ahead, she would need every ounce of courage she possessed. The trouble was that she had never felt so afraid in her life.

Chapter Three

Wulfrum rejoined Halfdan and Olaf Ironfist outside. His men were already moving among the bodies of the slain, collecting weapons and armour along with any valuables they might find. The fighting had been fierce while it lasted—the Saxons had put up a brave defence even though they were heavily outnumbered. He admired courage and it had been shown here this day. Their leaders had fallen and many besides, but a goodly number had been taken prisoner. They stood roped together under heavy guard. From their sullen expressions he knew them unbowed, though they feared for their lives even now. It was well. It meant they would do nothing foolish. He had no intention of shedding any more blood for he would need able hands to work these lands in future. However, it would not hurt his cause to leave them in doubt a while longer.

Wulfrum turned away from the prisoners and met the keen gaze of his sword brother. Halfdan lowered his voice.

'Hold this place well, brother. Lying as it does on the road to the north, it is of strategic importance to us.'

'You may depend on it.'

'I know it.' Halfdan clapped him on the shoulder. 'I could

think of no better hands to leave it in. Even so, it will keep you busy. The place seems to be strangely neglected.'

Wulfrum glanced around. 'It looks to have seen more prosperous days, but they will come again, I promise you.'

'Why would any man worthy of the name allow his holdings to fall into such disrepair?'

'I know not.'

'Unless of course there was no man in view,' said Halfdan, his tone thoughtful.

'Perhaps, yet the Saxons were organised and fought valiantly. It suggests a leader, does it not?'

'Belike he fell in the fighting, then.'

'Most likely. The Saxon losses were heavy. I shall make enquiries.'

Before further conjecture was possible they were interrupted by the approach of two of their fellow Danes, dragging a captive with them. The man's hands were bound before him and his face beneath a layer of grime was ashen. From the shaven crown and long robe Wulfrum recognised one of the Christian priests. He glanced once at Halfdan and then watched in silence as the trio came to a halt before them.

'Look what we found, my lord.' The guard's lip curled as he glanced at the prisoner. 'The craven swine was hiding in the barn.'

'Hiding, eh?' Halfdan's expression mirrored the guard's as he looked the priest over. 'Scarcely surprising, I suppose. He's a poor specimen by the look of him. Must be fifty if he's a day.' He turned to Wulfrum. 'What do you want to do with him? Shall we have him spitted and roasted like an ox? Or shall we flay him and nail his hide to the door of his accursed church?'

'Beg pardon, my lord,' said the guard, 'but we burnt the church down.'

Halfdan followed his gaze towards a distant plume of thick dark smoke. 'Ah, yes, so we did. Pity. We'll spit him, then.'

Grinning, the men moved to obey.

Wulfrum held up a hand. 'No, not yet. He may prove to be of use.' He fixed his gaze on the trembling form. 'How are you called, priest?'

'Father Willibald, my lord.'

Halfdan stared at the earl in disbelief. 'You want this shaven ass?'

'Aye, I do.'

'Very well, as you will. Put him with the others, then.'

With ill-concealed disappointment the guards dragged the priest away.

Halfdan watched them a moment before turning back to his companion.

'Have some of your men search the forest hereabouts. 'Tis likely some of the serfs have taken refuge there. We should not lose valuable slaves thus. Besides, if left on the loose, they may foment trouble later.'

Wulfrum nodded for it had been his thought also. 'It shall be done, my lord. If any are hiding, they will be found and brought back.'

'Meantime, let the injured be carried into the hall and treated. There must be those among the Saxon women versed in the knowledge of healing. They must be identified and put to work.'

'It should be easy enough. I'll wager that priest will know.'

Wulfrum was right. Two minutes was all he needed to elicit the relevant information. Hearing the names, he hid a smile. It seemed that his beautiful future bride had other talents to her credit. He strode back to the hall and collared one of his men.

'Have the guards bring the Lady Elgiva down here,' he ordered. 'And the woman called Osgifu.'

Wulfrum seated himself casually on the edge of the long table and waited. A few minutes later the guards reappeared, ushering the two women in front of them. They came to a halt a few feet away, eyeing him warily.

'I'm told you have skill in healing,' he said without pre-amble. 'You will help to tend the injured.'

He saw the flash of defiance in Elgiva's eyes, but he was not alone; her companion put a gentle hand on her arm and the two exchanged looks. Then the older woman spoke.

'We will do so, lord.' She paused. 'I will need my things.'

'Fetch them.' Wulfrum turned to one of the guards. 'Go with her.' Then he turned his attention back to Elgiva, who was regarding him with a distinctly hostile gaze. He let his glance travel the length of her and saw her bridle in an instant. 'Do not think of trying any tricks, Elgiva.'

'Do you think I would harm injured men? I have a greater regard for human life.'

'Then give them all tending.'

'Does that include Saxon, as well as Dane?'

'Of course. Slaves are of value to me too.'

'A pity, then, that you have slain so many.'

'The fortunes of war.' He paused, smiling faintly. 'They could always have surrendered.'

'To a life of slavery? You cannot seriously think so.'

'I don't. I merely offer it as a possibility.'

The amber eyes blazed, but her anger appeared to leave him unmoved. A few moments later Osgifu returned with the box that held her herbs and potions. She eyed Wulfrum and hesitated.

'Well?' he asked.

'I will need hot water and clean cloths too,' she said, 'and some help to bring pallets for the injured.'

He glanced at the guard standing nearby. 'Arrange it.'

The man nodded and went with Osgifu to do his bidding. Wulfrum turned back to Elgiva, who had made no move to obey. He raised an eyebrow and saw her chin come up. She lingered a moment more and then, in her own good time, turned away. Had she seen the glint in his eyes she might have made more haste for an instant later the flat of Wulfrum's sword caught her hard across the buttocks. With a gasp of indignation, she spun round.

'Defy me again, wench, and you go across my knee.'

The words were quietly spoken, but, looking at that imperturbable expression, Elgiva was left in no doubt he meant it. She was also aware of several grinning faces around them from those who had witnessed the little scene, no doubt hoping for further entertainment at her expense. For a moment she hesitated, caught between anger and indecision. Then Wulfrum stood up and took a pace towards her. Elgiva fled.

The afternoon was wearing on when the Viking hunters returned with some dozen bound captives, those who had fled when defeat became inevitable. Some were wounded, all dirty and dishevelled. Wulfrum surveyed them for a moment and then turned to Ceolnoth, who had formed one of the hunting party.

'These were all you found?'

'Aye, my lord.'

'Very well. Keep them apart from the rest. I'll deal with them later. Meanwhile, take some of the women to the kitchens. They can start preparing the food. Lord Halfdan and his earls will be hungry tonight. See to it.'

'Yes, lord.'

Ceolnoth swung down off his horse and moved towards the captive women, who eyed him with fear. Enlisting the aid of a warrior companion, he cut half a dozen free, including the girl, Hilda. Wulfrum noted the young man's gaze lingered far longer on her than on the rest, and he smiled to himself. It seemed he was not the only one to have an eye for a comely Saxon wench. He watched as the women were taken off towards the hall. Then his gaze went to the upper storey of the building and in his mind's eye he saw again the chamber where he had first met Elgiva. It was a fine room. Henceforth it would be his, as would she. Their union would set the seal of his ownership on these lands and these people. Whether they liked it or not, the Danes were here to stay.

He had no doubt as to Elgiva's mind on the matter. In truth, she was a spirited piece as Lord Halfdan had said, and brave too. Her defiance of Sweyn demonstrated that beyond doubt. Not that he blamed the man for wanting her. She was a rare beauty and it must have cost him a pang to lose her so soon. Wulfrum had not forgotten the look in his eyes when the girl had spurned him, nor again when Wulfrum claimed her for his own. If Ironfist and the others had not been there, Sweyn might have disputed the matter further. Even if he had, Wulfrum knew he would have fought to keep her for, from the moment he set eyes on the wench, he knew he wanted her for himself. Wanted her and intended to have her. Halfdan had seen it too. It was why he had urged Wulfrum to take her to wife and settle the matter once and for all. Wulfrum knew that a week ago he would have dismissed the suggestion out of hand. Today he had embraced it. After all, he was five and twenty and should have taken a bride long since. He would have if he'd ever found one he wanted. It had seemed a hopeless quest. That situation had just changed. Besides, he could think of many a worse fate to befall a man. Recalling the kiss he had stolen from Elgiva earlier, he grinned. If looks could kill, he knew he'd be a dead man now. Too bad—he was determined that kiss would be the first of many. Let her fight him tooth and nail; it would avail her naught. She would yield in the end. He would strip away her defences as he intended to strip away her clothes.

'My lord?'

Jolted back to the present, Wulfrum focused his attention on the man before him.

'Well?'

'Lord Halfdan requests your presence in the hall.'

'I will come.'

* * *

When he returned, he made his report and then looked about him with curiosity. He could see that the Saxon healers had not been idle. They had organised matters so that those men who had been badly injured had been lifted onto makeshift pallets and, having been tended, were watched over now by some of the serfs. Elgiva and her companion continued on to see to the walking wounded, of whom there was a goodly number.

'Those women know what they are about,' observed Halfdan, noting the direction of Wulfrum's gaze. 'It is useful to have experienced healers to call on. They will serve you well.'

He turned aside then to speak to one of his men, leaving Wulfrum free to observe. Across the hall he could see Elgiva with her latest patient, bandaging his arm. It seemed that Halfdan was right—she worked with assurance, her hands moving swiftly and competently about their task. From her hands he let his gaze travel on across the graceful curves of her figure, from the swelling bosom and narrow waist to the gently flaring hips. A thick golden braid hung down her back, though several tendrils of hair had escaped to curl about her neck and cheek. Just then her profile was towards him and he missed nothing of the delicate bone structure beneath that flawless skin. She was lovely, a prize indeed. As if sensing herself watched, she turned her head and looked round, perceiving him immediately. He saw the dainty chin tilt upwards before she looked away, and smiled to himself. She was safe enough for now; there were many more wounds to stanch and bind and he had still many matters to attend to, including a trip to the Danish encampment.

'After that, my lady,' he murmured, 'we shall see.'

Elgiva and Osgifu worked on. It was late in the day when the last of the wounded were carried in. Among them was

Aylwin, his face waxen beneath the dirt and gore. He had taken a deep sword thrust in the side and his tunic was dark with blood, yet a faint pulse testified that he lived. Swiftly they cut away the tunic and the shirt beneath. The wound gaped, wide and ugly, but it looked clean. Several superficial cuts marked his arms and livid bruises attested to the ferocity of the fighting. Elgiva set to work to stanch the bleeding. As she did so a shadow fell across them and she glanced up. Her heart skipped a beat to see Halfdan standing there. He surveyed the injured man a moment and then the pile of discarded clothing. Even soiled, it could never pass for the garb of a peasant.

'Who is he?'

Elgiva felt her throat dry. Then she heard Osgifu speak.

'This is Lord Aylwin.'

'A Saxon lord.' Halfdan looked from her to Elgiva. 'Your father, perhaps?'

'No. My father is dead.'

'Ah, your husband, then?' His hand moved to his sword hilt.

Elgiva bit back a cry of alarm, her mind racing. If Halfdan's earl intended to marry her as he had said, then she could not have a husband living. If he thought that the case, he would rectify the matter.

'He is not my husband, but I am betrothed to him.'

The Viking relaxed his grip on the sword and he laughed. 'Not any more.'

As she watched him walk away Elgiva let out the breath she had unconsciously been holding. Exchanging a brief glance with Osgifu, she set to work again with trembling hands to stanch the wound and bind it. She wondered if Aylwin would last the night and thought it unlikely. It might be better if he did die. The alternative was a life of slavery beneath the Viking yoke, something he would never submit to. Nor would he suffer another man to take his betrothed without a fight. Elgiva swallowed hard. Aylwin had been allowed to live for now, but for how much longer?

* * *

She and Osgifu worked until all had been attended to. The sun was going down before they finished and both women were exceedingly weary. Elgiva wondered if she would ever get the stink of blood and death from her nostrils. Every part of her ached from the effort of bending or stretching and her gown was soiled with blood and dirt. She retired with Osgifu to the women's bower and, having assured herself that the children were safe in the hands of one of the older women, she turned her attention to herself, bathing her hands and face in an attempt to cleanse away the memory of the past hours.

'Oh, Gifu, so many good men slain.'

The battle today had been a rout in the end despite all the Saxons had been able to do. No one could have withstood the invaders for long. Now they were the masters here and every last Saxon soul who survived was in their power. One taste of it was enough to strike terror into the heart.

'Aye, yet not all our warriors fell in the battle. The Vikings have already sent men out to search for fugitives, but they will not find them all.'

'I fear it will be too late to be of help here.' Elgiva met her gaze, unaware of the desperation in her own eyes as, unbidden, the memory of a man's face intruded into her thoughts, a strong, chiselled face and disconcerting blue eyes. She forced it down and strove against rising panic. She would not wed the Viking.

Osgifu broke into her thoughts. 'The forest is large and there are many places of concealment.'

'Aye, there are for those who know its secrets.'

Elgiva moved away as, through the haze of fear and desperation, the germ of an idea formed in her mind. She knew the forest paths well for, with Osgifu, she was used to spending time there, gathering the plants she needed for her medicines. She could not wait to see if Aylwin survived, if there would ever be a Saxon uprising. All that would take time, and time was the one thing she didn't have. Elgiva found suddenly that she was shivering with delayed reaction and the atmosphere seemed stifling. She moved to the doorway.

The place seemed quieter now—the evening meal was preparing in the hall and beyond the palisade the majority of the Viking host had encamped for the duration. The smoke from their cooking fires was already rising into the evening air. The women's bower was situated behind the hall where over the years various rooms had been added according to need. Looking around now, Elgiva could see the bodies of the slain lying where they had fallen and beyond them a few of Halfdan's men moving around outside stables and barn. However, there seemed to be no one at the gate just then and the broken timbers hung wide. Not far away the forest beckoned. Elgiva bit her lip. If she could somehow reach the gate without being spotted, there might be a chance of reaching the trees. The Viking encampment lay in the opposite direction and, while it would mean skirting the edge of the village, she could be fairly certain no Saxon would give her away. Once in the forest she would stand a reasonable chance of eluding pursuit. What she would do then she had no clear idea, but it seemed to her that there must be Saxons who had escaped the Viking host. If there were enough of them, they might return by stealth and put the invaders to the sword in their turn. Failing that, she might be able to find help elsewhere in those lands where the Danes held no sway. Anything was better than remaining here to become the bride of a conqueror.

Looking round the room, she saw the empty bucket and with it the idea. A trip to the well would serve as a plausible excuse for leaving the bower. She made for the door.

'What are you doing?' Osgifu looked at her in concern.

'I can't stay here, Gifu.'

'Elgiva, think.'

'I have thought. I will not do what they want.'

'If you run, they will find you and bring you back. These men are ruthless. Who knows what punishment they may inflict?'

'It cannot be worse than what they're already planning.'

'Don't do it, I beg you.'

'I will not stay here to be married off to a Viking warlord. I must get help. You said yourself that some of our men have fled into the forest. I will find them.'

'Elgiva, wait!'

The words fell on empty air for Elgiva was already heading for the well. Picking her way among the bodies all around, she tried to ignore the rising stench and darted covert glances all about her, fearing at every moment to hear someone raise the alarm. However, no one did challenge her and she reached the well a short time later. Putting down the bucket, she took another furtive look around but could still see no one at the gate. Summoning all her courage, Elgiva made towards it at a steady pace, not wishing to draw eyes her way by careless haste. At every step her heart hammered; she expected at each moment to hear the shouted challenge and the sound of pursuit. It never came and she reached the shattered entry. Cautiously she walked through the gateway and looked about her. The way was clear. Picking up her skirts, she ran, sprinting across the open ground betwixt her and the edge of the trees, ignoring everything but the need to escape and put as much distance as possible between herself and Ravenswood. Focused on her goal, she did not see the horseman approaching fast at an oblique angle to cut off her route.

By the time she heard the thudding hoofbeats, he was much closer. One horrified glance over her shoulder revealed the approaching danger in a brief impression of a great black horse and the warrior who rode it. Elgiva summoned every remaining vestige of energy and put on a last desperate spurt. The trees were no more than a hundred yards away now. If she could but reach them, she would have a chance of escape. Behind her the hoofbeats sounded louder, thudding in her ears like the sound of her own heartbeat as she willed herself on. It was a vain effort. The rider leaned down and a strong arm reached out and swept her off her feet. Elgiva shrieked as she was thrown face down over the front of the saddle, held firmly across the rider's knees. For some further distance every bone in her body was jarred before the horseman reined to a halt. Fury and fright vied for supremacy as she fought to recover her breath. Then she heard a familiar voice.

'Whither away, Elgiva?'

Her stomach lurched. Wulfrum! Frantically she strove to push herself upright, but a firm hand between her shoulders kept her where she was, his well-trained mount standing like a rock the while.

'Let go of me, you clod. You Danish oaf.'

'Clod? Danish oaf? These are grave insults indeed.' Wulfrum regarded his struggling captive with a keen eye. 'It seems to me that you need to learn better manners.'

'You have the nerve to lecture me about manners, barbarian?'

'I think you were not attending to me earlier, wench, for I warned you what would happen if you defied me again.'

Suddenly she did recall the words and her face grew hotter as she divined his meaning and realised the extreme vulnerability of her present position.

'You wouldn't dare.'

'Is that so?'

The flat of his hand came down hard, eliciting a yelp of indignation and further futile struggles.

'Let me go, you bastard! You swine! Let me go!'

It was an unfortunate choice of words for half a dozen sharp whacks ensued. Elgiva yelled in rage but bit back any further insults, knowing he would avenge himself if she uttered them.

'You're not going anywhere,' was the pleasant rejoinder. 'You belong to me now and I will hold what is mine.'

Fuming, she forgot her former resolve in the face of this breathtaking arrogance. 'I will never belong to you, you loathsome Viking filth.'

That last was a mistake—the hand descended several times more and much harder. Elgiva gasped.

'Anything more?' he asked. 'I can keep this up indefinitely if you can.'

Indeed there were plenty more things she could have found to say, chiefly concerning his lowly birth, probable ancestry and certain destination in the hereafter, but with a monumental effort she forced them back. Only a very small exhalation of breath escaped, a sound that reminded him of an infuriated kitten. Wulfrum waited a moment, but there was nothing more. His lips curved in a sardonic smile; touching his horse with his heels, he let it move forwards at a walk. Elgiva gritted her teeth in helpless fury as they headed back towards Ravenswood and a dreadful suspicion grew that his retribution wasn't over yet.

In this she was right. Wulfrum took his time about the return journey, knowing full well the helpless ire of his captive and her present discomfort. He had been visiting the Viking encampment earlier and was returning when he caught sight of the running figure heading for the forest. He had recognised her at once and knew a bid for freedom when he saw it. He also knew she must not be allowed to get away. How she had got so far was a mystery, one for which the guards would get a roasting later. As for Elgiva, she would discover that it did not pay to disobey him. Right now he knew she was smarting, as much from the humiliation as from his hand. It had been most tempting to put all his strength behind it and beat her soundly, but he had resisted the notion and tempered the punishment.

As it was, she would think twice before crossing him again. Like all the Saxons she would learn that rebellion came at a price.

In consequence Elgiva was held across the saddle bow all the way back to the outer door of the women's bower. If she had thought then he would let her slide from the saddle and slink indoors, she was mistaken for Wulfrum dismounted first and dragged her off the horse after. Tucking her under one arm, he carried her inside in another casual and humiliating demonstration of superior strength. When at last he set her down she was hot and breathless and, to Wulfrum's eyes, most attractively dishevelled, for the golden mane had escaped its braid and fell in tumbled curls about her shoulders.

Furious, Elgiva glared up at him, wishing anew for a sword to cut the arrogant brute down to size. However, he was very big and to her cost she knew his strength. She hated to think what other retribution he might take if she angered him further for she was uncomfortably aware of the bed on the far side of the room and of the dimming light and of his dangerous proximity.

It was not hard to discern some of her thought but, far from being perturbed in any way, Wulfrum smiled, thinking that anger heightened her beauty for those wonderful eyes held a distinctly militant light. He was sorely tempted to take her in his arms and kiss her again, but he suspected that if he did, he would not be able to stop there. Better to let her think about what had happened, to understand the futility of attempting to escape him. She was no fool and the lesson would be well learned. Besides, time was on his side now.

For the space of several heartbeats they faced each other thus. Then, to her inexpressible relief, he moved towards the door, pausing when he reached it.

'You will remain here until I say otherwise. I should perhaps point out that there will be a guard outside from now on.'

He left her then, closing the door behind him. Weak with relief, Elgiva collapsed against it, listening with thumping heart to the muffled hoof falls as he rode away.

Chapter Four

In the days following an atmosphere of deep gloom hung over Ravenswood along with the stench of death and corruption. Carrion birds flapped among the bodies or perched in readiness on the palisade as the demoralised Saxons, with an air of bitter resignation, went about the business of digging graves. Since the church had been burned and the priest taken prisoner there was little chance that he might bless the graves, a grievous lack that added to the pain of loss. The living had perforce to be content with murmured prayers and the laying of flowers.

Osgifu and Elgiva helped with the laying out of the dead, working in silence and in grief for the lives snuffed out so soon. Aylwin lived yet, though he was much weakened from loss of blood. The Vikings kept a close watch, but they made no move to harm him. Elgiva did what she could for him, but there were many others requiring her attention too, and her time was spent in tending the wounded, changing dressings, applying salves and balms, dispensing the medicines that dulled pain. Some men were beyond help and died; others like Aylwin clung desperately to life. His troubled gaze followed Elgiva as she moved among her patients, an attention that had not gone unnoticed.

Waiting until Elgiva was not by, Wulfrum made his way towards the pallet where the Saxon lay, regarding him dispassionately. He made no attempt to sit, thus putting the other at an added disadvantage by compelling him to look up at his visitor. At first neither man spoke. Then Wulfrum broke the silence.

'Your wound heals?'

'It heals.'

'Elgiva is skilled.'

At the mention of her name, the older man's eyes narrowed and his hand clenched at his side.

'What is it you wish to say?'

'That I know of your former betrothal to her...' Wulfrum paused '...a betrothal you would now do well to forget.'

'Elgiva is mine.'

'Not so. She belongs to me, as does this hall and these lands, and I shall take her to wife.'

'By God, you shall not!' The injured man started up, then winced as his wound protested.

Watching him fall back upon the pallet, Wulfrum raised an eyebrow. 'Indeed? And how will you prevent it?'

Aylwin remained silent, knowing too well the futility of any reply he might make. More than anything he wanted to be left alone, but his tormentor lingered still.

'You should have wed her when you had the chance.'

'Would that I had.' Aylwin regarded him with hatred. 'But she asked me to observe a decent period of mourning for her brother. I would not expect you to understand, Viking.'

Wulfrum laughed. 'I think I understand. The lady was not so keen as you to marry.'

Aylwin reddened for the words had touched a nerve. The same thought had occurred to him too.

'You should be thankful—if you had married her, you would be dead now,' the other went on, 'for I would still have taken her from you. As it is, your claims on her are void and you had best accept it.'

'Never!' The word exploded between them.

Wulfrum smiled and, throwing the Saxon one last contemptuous look, walked away.

Two days later Aylwin disappeared. At first no one thought it significant. A man so badly wounded could not have gone far. However, an exhaustive search revealed nothing. Elgiva heard the news with deep concern. Even if he escaped as far as the forest, Aylwin's weakened condition made him ill suited to such rough living and, without careful tending, he might well die. Angered that so prestigious a prisoner had slipped through their hands, the Vikings questioned everyone who had contact with him, including Elgiva and Osgifu.

Seeing their captors so disturbed, Elgiva knew only intense satisfaction. When Wulfrum questioned her, she was able to say with perfect truth that she knew nothing of the matter. However, she was unable to hide her feelings with complete success, a fact that he did not fail to note.

'He could not have gone far alone. He must have had help.'

'That is possible, lord,' she replied.

'Who was it?'

'I don't know.'

'But you wouldn't tell me if you did know.'

'No.'

It was a reply that was both honest and impudent in equal measure. With an effort, he curbed the urge to seize and shake her soundly. For all that air of quiet calm, the vixen was enjoying this. He didn't think for a moment that she was personally responsible for Aylwin's escape—she was under guard in the women's bower at night—but her relief when they failed to find him had been quite evident. Perhaps she wasn't as indifferent to the Saxon as he had first believed. The thought did nothing to improve his temper and he dismissed her before he did something he might later regret.

Relieved to be out of that unnerving presence, Elgiva returned to her work among the injured, conscious the while of the brooding blue gaze that watched her every move. The Viking would not find Aylwin now, she was sure of it. If he died, his friends would bury him in secret: if he lived, they would get him away to a place of greater safety—somewhere the Danes held no sway. The thought filled her with fierce pleasure and only with difficulty could she hide her elation. She might not have loved Aylwin, but she did rejoice in his freedom.

Unwilling to dwell too long on the chances of her former betrothed, Elgiva put her mind to more immediately pressing matters. Chief of these was the welfare of her nephews. After their recent treatment at the hands of the invaders she kept a watchful eye on them. Pybba was too young to know how near he could have been to death but, for some days after the coming of the Vikings, Ulric clung to Hilda, his nursemaid, staring wide-eyed and silent from behind her skirts if any of the men appeared. Elgiva, touched by his vulnerability, would take him on her knee and sing to him and he would snuggle against her, seeking her warmth and gentleness. With her and Hilda he knew he was safe.

In spite of her other responsibilities Elgiva spent time each day with the children. She also kept an eye on Hilda for the girl had suffered at the hands of the conquerors. In particular the young man called Ceolnoth sought her out as a companion for his bed. All her struggles and protests had availed her nothing. Elgiva knew there was nothing she could say to soothe that hurt and the girl's strained expression was a cruel reminder of the fate she too might have suffered had their positions been reversed.

Thus far Wulfrum had not intruded into the nursery. It was women's work and he was content to leave it so, and since he had become Lord of Ravenswood none of his men had laid a hand on any child, noble or base. However, one morning as he took a short cut through the rear of the hall, he was arrested by the sound of women's laughter and the playful squealing of a child. Moving towards the source of the noise, he paused in the doorway. Elgiva was kneeling on the floor. In front of her the oldest child was lying on the rug, laughing and giggling as she tickled his ribs. Across the room the girl Hilda watched and smiled from her place beside the baby's crib. It was a scene of innocent delight so different from anything he had known that Wulfrum was drawn and held in spite of himself. This was an Elgiva he had never seen, laughing and relaxed as though without a care in the world. The children were her nephews, but she tended them as though they were her own, with a gentle and loving hand. Watching, he smiled unawares as a new dimension opened up before him. One day he would have sons. His gaze warmed as it rested on his future wife. It would be good to have children with Elgiva. His smile grew rueful. One day.

Though he made no movement or sound, some instinct warned the occupants of the room that they were not alone. It was Hilda who saw him first. Her smile faded and a look of fear replaced it. Elgiva looked up and followed the direction of her gaze. Then she too froze. The child stared at him wide-eyed. In a moment the atmosphere in the room changed and became tense. He saw Elgiva rise and draw the child close.

'My lord?' The tone was anxious, even wary.

He surveyed her for a moment in silence, wanting to speak, but not knowing what to say. Then, 'The children are well?'

'They are well,' she replied.

'Good.' He paused, then glanced at the toddler. 'The boy is afraid.'

'Has he no cause?'

'None.' He met and held her gaze for a moment. 'He shall not be harmed if I have power to prevent it. Please believe that.'

Elgiva stared at him in surprise, but said nothing for her

heart was unaccountably full. His expression and his words had
seemed sincere. His former actions too had prevented harm
coming to the children. He was their enemy but, perversely, in
that moment she wanted to trust him in this.

Unable to follow her thought and seeing she remained silent,
Wulfrum felt suddenly awkward. What did he expect her to
say? That she believed him? Trusted the children to his care?
Aware of how ridiculous a notion that was, he turned abruptly
away. Trust could not be commanded, it had to be earned; thus
far, he could see he had done little to earn hers.

As he left the hall, the memory of the scene stayed with him.
It stayed throughout the morning as he supervised the work of
the serfs. He could not forget the fear of Hilda and the child
when they saw him or Elgiva's wariness. What did they take
him for? Then he remembered Sweyn and what he had been
about to do before he was stopped. Wulfrum sighed. True
enough, the child had cause to be afraid and the women too. It
would not be easy to overcome it, either, but Sweyn would soon
be gone and then they might learn there was nothing to fear
from him or his men. While he lived no harm should come to
them. He was their lord and their protection was his respon-
sibility. For the first time he began to feel its weight.

It had taken several days to bury the dead for goodly
numbers had fallen on both sides, but eventually it was done.
Elgiva stood by the Saxon graves a while and said her own
silent prayers since Father Willibald had not been permitted to
officiate at the burials or to say a mass for the souls of the dead.
To her surprise Earl Wulfrum had raised no objection to her attending the funerals or made any attempt to interfere. In any
case, his men were taking care of their own dead. A few of the
Viking warriors stood at a distance watching the events with a
careful eye, their presence a reminder of the new order.

A cold breeze stirred the branches of the forest trees around and Elgiva shivered, drawing her mantle closer, fighting down the fear in the pit of her stomach. Like a leaf swept along on the current of a stream, she had no control over the events that would shape her future. Everything she had known and loved was gone as though in a past life. True enough, she thought, she had been someone else then. And now? Now she was a prisoner like all the rest, little better than a slave. Not quite, she amended. Ever since Wulfrum had announced his intention to marry, his men had regarded her as his domain. She had not been troubled or molested in any way, though they looked their fill whenever she appeared. Neither had a hand been raised to Osgifu, who came and went to her mistress's bower without hindrance. To the best of her knowledge, the earl's promise that there should be no more killing had been kept; now most of the Saxons serfs had been put to work, albeit under the watchful eyes of their conquerors. Only the fugitives rounded up in the forest remained chained and under guard. Rumours abounded as to their eventual fate, though Elgiva had been cautiously optimistic.

'Surely he will not kill them—he has need of them to work the land and tend the stock.'

Osgifu had been more sceptical. 'He doesn't need to kill them to make an example of them.'

However, a day went by and another and nothing happened, but each time the Saxons had looked at the prisoners they had felt only deep disquiet for the reputation of the Danes went before them and had been well earned. Since their coming all the certainties of life had vanished, leaving only a dread of tomorrow.

Recalling that conversation with Osgifu, Elgiva wondered if her optimism had not been misplaced. She drew in a deep breath. Whatever the Danes decided, the prisoners would have no choice but to obey. Like the rest she had been kept under guard but she had been grateful for her relative isolation, not wishing to have any greater contact with the conquerors than was absolutely necessary. Now, outdoors again, she was restless, and her gaze went beyond the burying ground to the forest. Its quiet glades and green solitudes beckoned, inviting and forbidden, particularly after the confinement of the bower. It recalled happier days when she had accompanied her father and brother on the chase; recalled the sheer exhilaration of the gallop, the power of the horse beneath her. Thinking of the game little mare in the stables, Elgiva knew that was something else forbidden to her now.

Forcing down her resentment and her anger, she laid her flowers on the graves. All around her groups of people began to disperse, mostly in silence, and sorrow hung heavy in the air. Elgiva followed, wrapped in her own thoughts. Then she became aware that two of the Saxons had been keeping pace with her and glanced up to see Leofwine, the smith, and Elfric, his son. The smith shot her a swift glance.

'My lady, we must speak with you.'

Elgiva nodded discreetly, aware that she was watched. 'What is it, Leofwine?'

'My lady, there are men hiding in the forest, in the cave by the old dolmen stones.'

Elgiva caught her breath. 'How many?'

'Two.'

'They must get away. Why do they linger?'

'One is hurt, lady. My brother, Hunfirth. He has a bad wound in his side and an arrow lodged in his shoulder. Our cousin, Brekka, got him away after the battle and hid him in the cave. I urged him to save himself, but he will not leave Hunfirth in such sore case. We have kept them supplied with food, but I fear my brother will die unless he can get proper tending.'

Elgiva bit her lip. She was watched day and night and so was Osgifu. If they tried to get out, they would likely lead the earl's men straight to the hiding place. Yet they could not stand by and let men die.

'I will think of something, Leofwine, I promise. When I do,
I will send word with Osgifu.'

'God bless you, my lady.'

'I think we all have need of blessing,' she replied.

He nodded and walked away, unwilling to draw any unne-
cessary attention. Elgiva continued on. Her path led through the
hamlet, or what was left of it. The smell of charred wood lingered still and everywhere was evidence of destruction in the
piles of ash and blackened skeletons of burned-out dwellings.
Hard by stood the sombre ruins of the church. At intervals dark
patches stained the turf, marking the places where men had
fallen and died. Where once a thriving village had stood, all
around was a scene of desolation and death. Now it looked as
though more men would die. Suddenly she was determined that
it must be prevented. She must speak to Osgifu as soon as possible.

She came at length to the hall where the shattered portal still
hung askew, another painful symbol of defeat, and hurried on.
It was safer by far to walk round than through for more of
Wulfrum's men were about and she had no wish to draw their
attention. Every thought of the Viking marauders was anathema.
By day Halfdan sent out groups of men to hunt for fugitive
Saxons to return to their new master and for game, for such a
large force must be fed, the men demanding meat to supplement
what they had stolen on their passage through the countryside.
By night they feasted. The great hall rang with the sound of their
laughter and jesting over flowing mead horns. Then the female
serfs faced another fear as the thoughts of the men turned from
fighting to other things. She shuddered, the chill of one realising all too well that she lived on borrowed time.

Hastening towards the bower, so engrossed in thought, she
failed to notice the man standing nearby. She was almost on
him before she saw him and stopped short with a sharp intake
of breath when she recognised the cruel predatory smile.

Sweyn's gaze travelled over her appreciatively. Elgiva regarded him with coldness and said no word, but as she made to pass him, he blocked her way.

'Not so fast, wench.'

He lifted a hand towards her, but she stepped out of reach, her eyes raking him with scorn.

'Get out of my way.'

His thin lips twisted in a smile, but it never reached his eyes. 'Still high and mighty, Elgiva?'

'Let me pass.'

'We have some unfinished business, you and I.'

Elgiva's heart beat faster but she lifted her chin and stared him down.

'You and I have no business of any kind.'

'You think so?'

She tried again to pass him, but this time he held her arm to prevent it. His fingers dug into her flesh as he drew her closer. Wincing, Elgiva shrank back. His grip tightened and he smiled.

'Afraid, my lady?'

'You flatter yourself.'

'Do I so?'

'Let go of me, oaf.'

'You heard the lady,' said a voice behind them.

Both of them turned in surprise to see an imposing figure standing there, a grizzled giant carrying an axe. He surveyed them calmly enough, but his expression was utterly uncompromising. Elgiva had not thought ever to be thankful for the presence of a Viking, but now she breathed a sigh of relief. However, Sweyn was unwilling to give up his prey so easily.

'Mind your own business, Ironfist.'

'This is my business. The woman belongs to Wulfrum. Now let her go.'

For a few moments his steady gaze held that of Sweyn. The cold eyes spoke of anger, but he released his hold on her arm.

'You should return to your bower, lady,' said Ironfist.

Elgiva wasn't about to argue. Throwing him a brief glance, she hastened away, aware that both men watched her departure. She had scarcely taken a dozen paces when another familiar figure hove into sight. Startled, she checked mid-stride, unable to go forwards or back.

Wulfrum surveyed her in surprise, noting her evident unease, and then glanced over her shoulder towards Ironfist and Sweyn, now some yards distant. The berserker threw him a mocking smile and then turned and strolled away. The giant watched him go.

Wulfrum frowned and his gaze returned to the girl, looking closer now. 'Are you all right, Elgiva? Has Sweyn been bothering you?'

Her face, pale before, turned a warmer shade. 'No.'

'You're a poor liar, my lady. What happened?'

'It was nothing. Hot air.'

'Did he lay hands on you?'

Elgiva forced herself to meet his eye. The last thing she needed now was a confrontation between Wulfrum and Sweyn. 'Ironfist dealt with it, my lord.'

'Did he so?'

'Please…it was nothing.'

'I'll decide that.'

'Hasn't there been enough strife already?' The words came out with unwonted force. She drew a deep breath. 'I beg you, let there be no more of it.'

He heard the distress in her voice, but it was the power of those amber eyes that arrested him most. In them he read anxiety and distrust. Did she fear that he might lay the blame at her door? Knowing what Sweyn was capable of and knowing of Elgiva's detestation of him, Wulfrum did not think for a moment that she would have anything to do with the man. Whatever had occurred had shaken her, but it was clear she didn't

want him to pursue the matter and that to do so would add to
her distress. He was loath to do that. Rather he wanted to say
something to alleviate it, but the situation was new to him and
he found himself at a loss. Better to let the matter lie, at least
as far as she was concerned. He could always speak to Ironfist
later.

'It is not safe to be abroad. Go back to the bower, Elgiva,
and stay there.'

For all it was a command, the tone was gentler than she had
expected and surprise rendered her silent, merely inclining
her head in acknowledgement of his words. Then she walked
away. With a wry smile he watched her go, well aware of the
alacrity with which she left. He would have liked to find a reason to detain her and it was in his mind to call her back, but if
he did she would obey only because she must. It was clear she
took no pleasure in his company. But, then, why should she?
He sighed, wondering why it should matter. It never had before.

Glad to be out of that unsettling presence, Elgiva let out the
breath she had been holding. Wulfrum had been quite gentle
on this occasion but he was still a conqueror, a fact that must
not be forgotten. As for the other, she could still feel the imprint
of Sweyn's fingers on her flesh. Chilling to think what might
have happened if Ironfist hadn't appeared on the scene. She recalled his words: *The woman belongs to Wulfrum.* The thought
occurred then that Ironfist hadn't come along by chance. The
earl guarded what was his. She had no doubt he would fight to
keep it too, fight and kill. Shivering now, she hurried back to
the sanctuary of the bower and closed the door, wanting to shut
out the Viking presence at least for a while.

A few minutes later Osgifu appeared and Elgiva explained
what Leofwine had told her. The older woman heard her with
mounting concern.

'Somehow we must help those men. There have been enough deaths here.'

It was exactly what had been going through Elgiva's mind. 'How are we to get out though? The earl's guards are vigilant.'

Men had been posted outside the women's bower, as well as at the gate to Ravenswood and at intervals along the palisade. No one now could come or go undetected.

'In truth, I don't know.'

'There must be a way.'

Elgiva was thinking hard. The plan had better be a good one. She had no desire to lead Wulfrum's men to the fugitives or to be caught and dragged ignominiously before him to face another interrogation.

Osgifu broke into her thoughts. 'A simple disguise might serve.'

'A disguise? How? Surely the guards would never fall for it.'

'They might, if it were done subtly. People generally see what they wish to see. The guards are no different in that respect, I think.'

'What is in your mind?'

Osgifu explained. Elgiva listened and smiled. It was a simple idea but for that reason it might just work.

'I will speak with Hilda,' Osgifu went on. 'We'll need her help. In the meantime let us hope Wulfrum doesn't decide to visit the women's bower. That would be more than a bit inconvenient. He's not a man to cross.'

'What the earl doesn't know won't hurt him.'

'True.' Osgifu donned her old grey mantle and pulled up the hood. 'Happily this weather suits our purpose.'

The spring had been cool and showery and it had been raining intermittently all day. It was a perfect reason to wear a hood and one drawn forwards over the face as now. Elgiva watched her leave and then set about gathering up those things they would most likely need.

* * *

A short time later Osgifu returned with Hilda also clad in a grey mantle with the hood drawn up. She doffed the outer garment and helped Elgiva to put it on.

'God send you can help Hunfirth, my lady.'

'Amen to that.' Elgiva slipped the leather bag containing her things beneath her cloak. It was small enough to escape detection. Then she drew up her hood. Even a cursory glance would not mistake Hilda's tawny locks for her own gold ones. Pulling the cloth forwards to hide her face, Elgiva nodded to her companions.

Osgifu turned to Hilda. 'You must wait here till we return.'

'I shall. The children will be safe enough meanwhile. I've left them with Acca.'

It was a happy choice. Acca might be getting on in years, but she was kind and a most trustworthy servant besides.

Elgiva smiled. 'It is well.'

'My lady, you must use this chance to get away.' Hilda regarded her earnestly. 'Get far away into the forest where the conquerors will never be able to find you.'

'And leave you to their tender mercies in my place?'

'It does not matter.'

'It matters to me, Hilda. We have seen what cruelties they practise and I would not have anyone suffer at their hands again.' Elgiva squeezed the girl's arm. 'I will give what help I can to Hunfirth and return as soon as may be. Do you stay here meanwhile?'

Hilda nodded. Then, with swift-beating heart, Elgiva followed Osgifu from the bower. The guard outside glanced their way, but made no move to stop them, having seen two identically dressed women go in before. They walked away, resisting the temptation to hurry, and made for the gate. It was open to allow the normal traffic in and out and, though the guards kept an eye on those who came and went, they saw nothing suspicious in two more servant women going about their business.

Only when they were past these first obstacles did Elgiva breathe more easily. However, they could not afford complacency, for the Vikings kept a presence in the village too. At the smithy Elfric joined them and from there they followed the path that led towards the woodland. The rain had slackened a little, but the chill was penetrating and for that reason most people had sought shelter. Elgiva took a covert look around but could see no sign of any Danes. Belike they were within doors too. Fortunately the smithy was on the edge of the village; from there it was but a short distance to the trees. As they walked they looked about the while to ascertain that they were not followed.

In spite of the potential danger Elgiva felt her heart lift to be in the open air again, to breathe the welcome scent of damp earth and leaf mould, to see on every bough the glad new leaf appearing, wreathing the branches in a mist of green. The forest held a promise of freedom. She knew its secret places, knew she could hide herself there with ease and, equally, knew she never would. Her word was given and she would not break it. Thus with unerring steps she made her way along the familiar paths towards her goal.

It was perhaps a matter of half a league to the ancient dolmens, three great monoliths topped by another, stained and weathered, greened with moss and lichen, and so old none could say how they came there. A little further on was a rocky outcrop in the trees, where lay the cave they sought.

As they neared the place they slowed and she heard Elfric whistle softly twice. At his signal a man emerged from the cave, a drawn sword in his hand. When he saw who it was, he lowered the weapon.

'Elfric. God be thanked.'

Elgiva recognised the speaker, the man called Brekka who had been one of her brother's retainers. He turned to her now and inclined his head respectfully.

'My lady, you take a great risk in coming here, but I thank you and Osgifu too. Hunfirth is in a poor way. I have done what I can for him, but it is little enough.'

They followed him through the narrow entrance into the wider cave beyond. In the dim light they could see the injured man lying on the hard earth floor. Elgiva knelt beside her companion and they made a careful examination of their patient. She knew Hunfirth by sight, but her heart misgave her as she looked at the man's pallor and heard his ragged shallow breathing. An examination of his wounds did nothing to restore her confidence. Apart from a deep sword thrust to his side, there was the arrow lodged in his shoulder and the signs were that the wound was already festering.

'This arrow must come out or he has no chance,' said Osgifu. 'Even then the outcome is doubtful given how much blood he has already lost.'

'He will die if you do not treat him,' replied Brekka.

Osgifu nodded. 'That is so.' She took the leather bag from beneath her cloak and began to get out her things.

It took some time to perform the task, given the limitations of the place and the basic nature of the equipment they had been able to bring, but eventually it was done. The patient had lost consciousness long since. In her heart Elgiva doubted whether he would survive the night. She turned to Brekka.

'If Hunfirth dies, you must not linger here.'

He shook his head. 'If it comes to that, my lady, I shall seek the other Saxon fugitives and join with them.'

'Enough blood has been spilt. I beg you to save yourself.'

'If I do, it will only be to fight another day.'

Seeing it was useless to argue, she and Osgifu gathered their things and prepared to leave. Outside the air was colder and the grey sky darkening. Elgiva realised then how much time they had spent in the cave. It was imperative now to get back before they were missed. They said their farewells to Brekka and retraced their steps, coming at last to the edge of the trees. Elfric looked around to check that the coast was clear. He need not have worried: it had begun to rain again and the place seemed deserted. In a little while it would be dark.

They reached the smithy, expecting to see Leofwine waiting there. However, the lean-to was dark with no sign of the smith. Elgiva frowned, feeling suddenly uneasy. It was too quiet. Something of this had occurred to her companions too and she could sense their nervousness.

'Go, my lady,' said Elfric. 'It is not safe to linger here.'

She was about to reply when a muted sound stopped the words, the sinister scrape of metal on stone. Before she could utter any warning, half-a-dozen dark shapes detached themselves from the shadows of the building and in moments the three of them were surrounded by armed men. Elgiva drew in a sharp breath as she recognised Ironfist. Taking a firm hold on her arm, he turned to his companions.

'Take those two and chain them with the others.'

Elfric and Osgifu were hustled away. With beating heart Elgiva looked up at her captor, but the giant's face was impassive as he drew her inexorably with him. Instead of following the rest, he peeled off at a tangent towards the women's bower. When they reached it, he shoved open the door and pushed her inside. In the dim light she could see the tall dark-clad figure before the fire. On hearing them enter, the figure turned round. Elgiva's mouth dried. Wulfrum!

'Good evening, my lady. I have been looking forward to your return for some time. Perhaps you would care to tell me where you have been.'

For a moment they regarded each other in silence, but even in the firelight she could see the anger in his face. She paled, heart thumping hard against her ribs, but she was thinking fast. How had he found out? What unlucky chance had led him here? There was no way of knowing what information he had already extracted from Leofwine and Hilda, but some instinct warned her not to lie to him, that to do so would make matters worse. Behind her she was aware of Ironfist's bulk blocking the door, cutting off all possibility of escape. She took a deep breath.

'Osgifu and I went to help a wounded man.'

'What man? Where?'

'Leofwine's brother, Hunfirth. He was wounded in the battle for Ravenswood and he took refuge in the forest.'

'How many are with him?'

'Just one.'

'Where are they?'

'Where we left them.'

'Don't test my patience further, Elgiva. Where are they?'

'I cannot tell you that.'

'Cannot or will not?'

'These are my people. I will not betray them.'

'You'll tell me,' he replied.

For the first time she noticed the coiled whip at his side and felt her legs tremble beneath her. Wielded properly, the lash could cut a groove in solid wood. She had seen what it could do to human flesh. He could not really be intending to use it. Her eyes sought for any clue in his expression that might suggest otherwise, but they found none. Then she remembered his response the day she had tried to run and a faint sheen of perspiration broke out on her forehead despite the cold without. The Viking knew how to punish and wouldn't hesitate, either. Elgiva bit her lip, clenching her fists at her sides to stop them from trembling. Come what may, she could not betray Hunfirth and Brekka. Let the warlord do his worst—she would never tell him. Her chin lifted and she met his gaze.

'I am a healer, lord. It is my part to save men, not to destroy them. Leofwine asked for my help and I gave it willingly. As

I gave it to your men too. As I would to any human being who needed it. If that is a crime, I am sorry for it.'

'No, that is not a crime. Disobeying my orders is.'

'I was not aware you had given any orders about letting wounded men die.'

'Don't try to twist my words, wench.'

'I had no thought of doing so, lord.'

'It seems you have plenty of willing accomplices too.'

'Leofwine sought to aid his brother. Osgifu and Hilda helped me because I asked it. They are not to blame. If your anger must fall on anyone, let it fall on me.'

Wulfrum's gaze burned into her own, but Elgiva did not flinch. Inwardly she thought he might kill her.

'You may live to regret those words.'

'I beg you, lord, do not hurt them. They could not have done other than they did.'

'They show a reckless loyalty to you, that's for sure.'

'Loyalty is not a crime, either.'

Wulfrum's jaw clenched even as he admired the breathtaking audacity of the reply. He had to admit the little vixen did not want for courage. Even though she knew her present peril full well, she had answered him calmly enough and he had discerned no trace of fear in the unwavering amber eyes. She hadn't lied to him, either, although she was undoubtedly smart enough to realise he would have learned the truth long since from her confederates. By rights he should thrash her now along with all the others in this latest exploit. He was still tempted.

When he had visited the bower earlier and found her gone, his anger had known no bounds. Hilda, on the receiving end of it, had very soon told him the plan, a tale corroborated in part by the guards. Then Ironfist had remembered seeing her speaking with the smith earlier that day, on her return from the Saxon funerals. Wulfrum had gone to the smithy with half-a-dozen men and, in a very short time, had all the information he wanted from Leofwine. He had been able to believe the tale about the injured man, but certainly not the part about Elgiva's intention to return. She had got out of Ravenswood with a head start and would surely make good her escape. Yet both Hilda and Leofwine evidently had complete faith in her word. Even with his anger at white heat it gave him pause. Against his better judgement he had not ordered immediate pursuit, but instead had waited. In the meantime he had had the two Saxon miscreants chained with the dogs in the kennel where they could do no more mischief and could think at leisure of their probable fate.

Unable to follow his thought, Elgiva quaked.

'We will test that loyalty,' he said. 'We shall try how far it will go under the lash. I think it will not be long before your friends tell me what I wish to know.'

Elgiva's colour ebbed and tears welled in her eyes. 'Please don't hurt them. They have done nothing....'

'Then tell me where the fugitives are.'

'I cannot. You must know that.'

He took a step closer. Elgiva swallowed hard, but remained still, aware of Ironfist just behind.

'This is the last time I shall ask you. Where are they, Elgiva?'

Seeing she remained silent, Wulfrum looked beyond her to Ironfist.

'Go to the hall and find out,' he said, handing the giant the whip.

'Consider it done, lord.

With sinking heart Elgiva heard Ironfist leave and then she was alone with Wulfrum, who regarded her with that in his face which made her heart thump unpleasantly hard.

'Please don't do this,' she said then.

'If you were truly concerned for the welfare of others you would have considered the consequences of disobedience.'

'Then punish me, not them.'

The amber eyes glistened with unshed tears. He wondered if she would weep and doubted it somehow. He had cause to know her courage and her pride.

'Believe me, Elgiva, you will learn to obey me.' He paused. 'The lives of your accomplices will be forfeit if you attempt to leave Ravenswood again without my knowledge. There will be no other warning.'

Her face was very pale, but she faced him, dread vying with resentment, choosing her words with care. 'Then you do not propose to kill them?'

'Not this time, but their future well-being depends on you.'

'I understand.'

'Do you?' He drew closer. 'I hope so.'

It took every bit of self-control for her not to take a step backwards. He towered over her, seeming even larger in the confined space. His expression sent a chill through her.

'In the meantime you will be confined to the women's bower until further notice.'

The implications began to dawn. 'But what of the injured? And Ulric and Pybba?'

'You should have thought of that earlier,' he replied.

'But, my lord, I—'

'I have said. You will do as you're told.' His keen gaze saw the glint of anger in her eyes before they were veiled. 'Otherwise I shall thrash you to within an inch of your life.'

Her hands clenched with helpless ire, but she knew it would avail her nothing to argue. In his present mood he might well carry out the threat and she knew already the weight of his hand.

'How long must I remain here?'

'For as long as it pleases me.'

Elgiva fought the temptation to tell him the thoughts uppermost in her mind. However, it did not need a seer to read them for anger was writ large on her face.

He lifted an eyebrow and regarded her with a speculative eye. 'Perhaps I should take your clothes too, just to make sure.'

Elgiva's face registered an interesting variety of emotions. Wulfrum smiled, watching a wonderful rosy blush rise from her neck to her cheeks. Then he waited. Seeing that smile, she knew beyond doubt that the knave was enjoying this. It was in her mind to call him every kind of scurvy rogue in creation, but she bit back the words that rose to her lips—in truth, she dared offer no more provocation, knowing now he would do just what he threatened. The brute had no shame.

As a matter of fact, Wulfrum had himself well in hand. The idea of Elgiva without her clothes was a heady one, but he put it aside, for now. His time would come. In the meantime he would leave her to think about the folly of wilful disobedience. He strolled to the door.

'I'll bid you a good evening, my lady.'

Elgiva glared after the departing figure and saw the door close after him. There followed muffled words as he spoke to the guards outside, and then silence. For some minutes she paced the floor in helpless fury and frustration. Her heart was filled with dread to think of the possible fate of her companions, but she dared not try to find out. She had been so preoccupied with helping Hunfirth and Brekka that she had put others at risk. Pacing the floor, she tried to think. When she had calmed a little she realised she need not fear for Ulric and Pybba. They would be safe enough for surely Wulfrum would not punish the helpless for her fault. Wulfrum again! Everything came back to Wulfrum. Could she trust him in this regard? She had to hope so. Throwing herself on to the bed in helpless ire, she felt the awful truth sink in. She was exactly where he intended her to be and she would be there at his pleasure. Elgiva punched the mattress hard, unsure whether she was angrier with him or herself.

Chapter Five

She had plenty of time to think of all the things she would like to do to Wulfrum in the days that followed. A guard brought her food and drink and emptied the slop bucket, but other than that she saw no one. As time passed the bower seemed to grow smaller and incarceration chafed her spirit. With growing anxiety, she pondered the fate of Osgifu and the others, praying that they were unhurt. Had Leofwine led the Vikings to the hidden cave? Had they captured Hunfirth and Brekka? Was Aylwin still alive? Were her nephews being cared for? Tormented by the lack of news, she could not settle to anything and paced the floor, inwardly cursing Wulfrum and all his fellow Vikings. She had no regrets about trying to help Hunfirth. It had been the right thing to do. If only she could be certain that her people had not suffered as a result. The enforced idleness was as bad as the lack of knowledge. Wulfrum knew it too, of that she had no doubt.

'Damn him!'

The very thought of the man was enough to stir her anger again. He knew how to punish. Yet in her heart she knew this was but a small taste of his power. Had he chosen to, he could have flogged her until the flesh hung in ribbons from her back. She shivered. In truth, she had been surprised that he had not, surprised and mightily relieved too. He held all their lives in his grip now and they were his to do with as he pleased. Why had he stayed his hand? He could have made an example of her, of all of them. Perhaps he already had. Perhaps he had lied to her when he said he would not kill her companions, and Osgifu and Hilda were hanging from a tree even now along with Leofwine and Elfric. Perhaps her incarceration was but a prelude to something far worse. The uncertainty was what she hated most, as of course he knew she would.

'Damn him!' she said for perhaps the hundredth time.

Her imprisonment was running into its third day when the door opened to admit Osgifu. Elgiva leapt up, staring at her in disbelief. Then she was running across the intervening space and they were hugging each other fiercely.

'Oh, Gifu. Are you all right? I've been imagining all kinds of terrible things. Did they hurt you?'

'No. I am quite well.'

'What of Hilda and the others?'

'Well, too.'

'And the children?'

'Both fine.'

Elgiva closed her eyes and gave silent thanks to God. The relief was so intense she found herself shaking.

'What of you, child? Has he hurt you?'

'No. Things are as you see.' She glanced with distaste around her prison. 'But I am not hurt.'

'Thank heaven. When you were taken away that night, we feared the worst. No one has set eyes on you since and rumours are rife.'

'How did you get in here?'

'The guards let me pass, on Lord Wulfrum's orders.'

'When did he release you?'

'The very next day.'

'What!'

'It's true. At dawn he and his men came for Leofwine and took him away. Hilda and I thought we'd never see him alive again. As for Elfric's fears, you can imagine.'

Elgiva could, only too well. 'What happened?'

'A few hours later the Vikings returned. Leofwine had taken them to the cave, but when they arrived, all they found was Hunfirth's body. It was cold. He must have died in the night. Brekka was gone.'

Elgiva digested the news.

'Where will he go, do you think?'

'South, probably, to try to reach Wessex or somewhere the Danes do not hold sway.'

'I wish him God speed.'

'And I.'

'Will the Vikings try to find him?'

'I don't think so. From what Leofwine said, they showed no interest in pursuit. They brought Hunfirth's body back for burial too.'

'Wulfrum let Leofwine bury his brother?'

'Yes. And he freed the rest of us. He sent me straight back to tending the remaining wounded from the battle.' Osgifu shook her head. 'I thought we were dead for sure that night we were caught returning from the forest. He is a strange one.'

'Strange indeed,' replied Elgiva, turning the story over in her mind. Wulfrum had shown mercy to an extent she could never have imagined.

'We thought you were dead at first. Then we learned you were shut up in this room. I begged to be allowed to see you but he refused, until now.'

'Oh, Gifu. I've been so afraid. I thought I would never see you again.'

Elgiva's tears spilled over now and ran down her cheeks. Then Osgifu's comforting arms were round her.

'Don't cry, child. You have been so brave. Your strength has given us all the will to go on.'

'I was terrified, Gifu.'

'No one would ever have known it.'

'I thought he would kill us all.'

'The Viking respects courage and you have shown that in good measure.' Osgifu smiled. 'I think it is why he has not exercised his power as he might have done. In truth, I expected a very different outcome to the events of the past few days. You must have made quite an impression.'

'I've paid for it since.' Elgiva dashed her tears away with the back of her hand. 'He has let me sweat in here, not knowing anything. He knew it would be almost as bad as a flogging.'

'The man is cunning.'

'He's a devious swine. I would give much to tell him so.'

Osgifu looked at her in surprise. 'Have you not seen him then since he locked you up?'

'No, only his guards. He means to teach me a lesson, you see.'

'Surely he will free you soon.'

Elgiva sighed, wishing rather than believing it might be so. The knowledge that he had freed the others long since made her continued punishment all the more pointed. This was not about helping an injured man, it was about defiance. He did not need to beat her bloody to let her know his power. A more subtle demonstration had worked just as well. Elgiva gritted her teeth.

'How I hate that man!'

'He has made his point. He can't keep you locked up much longer.'

However, it seemed Osgifu's prediction was wide of the mark for that day passed and the next and still Wulfrum made no move to release her or even to speak with her. Elgiva could only feel thankful for his continued absence. Though it was most irksome to be confined, it was infinitely preferable to the plan originally proposed for her future. Perhaps he had changed his mind now. Indeed, it looked as if he had forgotten all about her. She prayed it might be so.

The hope was short-lived for the following day he did come to the women's bower. Hearing the door open, Elgiva assumed it was Osgifu, but turned to see Wulfrum standing there. For several moments they faced each other in silence. He surveyed her critically. She was a little paler than usual but he put that down to her enforced stay within doors. Otherwise he could detect no ill effects from the experience. She was as beautiful as he remembered and, from the look in those glorious eyes, quite unrepentant. He was amused. Shutting Elgiva up might have restricted her freedom, but it had not cowed her spirit for her chin lifted in a manner that was becoming familiar to him. Would she plead with him now to set her free? He suspected not. Pleading was not something that came readily to her, at least not for herself, however eloquent she might be on behalf of others. If he knew anything about her, it was that she would cut out her own tongue before asking any favour of him. She was proud and she was brave and he was becoming hourly more reconciled to the thought of their wedding. Far from having changed his mind, she would have been unnerved to learn that recent events had but confirmed him in the decision. Unable to follow his thoughts, Elgiva grew restive under that keen scrutiny and it was she who broke the silence.

'There was something you wished to speak of, lord?'

'Indeed. I have had no chance before now, being occupied with other matters.'

'Such as the burial of the slain?'

He heard the ironic tone, but let it go. 'That was a part of it,' he acknowledged. 'However, 'tis done, and now other things take precedence.'

Elgiva threw him a cool quizzical look but ventured no comment and remained where she was, watching him cross the floor towards her. She had forgotten how tall he was, how powerful a presence.

'It is of our marriage I speak,' he said.

Some of the colour faded from her cheeks.

'Never tell me you had forgotten, my lady. Or perhaps you were hoping I had?'

She bit her lip but said nothing, for it was a most accurate shot.

'I regret to disappoint you, Elgiva. You and I wed on the morrow.'

The words hit her like a blow, but she recovered fast enough. 'I will not.'

'Your consent would be better. More dignified.'

'Do you intend to use force, then?'

'If I have to,' he returned mildly.

Amber eyes glared into cool blue, Elgiva the while much tempted to hit him and remove some of that infuriating self-assurance. Then she reflected that it wouldn't even dent the surface. His arrogance was as impenetrable as his armour.

'Do you think I would stoop to wed a Viking thief? I would rather die.'

Wulfrum held his temper. 'You are overproud, my lady, and pride goes before a fall.'

He drew closer. Elgiva took a step back and then could have kicked herself for it, seeing the mocking expression reassert itself. His gaze swept her from head to foot and he frowned.

'I would see you in something more festive for our wedding.'

She had donned her plainest gown in token of mourning and the sober brown shade was unadorned save for the girdle that rode her waist. Evidently it found little favour with him. Bridling under that keen scrutiny, Elgiva wondered if he thought she would don her finery in his honour. If so, he was sorely mistaken. She would not make herself attractive for him. Then she became aware that Wulfrum was looking beyond her to the chest by the far wall. Without further ado he crossed the room and threw back the lid, revealing the garments within. Seething, she watched as he lifted them out one by one, surveying them critically before tossing each one aside on the bed. Blue, green and mauve followed in swift succession until he came to the gold gown with the embroidered neck and sleeves.

'You will wear this on the morrow.'

'I am in mourning and therefore cannot.'

'Tomorrow you become the wife of an earl and you should be dressed as befits your rank.'

'I cannot forget the slain so soon.'

'I do not expect it,' he replied, 'but I shall expect you to wear this gown.'

'I won't.'

The blue gaze never left her but there was no shade of humour in it now.

'You will wear it, Elgiva, if I have to dress you myself.'

It was on the tip of her tongue to say that he wouldn't dare, but a second's reflection stopped the words there. She knew with certainty that he would make good the threat. Forcing back her fury, she returned his gaze.

'Is there anything else?'

'Aye, there is.'

Wulfrum drew her close. Elgiva stiffened. Amusement returned as he looked down into her face.

'You can fight me all you like, lady, but you will kiss me.'

'Why, you arrogant, conceited—'

The words were lost as his mouth closed over hers. Elgiva struggled, but there was no chance of escape and he took the kiss in his own good time.

'Let go of me! How dare you treat me like this?'

'I shall not let you go. As to what I dare…'

Elgiva's cheeks turned a deeper shade of pink for the warmth and the nearness of the man, the faint scent of leather and musk. Out of the corner of her eye she was more than ever aware of the bed, now strewn with her gowns. If he chose to force the issue she would never be able to hold him off, being well aware he was using only minimal effort to restrain her now.

He kissed her again, the pressure of his mouth forcing hers open. Thereafter the kiss grew gentle and lingering. Elgiva shivered, but her hands ceased to push him away. The thought returned: no man had ever kissed her like this. No man had ever caused that unsettling flicker of warmth deep inside her, either. When he eventually drew back, she saw him smile; all at once her response appalled her. This man was an enemy. That she should have yielded to his kiss made her sick with self-loathing. Worse, what had left her shattered was clearly a source of amusement to him.

'Please...'

'What would you have of me, lady?' His lips brushed her hair, her ear, her cheek.

In desperation Elgiva tore away from him. 'Nothing! I want nothing from you! I want no part of you. I loathe you.'

Wulfrum regarded her steadily but made no attempt to hold her. 'Now I had a very different impression a moment ago.'

'You imagined it, then.'

'You deceive yourself, Elgiva.'

'I do not.'

'Shall I prove it to you?'

'No! Get out!'

He laughed out loud. Dry mouthed and with beating heart, she watched him cross to the door.

'Until tomorrow, then, lady. I feel sure you will understand when I say you will remain confined until then.'

Incensed, Elgiva watched him go, looking round for something to throw. There was nothing immediately to hand. The nearest item was a wooden stool some feet away. By the time she had grabbed it he was gone, but she flung it anyway and with all the force she could muster. It hit the door with a crash that reverberated through the bower, but as the noise faded she could hear the unmistakable sound of his laughter.

Seeing Wulfrum enter the hall, Ironfist looked up quizzically. Halfdan followed his gaze and grinned.

'And how is the fair Saxon?' he demanded. 'Burning with impatience for her wedding day?'

Wulfrum returned him a wry smile. 'Burning with impatience to stick a sword in my guts.'

'Aye, she has spirit, that one,' said Ironfist.

'Spirit and beauty,' replied Halfdan. 'It will take some taming but you will bend her to your will—in time.'

He glanced across the hall to where Sweyn sat with a group of men and his tone grew more serious.

'Keep her close, Wulfrum. Sweyn is still smarting from losing her.'

'Then he should have taken more care. She is mine and I will guard her well.'

'See you do.' Halfdan threw another glance across the hall. 'There is no point in inviting trouble. When I leave, I will take Sweyn with me. We shall see if the lure of land and gold will turn his mind to other things.'

'It is a good plan,' said Ironfist.

Halfdan grinned. 'He will find Saxon maids aplenty to keep him occupied and turn his thoughts from this one.'

'Let us hope so.'

'You doubt it?'

'Some women are not easily forgotten.'

'Never tell me you're soft on the wench too?'

Ironfist threw him a speaking look. 'I am long past such foolishness, but I can see straight. The girl is fair. She draws men's eyes as a flame draws moths.'

'It is no crime to look, eh, Wulfrum?'

'No, my lord. They may look their fill.'

'But no touching?'

'Ordinarily I am not one to quarrel over a wench or two,' said Wulfrum, 'but this one I share with no man.'

Elgiva looked with loathing at the gold gown and every fibre of her being rebelled.

'How can I do this, Gifu? How can I wed that barbarian?'

'I think you have no choice.'

'There must be some way out of this.'

Elgiva paced the floor, cudgelling her brains for some means to prevent the disaster looming on the morrow. Osgifu's grey eyes were resigned.

'There is none.'

Something in the tone gave Elgiva pause and she stopped pacing, regarding her keenly. Her heart began to beat a little harder and she remembered an earlier conversation.

'Was this what you saw in the runes?' Seeing Osgifu remain silent, Elgiva swallowed hard. 'Was it? Answer me.'

'Yes.'

'It cannot be true. It cannot be.' Elgiva's eyes filled with tears. 'I will not wed the Viking. He will not take me as he has taken these lands. I must get away somehow, tonight, and go somewhere he will not find me.'

'There is nowhere to run, child. The Danish marauders are everywhere, and renegade Saxons too,' Osgifu replied. 'It is too perilous for a woman to be abroad unprotected. Even if you did escape, Wulfrum would send out men and dogs and he would find you. I think you would discover then the full weight of his wrath.'

Elgiva swallowed hard. It was the truth. She dreaded to think what Wulfrum might do if she tried it and yet the alternative seemed every way as bad.

'I cannot just submit! Shall I wed an enemy of my people? A pirate?'

'You have no choice but to submit. If you do not, he will use force.'

It was so precisely an echo of what Wulfrum had said that Elgiva shivered.

'Yes, and not against me, against those I should protect.'

'He said so?'

'As good as. He let it be known any disobedience on my part would result in others bearing the brunt of his anger.'

'He is clever and devious.'

'You said it.'

'I think they truly mean to stay this time,' Osgifu continued, 'not just to plunder and kill. They want the land.'

'Our land. Land they have no right to, that they slew Saxon people to get.'

'Aye, and will slay more to keep if they have to.'

Elgiva felt a sudden pang of guilt. Aylwin had been prepared to lay down his life for her and hers, but she had held him lightly. He had deserved better. In all likelihood he was dead of his wounds and lying in an unmarked woodland grave. Hot tears pricked her eyelids as the memories returned unbidden. She would have married Aylwin and tried to make him a good wife as her duty dictated. Now he was a fugitive and she was the prize of a conqueror.

In her mind's eye she could see Wulfrum's face again, with those piercing blue eyes and the mocking smile. The very thought was enough to stoke the fires of her anger. Did he really have the arrogance to think she would give herself to him? Then she remembered how big he was and how strong. He could take her whenever he wished. It occurred to her that he could already have done so, yet he had stayed his hand. Did he think that by making her his wife he would earn her gratitude? That she would submit meekly and tamely in his bed? Elgiva clenched her fists. She would see him in hell first, along with his entire accursed race.

'Do not torment yourself, child.' Osgifu's voice broke into her train of thought. 'It will serve no purpose.'

'I could not offer Aylwin my heart, Gifu. Yet he defended Ravenswood with his life.'

'He was a good man. Whether Wulfrum is another only time will tell.'

Elgiva stopped in her tracks. 'Wulfrum is a Viking, a pirate, a marauder. How can he be a good man?'

'I know not, but it seems to me that he is not like that other, Sweyn.'

Elgiva knew it was true. There was a streak of cruelty in the man that she had not found in Wulfrum or in his giant companion.

'Sweyn is evil,' she replied. 'Evil and brutal.'

'He desires you, it is plain.'

'I'd slit my own throat first.'

'As the wife of Wulfrum you will be beyond his reach. That one has the ear of Halfdan. Aye, and his favour too, as he has granted him the gift of land.'

'Stolen land.'

'But who is there now to make them give it back?'

Elgiva sighed, knowing the answer. For years Northumbria's rulers had been involved in petty disputes, Osbert north of the Tees and Ella in the south, each vying for the crown. The kingdom was ill prepared to withstand invasion, a situation the Vikings had exploited to the full. Now Osbert and Ella were dead and, since Mercia and East Anglia had fallen, there was nothing to stop the invading army. Northumbria was as good as theirs. They would never yield it up, nor would they return to their cold northern shores. Halfdan and his brothers would take what they wanted and reward their faithful earls with lands and serfs to work it. The Viking horde was there to stay.

'There is no escape, is there?' she said at last.

'No.'

'I'd rather be dead.'

'Then who would protect your people from the vengeance of the Vikings?' demanded Osgifu.

'It will make no difference to them whether I live or die.'

'It will make all the difference. As Wulfrum's wife you will have great influence.'

'I will have no influence.'

'Then you are not the woman I took you for.'

Elgiva stared at her, but Osgifu's gaze remained steadfast.

'The man is clearly besotted. You must use your power over him.'

'Besotted?' Elgiva gave a hollow laugh. 'Hardly.'

'I have seen the way he looks at you.'

'He looks at me with lust, that is all.'

'Then why does he take you to wife? He could have had you the day the Vikings took this place and then kept you as a concubine or handed you over to his men for a plaything. Instead he offers you a place of honour at his side.'

'Honour? You call it an honour?'

'In his view, aye. By doing so, he puts you beyond reach of all others, beyond danger. Consider the alternative.'

Elgiva lapsed into a confused and angry silence. Seeing it, the older woman pressed her point.

'This situation is not of your choosing or of your making, but you can turn it to advantage. You have beauty and wit. Use them.'

'You overestimate my powers, Gifu. Wulfrum will do as he wills.'

'A beautiful woman can make a man do as *she* wills. A clever one can make him think it was his idea.'

In spite of herself, Elgiva smiled. 'Truly you are cunning.'

'A woman must be cunning to survive. You will survive because you are strong. Aye, and brave too. You will do what must be done.'

Elgiva knew she was right. Now that Osric was dead and

Aylwin a fugitive, it was her place to protect her people in so far as it lay within her power to do so. Just then she did not believe that amounted to much.

'And by that you mean I must marry Wulfrum on the morrow?'

'There is no other choice,' replied Osgifu.

Chapter Six

∽⧉∾

The ceremony was held outdoors in a forest glade hard by, the better to accommodate the number who would attend. Even if the church had been intact it could not have held so many. In the midst Father Willibald waited in resigned reluctance, surrounded by the warrior host. Unaware of the priest's discomfiture, the warriors talked and jested among themselves until the arrival of Wulfrum with Olaf Ironfist and Lord Halfdan. A cheer went up and the jesting increased. Wulfrum smiled, letting it wash over him, and cast a swift glance around. The priest, looking up at the three of them, swallowed hard and tried to conceal his nervousness. His gaze moved past them to the assembled Saxons whose presence the earl had likewise commanded, seeing in their expressions his own doubt and fear. Of the Lady Elgiva there was no sign.

'And the bride, my lord?' he asked diffidently.

'She is coming,' replied Wulfrum.

An imposing figure, he was dressed in a scarlet tunic of fine wool over blue leggings. A cloak of dyed red wool, embroidered at front and hem, was thrown over his shoulders and fastened by a silver dragon brooch. His shoes were made of good leather and by his side he wore a fine sword.

Halfdan and Ironfist were also attired in their best to do honour to their friend. They glanced once at Father Willibald and then ignored him, a state of affairs that suited him perfectly.

The minutes passed with still no sign of the bride and Halfdan exchanged glances with Ironfist, though he said nothing. Wulfrum felt a twinge of unease, but forced it down. It was, after all, a woman's privilege to keep her groom waiting on her wedding day. It occurred to him that Elgiva might consider flight, but, if so, she would soon have found it impossible: Ravenswood was well guarded and by his own men. A cat could not slip out unnoticed. No, this marriage would take place as planned. It was an important symbol, announcing that the Norsemen were there to stay and that they would ally themselves with Saxon blood. He knew too that if he intended to rule these people, it would be far better to show them that their lady was held in a position of respect. To see her demeaned as his whore would have added to existing resentments. In many ways it was a political move, though, if he were honest, not entirely. He did not deceive himself that Elgiva entertained any tender feelings on his account; given the chance, she might well drive a sword into his heart.

'Where is the wench? What keeps her?' demanded Halfdan.

Distracted from his thoughts, Wulfrum frowned. The assembled crowd was growing restless. If Elgiva was playing some petulant female trick, he would return to the hall and drag her forth himself. The flicker of doubt grew into a spark of annoyance. Would she dare to humiliate him before his men, before his overlord? By Odin's beard, if she tried it—

He never finished the thought, aware suddenly that the conversation around him had stopped and all eyes were drawn to the far edge of the glade. He turned and looked, then looked again, and all anger died in an instant. Elgiva, attended by Hilda and Osgifu, moved across the greensward towards him. For a moment he wondered if she were real or some sprite from the forest. Glancing sunlight caught her in its rays, enfolding her in a halo of light. Clad in the golden gown with her golden hair loose about her shoulders and restrained only by a circlet of flowers, she seemed some ethereal being, so graceful in her movements that she might have floated above the earth rather than walked on it.

'Thor's thunderbolts,' muttered Olaf Ironfist, 'but she is fair.'

Beside him Halfdan nodded. 'I'm starting to wonder if I wasn't too hasty in letting Wulfrum have the wench.'

Wulfrum forgot his anger and his doubt and felt in his heart the first stirring of pride that this Saxon maid was to be his wife, along with the knowledge that every man present wanted to be in his shoes.

Elgiva walked with unhurried step across the glade with head held high, looking neither to left nor right, giving no sign that she was aware of the attention focused on her. When she reached Wulfrum's side, she made a brief and graceful curtsy, meeting his gaze for a fleeting moment before he took her hand.

'You shine like the sun, my lady.'

There was no mistaking the admiration in his eyes, but Elgiva returned it with coolness.

'You are all kindness, lord.'

If he noted the ironic tone he gave no sign and led her forwards to the waiting priest. She concealed her surprise to see Father Willibald there, knowing that many of the Vikings had yet to embrace the Christian faith and worshipped their old gods. She realised she had no idea of Wulfrum's beliefs. Part of her had expected to endure a pagan ceremony, something that could never have been regarded as binding by the Saxon population. Had Wulfrum known that? One moment's reflection assured her that he had. This marriage was intended to be binding in every way. Her heart pounded. There was to be no escape.

The ceremony went without the least hitch. Contrary to all her hopes there was no timely interruption, no divine intervention, and no Saxon army to save her at the last moment. The words were spoken, the rings exchanged and the air was split by a rousing cheer from the assembled crowd as Wulfrum took his bride in his arms and sealed the moment with a kiss. Elgiva permitted that embrace but did not respond.

Wulfrum's lips brushed her hair as he whispered, 'You will kiss me, Elgiva. I shall hold you thus until you do.'

She knew it was no idle threat and had perforce to yield to a much longer and more intimate embrace. The roar of approval from the gathered crowd echoed through the forest and flocks of birds rose startled into the air. Wulfrum drew back a little and looked into her face, now a deeper shade of pink, and he smiled. Elgiva laid a hand on his breast.

'My lord, there is something I would ask.'

'Ask, my lady. I will refuse you nothing if it be reasonable and within my power to grant it.'

'It is that the graves of the Saxon slain should be blessed by the priest.'

He regarded her in silence and then nodded. 'Very well, it shall be done.'

Elgiva let out the breath she had been holding. It was a conciliatory gesture that would please her people and she suspected he knew it. It was part of the role he played, for all he was a Viking warlord and their conqueror still. She had no time for further reflection because Wulfrum's men pulled him away from her and she saw him raised shoulder high. Then strong arms swung her off her feet.

'By the breath of Odin, 'tis a woodland fairy after all!' exclaimed Halfdan.

'How so?' demanded Olaf Ironfist.

'See for yourself.'

He tossed her lightly to Ironfist, who caught her with ease.

'By the breath of Odin, you're right.'

Ironfist laughed and threw her up to sit on his shoulder, an arm about her knees, supporting her feet in one huge hand. Then, surrounded by the cheering throng, he carried her along beside her lord, back towards the hall for the feast. Elgiva was set on her feet before the door with Wulfrum beside her. He took her hand and led her across the stepped threshold to another rousing cheer. The bride had not stumbled and the auspices were good.

The feasting lasted all day and into the night, with songs and jests and tests of strength while the mead horns overflowed. Many a health was drunk to the newly-wed couple, along with toasts to the gods. Elgiva watched it all with a growing sense of detachment, aided in part by the amount she had drunk. It was little enough in comparison to the men all around her, but, taken on a stomach almost empty, it went to her head quickly and added to a growing sense of unreality. From time to time she felt herself being watched and would look up to see Wulfrum's gaze resting on her. From the number of times his horn was replenished she had hopes he might drink himself insensible before the night was out, but to her growing dismay the mead seemed not to touch him. To be sure he laughed and joked with his men, but the blue eyes remained watchful for all that.

Elgiva felt only increasing panic and a desire to slip away and run. It was impossible. She would be caught very quickly and returned to her husband. Her husband! It was inconceivable that she wore his ring, symbol of the eternal bond between them, a bond that would be sealed this night when he took her to his bed. Her jaw tightened. If he thought she would yield up her body, as well, Wulfrum was much mistaken. A decidedly militant light appeared for a moment in the amber eyes before being swiftly veiled. When she looked up again it was to see Sweyn watching her from across the hall, a fleering smile on his lips. Elgiva returned the stare for a moment or two and then looked away. He was the least of her worries now. Besides, in a day or two he would be gone and she would never see him more. With any luck he would perish in the fighting to come.

These thoughts were interrupted by Osgifu, who now approached her chair. Behind her were Hilda and some of the other women.

'Come, my lady. It is time.'

Elgiva's stomach lurched and she closed her eyes to steady herself. The women would lead her to the bedchamber and prepare her for the arrival of her husband. *That's what I'll never stand,* she thought. *I'll never give myself to him.* Her fingers brushed the hilt of her belt knife and its touch reassured her. There was another way. She opened her eyes to see Wulfrum watching her and the sight of his mocking smile stiffened her spine like nothing else could. With every bit of self-possession remaining, she rose from the table, following her women to the stairs, accompanied by a loud cheer from the assembled throng.

When they reached the chamber the silence was almost deafening; the usual laughter and jesting that should have accompanied the bridal preparations were absent. The women said nothing and their demeanour was anything but joyful. Elgiva stood like a rock while they removed her girdle and unlaced her gown, drawing it off, and leaving her in her kirtle. Someone poured water into a basin so that she could bathe her hands and face. Then Osgifu removed the flowers from her hair and combed it out across her shoulders. Finally she was ready. At the side of the room the great bed waited. The women looked from it to her. Elgiva remained where she was.

'My lady, you must—'

'I must nothing. Now leave me.'

The women exchanged uncertain glances, but Osgifu ushered them to the door. As it opened to allow their departure, it also admitted a great wave of noise from the hall below, a

mighty cheer from the warrior host as Halfdan and half-a-
dozen others hoisted Wulfrum on to their shoulders and carried
him to the staircase led by Olaf Ironfist with a lighted torch.
When they reached the chamber they set their burden down
with much laughter and many a ribald jest. Then their attention moved from Wulfrum to his bride, their eyes burning with
lust as they feasted them on the woman before them. The thin
kirtle did little to conceal the lines of her body, a form whose
hinted curves seemed made for a man's touch. Mentally each
gaze stripped the fabric away, leaving her naked save for the
mane of gold hair that flowed down her back. Elgiva forced
herself to remain still, to fight down the terror knotting her gut.
A sheen of perspiration started on her skin. She knew now how
a cornered deer felt before a pack of wolves.

As if he had divined her thought, Halfdan spoke. 'Oho, be-
ware, my lady! Here's a wolf will gobble you up!'

''Tis a tender morsel,' agreed Ironfist, grinning.

'We shall look to see the proof of his feasting.' Halfdan
clapped Wulfrum on the shoulder.

Elgiva felt her heartbeat quicken, but before anyone could
say more Wulfrum turned towards them.

'The wolf feasts tonight, but he will do so at his leisure and
in private.' He nodded to the door.

With mock grumbling and some final crude injunctions the
men turned and began to troop out. Those too slow to suit him
were forcibly ejected. Weak with relief to see them go, Elgiva
watched him bar the door. However, the relief was short lived,
for now he turned and all his attention was on her.

'I am not minded to be disturbed this night,' he said, 'no matter what the pretext.'

Elgiva said nothing, her gut knotting further as he divested
himself of his cloak and unbuckled his sword belt. Then the
tunic joined the cloak. One look at those broad shoulders gave
her little hope of holding him off by force. The lamplight

gleamed softly on his silver arm rings and revealed the lines of old scars on his flesh, several on his upper arms and a deeper one across his ribs. Seeing that she did not move, Wulfrum smiled.

'That kirtle becomes you well, my lady, but I am curious to know what lies beneath.'

'So the wolf can feast?'

'Something like that.'

'I am not minded to satisfy your curiosity, Viking.'

'Say you so?'

'Do you think I would give myself to one who has slaughtered my kin and enslaved my people?'

'Slaughtered? It seems to me that the menfolk of this hall put up a strong resistance. They died honourably with swords in their hands as men should. As for the serfs, they will work these lands as they did before, albeit for a new master.' He paused. 'And you, my lady, you too will yield.'

Elgiva felt warm colour flood her face but her eyes met and held his. 'I will never yield.' She took a deep breath. 'I will not lie with you.'

'You will lie with me tonight and every night.' He drew closer, pausing only when he was within arm's reach. 'Now, take off that kirtle.'

Elgiva's eyes flashed and he saw her chin come up. He raised an eyebrow.

'Must I do it for you?'

She bit back defiant words. He would do as he threatened and she had no way to stop him. Her eyes sought for some means of escape, but the window was shuttered fast and the door barred. Worse, she would have to pass him to reach it.

'I'm waiting, Elgiva.'

'How I hate you!'

'It will make our marriage the more interesting. Take off the kirtle.'

'I will not.'

Wulfrum bent on her such a look that she quaked. As she retreated, her leg brushed the edge of the chair where her gown and girdle lay discarded. She remembered the knife and, turning, grabbed it, drawing it from the sheath and bringing it up in front of her. Wulfrum saw the glint of the blade and grabbed her wrist, arresting the progress of the point. For a few moments it wavered between them. He increased his grip and heard her gasp. The blade clattered to the floor.

'For you or for me?' he demanded.

'For me.'

'You will not escape me so, Elgiva. You belong to me now and I will keep safe what is mine.'

'I am not yours, Viking!'

'Not yet,' he agreed.

Before she guessed his intent, he lifted her bodily off the floor and strode to the bed, tossing her on to the furs. Elgiva scrambled away, retreating until her back was to the wall, watching in horrified fascination as he unfastened his leggings and let them fall. Then he came on. She drew in a sharp breath. Having had a brother, she was no stranger to the male body, but every inch of that lithe and muscled form spoke of a warrior's strength. Struggling to her feet, she launched herself off the end of the bed and then uttered a shriek of despair as Wulfrum's arm locked fast about her waist. With insulting ease he tossed her down on to the fur coverlet. Strong hands grabbed the hem of her kirtle, ripping it upwards in one fluid movement. The thin fabric parted to the neck. Elgiva twisted away and struggled to her knees. For a moment they faced each other and her cheeks flamed as the Viking's insolent gaze raked her from head to toe. Then he grinned and the glint in those blue eyes became dangerous.

Again she backed away and again her back met the wall. Wulfrum came on, seizing her arms, drawing her towards him.

Somehow she got a hand free and hit him hard across the cheek twice. He laughed, catching her wrist before she could get in a third blow, and flung her backwards. Elgiva turned her head and bit him, the nails of her free hand raking his shoulder, raising scarlet welts on his flesh. It was a brief victory; in seconds he had hold of both her wrists and imprisoned them above her head. Cursing him, Elgiva writhed and kicked out, but he held her easily now, forcing her down into the furs with the weight of his body. With a sense of panic she felt the hardness of his manhood against her.

'You bastard! You cur! Let *go* of me!'

'No, my lady, I shall not do that.' His hand travelled down to her waist, over the curve of her hip, down her thigh in a long lingering caress. He felt her kick out again, try to raise her knee, and laughed softly.

'None of your tricks will work, Elgiva.'

'Give me a sword and I'll geld you like a steer!'

'Then I should fail in my duty as a husband, and I do not mean to fail.'

Before she could reply his mouth closed over hers in a kiss that was burning and insistent while his hand continued its exploration of her body. Elgiva tasted the sweet mead on his breath, breathed in the musky scent of his skin as he took the kiss at leisure. Then he drew back a little, letting his gaze travel the length of her, taking in every curve of breast and waist and thigh, the long slim legs and dainty feet. In the lamplight her flesh seemed golden.

'Truly, lady, you are beautiful.'

Elgiva's angry reply was lost in a thunderous banging that shook the chamber door and her heart leapt in terror to hear Halfdan's voice.

'Come, Wulfrum! Have you done your duty to your wife?'

'Odin's sacred ravens,' bellowed Ironfist, 'he's had long enough to do it half a dozen times!'

A roar of agreement followed from those without the door. Wulfrum grinned as he looked into Elgiva's bewildered face.

'They seek proof of our union, my lady.'

For a moment her mind was blank. Then, as she recalled the earlier banter, her cheeks flamed. The banging continued and the voices without became more insistent. The door shook on its hinges. A little more and the entire Viking war host would be witness to their wedding night. Elgiva swallowed hard and closed her eyes. Suddenly she felt Wulfrum's weight shift and the hold slackened on her wrists. When she looked again, it was to see him retrieve the fallen knife. In horrified fascination she saw him draw the blade across his arm and then the welling beads of blood as he gathered up the torn kirtle and opened it out before wiping the cloth across the wound.

Throwing a speaking look at his wife, he crossed the room and unbarred the door, opening it sufficiently to thrust the garment out to the waiting hands. For a moment there was silence, then a rousing cheer. Without waiting for more, Wulfrum slammed and barred the door again, letting out a long breath. Then he looked at Elgiva, who was kneeling on the bed, golden hair spilling wildly round her shoulders and over the pelt she was using to shield her nakedness. Her amber eyes were wide, her face ashen. Presently the noise outside diminished and retreating footsteps announced the departure of the intruders. Elgiva drew a ragged breath. They were going. Once again she became aware of Wulfrum. For a long moment their eyes met and she saw him smile. Then he became aware of the blood trickling down his arm and crossed to the basin to retrieve a cloth. She took a deep breath.

'You'd better let me bind that.'

'It's a scratch, no more.'

Elgiva tucked the fur around her and quit the bed to join him at the basin. She poured a little water and, taking the cloth from him, wiped away the blood. As he had said, the cut was not deep, but it bled profusely nevertheless.

Wulfrum watched with quiet amusement, but stood quite still while she bathed the wound and stanched the bleeding enough for her to bind it. He said nothing while she worked, but his eyes never left her. Elgiva kept her eyes on the improvised bandage, hoping he would not notice how her hands shook. When she had finished, he glanced at her handiwork and nodded.

'It is well.' He turned her to face him. 'Now, where were we?'

Elgiva shivered as his fingers brushed her shoulders and strayed across the tops of her breast, ill concealed by the fur pelt. Then his hand closed about her arm and he drew her back to the bed. This time she did not struggle, knowing there was little point. She knew his strength and hers could never match it. She lay beside him, felt him undo the pelt and then his weight as he leaned across her. He would take her now. It was his right. Elgiva closed her eyes and turned her head away. It would soon be over.

Wulfrum's lips seeking hers brushed her cheek instead. He could feel the tension in her body, even though she no longer fought him. Her face was turned away from his, but there was no mistaking the expression of fear and reluctance. He frowned.

'Look at me, Elgiva.'

Slowly she turned towards him and he could see tears welling in her eyes. It was the first time he had ever seen her afraid. Even when Sweyn wanted to kill her she had radiated courage. Now it seemed her store was exhausted. He was not altogether surprised, given the events of the past few days. She had shown greater resilience and determination than any woman he had ever known. With a gentle hand he smoothed the hair from her face.

'You need not be afraid of me, Elgiva. I will not hurt you.'

She remained silent, but the amber eyes registered confusion. He thought ruefully that, had it not been for Lord Halfdan's untimely interruption, he would have taken her. Ironic that his men had prevented the very deed they applauded. It was a good thing they were drunk enough to accept the proof he gave them. Even if they had been sober, it would have been inconceivable to them that he could be in bed with a beautiful naked woman and not possess her immediately and by any necessary means. Looking at the body lying next to his, he thought they had a point.

Seeing Wulfrum's smile Elgiva felt her confusion grow for she could not fathom his thought. Was he trying to lull her into a sense of false security, only to pounce when her defences were down? It would be just like him. He had no shame. Like all his vile race, he took what he wanted without regard to others. He had married her because he willed it, because she was as much a prize as these lands and this hall. As a captive her views had not been considered. The only choice had been to wed him or take Sweyn. Thinking of her likely treatment at those hands, Elgiva shuddered. She might not have survived the revenge he would have exacted. This marriage to Wulfrum had saved her from that fate. In his arms lay her safety. His men would not touch her and Halfdan's were leaving on the morrow, Sweyn with them. She would not be sorry to see them go. They would find other lands to conquer, other plunder to seize, other captives to take, but Wulfrum would not be with them. He was here and here to stay and nothing now could ever be the same.

Fatigue washed over her, along with the soporific effects of the mead, and Elgiva felt her eyelids grow heavy. She fought it. She must not relax her guard. However, pressed close to Wulfrum, the warmth of his flesh beneath the coverlets added to her drowsiness and her tired body relaxed of its own volition. Her eyelids drooped again, fluttered once and then closed.

Wulfrum glanced down, stroking back wisps of golden hair from her cheek. She stirred slightly, but did not wake, unaware of the gaze that drank in every line of her face. Truly, he thought, she was beautiful. And she was his, nominally anyway. The rest would come. She would yield as he knew she must. A body like that was made for love-making. Lightly he stroked the warm skin of her breasts, tracing a path down the curve of her waist and the gentle flare of her hip, breathing in her scent. It was powerfully erotic. However, he resisted the temptation to wake her. After all, he had time enough now.

Chapter Seven

Elgiva awoke to broad daylight. For a few confused seconds she could not remember where she was. Then memory flooded back and with it shame. Beside her lay the man who was her husband now. Wulfrum slept on and for a moment or two she watched. He was lying on his back, one arm thrown behind his head in an attitude that seemed both abandoned and vulnerable. Her gaze travelled from the dark tousled hair to his face, exploring its chiselled lines, then moving on to the lips and chin and thence to his naked torso where the marks of her nails showed a harsh red. The welts looked painful, but she felt no remorse. It occurred to her as she watched him sleep that anyone with a blade could kill him where he lay, driving the point between his ribs and thrusting it in to the hilt. It would be no more than he deserved. Even as the thought formed itself, she rejected it—she could never kill a man in cold blood. Besides, had he not spared her from dire humiliation last night? Aye, and rape too. Why had he? It was his right to take her and yet he had waived that right. Truly the man was an enigma: on the one hand, a fearsome warrior, and, on the other, capable of tenderness and compassion. He intrigued even while he repelled.

Throwing the coverlet aside, she eased herself to the edge

of the bed but was stopped short. Her hair was partly trapped beneath the weight of his body. With great care she eased it away. Wulfrum stirred, but did not wake. Elgiva drew in a deep breath as the strands came free. Cautiously she climbed out of bed, glancing around for her kirtle. Then she remembered what had become of it and her cheeks grew hot. Seizing a pelt from the bed, she wrapped it around herself and tiptoed to the window, peeping through a crack in the shutter. Nothing stirred, either in the courtyard or the meadow beyond the palisade where the majority of Halfdan's force was encamped. No doubt many would feel like death this morning after the vast quantities of mead and ale they had consumed. She turned back into the room, thinking to retrieve her gown. It would not be so comfortable without the kirtle beneath, but there was no alternative unless she wished to leave the chamber clad only in a wolf pelt. The rest of her garments were in the chest in her bower.

Looking round the room, she saw the clothing that Wulfrum had discarded the previous night and with it his sword. Elgiva moved towards it, her bare feet making no sound on the wooden floor. With care she lifted the heavy blade from its resting place and studied the hilt in curiosity. It was made of iron, gilded, and bound with copper wire, the pommel set with red jasper. Closing her hand round the hilt, she drew the blade part way from its scabbard. It was a fine weapon and beautifully wrought—a true melding of iron and steel. Where the hammer had fallen on the metal, it had left wondrous patterns like wreaths of frozen breath, fantastic shapes that seemed to change with the light. Down the centre were hammered grooves to channel the blood. She had no need to try the edge of the blade to know it was keen. She would have wagered too, that it was finely balanced. In truth, it was a warrior's weapon.

'Were you planning to use that, Elgiva?'

She spun round to see Wulfrum watching her from the

bed. Recovering her self-possession, she slid the blade back into the scabbard.

'No. You are more use to me alive. All the same, it is a beautiful sword.'

'It is called Dragon Tooth.'

'An apt name.' Elgiva laid the weapon back where she had found it.

'So it is,' he agreed. 'It was wrought by a smith of great renown among my people. He made it for Lord Ragnar, and he gave it to me.'

'A handsome gift. He must have favoured you highly.'

'He was like a father to me.'

Elgiva looked at the sheathed blade and thence at Wulfrum. The blue gaze that met hers was implacable. Elgiva shivered. Suddenly a lot of things had become clearer.

'And when King Ella slew Ragnar, you sought to avenge his death.'

'Of course. I swore the blood oath along with his sons. With my sword brothers. It was a matter of honour.'

'A matter of honour to slay King Ella, perhaps,' replied Elgiva, 'but to slaughter the innocent too?

'Kings are not as ordinary men. The decisions they make fall on all their subjects for good or ill. When Ella threw Ragnar into the snake pit, he not only murdered a great warrior he added grave injury to that insult—a warrior must die with a sword in his hand or he cannot enter Valhalla. Ella denied him that right and in so doing he sealed his own fate and that of his kingdom.'

Elgiva bit her lip, knowing there was more than a grain of truth in his words. Besides, for years Northumbria's rulers had been involved in petty disputes. Had they only joined forces, the Vikings might have been repelled. As it was, the land was overrun and its people conquered. Guessing the trend of her thoughts, Wulfrum frowned.

'There is no use repining. What's done is done.'

'Indeed, but do not expect a conquered people to enjoy their situation.'

'I do not, but I expect to be obeyed.' Wulfrum's voice was quiet, but every word carried weight. 'The conquered must bend to the yoke.'

'Aye, my lord, for who would dare do other?' The tone dripped sarcasm.

'I think you are not conquered, lady.'

Elgiva glared at him. Undismayed, he let his gaze travel over her appreciatively. The pelt she had wrapped about her left her arms and shoulders bare and stopped short mid-thigh, revealing a shapely pair of legs, and he was reminded of those other more intimate places beneath. He resisted the temptation.

'Come, do not deny it.'

'Whatever you say, my lord.'

'The man who would be your lord, Elgiva. Only I think another stands between.'

Genuinely puzzled, she could only stare at him.

'Don't pretend you don't understand. I refer to your former betrothed.'

'Aylwin?'

'He.'

'How can he stand between, my lord? He is gone.'

'And yet you have not forgotten him.'

'No. How could I?'

'Then you were fond of him.'

'He was a good man. I respected him.'

'More than that, I think.'

Elgiva began to feel uneasy, wondering at the tenor of his questions.

'He was a friend of my father's. Since his death, Lord Aylwin considered it his duty to help our family.'

'Indeed. And what of your brother?'

'He died in a hunting accident two months ago.'

'And yet the neglect I see around this estate goes back further.'

'Osric had no interest in anything save his hawks and his hounds.' She hesitated. 'You have seen how things are at Ravenswood. I could not bear to see it so neglected. The only way to change things was to marry a man who would restore the place to what it was when my father was alive.'

He heard the sadness in her voice and understood. He too knew what it was to lose a father. Yet her brother must have been a wastrel indeed, to let so fair an estate fall into rack and ruin. In that moment he had an insight into her predicament and knew it would have been hard on a woman alone.

'So after your brother's death you were left alone.'

'Save for Osric's sons,' she replied. 'The children whom Sweyn would have murdered.' The contempt was clear, but he could understand it.

'Did your brother make no attempt to find a husband for you?'

'No.' She did not qualify it, hoping yet to keep the conversation away from Aylwin. 'I told you, he had no interest in the matter.'

'Very remiss of him.'

Elgiva felt her blood race, more than ever aware of that searching blue gaze. Why should he care about her relationship with Aylwin?

'A woman alone would find herself in an unenviable position,' he went on. 'Particularly a beautiful woman with wealth and land.'

'I did not choose the circumstances.'

'No. What woman would?' He paused. 'You would seem to have been fortunate in your friends.'

'As you say, lord.'

'But this Aylwin was much more than a friend, was he not?' The blue gaze grew warmer. 'You loved him, didn't you?'

He saw the momentary flicker of surprise on her face and

knew a moment's triumph. His guess had been right, then. Her reluctance for him stemmed from her love for another.

'Some marriages are made for love, my lord,' she replied, 'but precious few.'

The irony was pointed and his jaw tightened in response.

'True,' he replied. 'And yet that has never been grounds for a wife to deny her husband.'

'You think I denied you because I loved Aylwin?' Elgiva wanted to laugh, but it caught in her throat like a sob.

'Is it not so?'

She shook her head, unable and unwilling to explain. Wulfrum smiled grimly.

'Then let us put it to the test.'

Without warning, he scooped her up and carried her to the bed, spilling her on to the coverlet and pinning her there with the weight of his body, clamping her wrists in strong hands. For a moment he was silent and Elgiva remained quite still, waiting, praying, striving to keep her breathing even, to ignore the pleasurable warmth along the length of her skin. It seemed as if every part of their bodies touched. If he pressed his advantage now, she could not stop him. For a fleeting second she wasn't even sure she would try. Appalled, she pulled herself up abruptly. He was the enemy. There could be no warmth between them.

Unable to follow the thoughts behind the smooth brow, Wulfrum frowned. For all that they afforded pleasure, women were subtle and devious creatures, not to be trusted like men. Elgiva's golden beauty made her more dangerous than most. He knew that she had told him some of the truth, but he was not naïve enough to think she had told him everything. However, it answered some of the questions that had been puzzling him in the past few days. He would discover the rest by and by. In the meantime he was in a highly desirable position.

Elgiva saw his expression change and tensed beneath him, putting up a token resistance to the kiss he took next. His mouth on hers was gentle, but it would not be denied, forcing hers open, demanding her response. It seemed to go on for a long time. Then he drew back a little, looking into her face.

'Give yourself to me, Elgiva.' The tone was more a plea than a demand, his voice husky with desire. Her body tensed further. Seeing her expression, he masked disappointment with mockery. 'No? I thought not.'

She met his gaze and tried to ignore the dangerous thumping of her heart.

'I will never give myself to you.'

The blue eyes burned. 'Did you give yourself to Aylwin?'

For a moment she was thrown. If she hadn't known better, she would have thought he was jealous. It was tempting to lie, to tell him she had belonged to his enemy, but somehow she couldn't quite bring herself to do it.

'No.'

'He was a laggard, then.'

'He showed restraint out of respect. I cannot expect you to understand.'

'I understand, all right—you didn't want to bed him.'

Her cheeks grew warm, partly for the accuracy of that shot and partly for the assurance with which it was delivered.

'Come, admit it.'

'I admit nothing except that I loathe you,' she retorted.

If she expected him to become enraged, she was mistaken.

'No, you don't.' He smiled and reached out, taking a lock of her hair between his fingers, testing its softness. 'And you will come.'

Her jaw tightened. Did this arrogant barbarian think she would fall into his arms just because he willed it?

'You are thinking you will never do that, isn't it so?'

The blush on her cheeks was sufficient answer and his smile widened.

'Never is a long time, Elgiva, and time is all on my side.'

Then she felt his weight shift and she was no longer pinned. In trembling relief she massaged her bruised wrists and watched him leave the bed to cross the floor and retrieve her gown. Then he tossed it to her. She caught it awkwardly.

'Put it on.' He saw the fleeting expression of surprise in the amber eyes. 'Yes, I'm letting you go—for now.'

Nothing loath, Elgiva rose and struggled into the gown, conscious the while of his watchful gaze, but she could think of nothing to say. Then, having dressed, she moved to the door. It was still closed and the wooden bar heavy and awkward. As she struggled to lift it, Wulfrum moved. Two large hands covered hers. Elgiva froze. Had he changed his mind? She looked up at him to find out. The mocking smile was back, but he lifted the heavy bar. Weak with relief, Elgiva swallowed hard. However, he held the door closed a moment longer.

'I will give instruction for your things to be moved in here.'

'I have my own bower.'

'Henceforth you will share this room with me,' he replied. 'Love me or loathe me, you will discover how real this marriage is going to be.' The tone was soft enough, but utterly implacable. Unable to withstand his gaze longer, Elgiva looked away. Wulfrum smiled. Then, to her unspeakable relief, he opened the door and let her pass.

Elgiva made her way back to her bower and sank weak-kneed and shaking on to her bed. The tears she had been holding back spilled over and fell unchecked, all the fears and tensions of the last week pouring out in great racking sobs. She cried for the loss of her kin and her home and for the knowledge of a past life that could never be regained. She cried for a long time. Osgifu, peeping in unnoticed, saw her and retreated again to let her have her cry out. The grieving was long overdue.

When it was over, she brought hot water and helped her mistress wash away the scent of the bedroom. Then she helped her to dress again in a clean kirtle and the blue gown. She combed out the golden hair and braided it down Elgiva's back in a neat and sober plait. When she was done, it seemed to her that no trace remained of the frightened girl at the end of her tether and that in her place was a poised and lovely woman.

By now life was stirring in the hall and Elgiva had no wish to meet any of the Viking war band. She slipped out and, after checking that the coast was clear, went to the stables where her bay mare was stalled. Hearing her footstep, the horse whinnied softly, turning her elegant head to look at the approaching figure. Her soft muzzle snuffled the proffered palm and Elgiva wished she could have found an apple to bring. She stroked the glossy neck and looked the animal over with an expert eye, but to her relief the horse was unscathed by recent events. A look around the stables made it clear they all were. It was evident the Vikings held livestock too dear for indiscriminate slaughter. The mare's bridle still hung on the peg at the stall's entrance and for a moment Elgiva was swept with longing to get out of Ravenswood, to ride away from everyone and everything. Another moment's reflection assured her it would never be permitted. She might be Wulfrum's wife now, but she was a captive for all that and would not be allowed out of sight. The war band would leave soon and Ravenswood would be in Wulfrum's hands, as would she. He would certainly never permit her to ride and so provide the means for her escape. Elgiva sighed. The horse was a symbol of the freedom she had lost and would never have again. Ravenswood was no longer her home, it was her prison and she shackled irrevocably to her gaoler. Nothing could change that now except death. In that bleak moment it seemed in many ways preferable to the future that awaited her. Then she remembered Osgifu's words and knew she could not abandon her people. That dark future beneath the Viking heel was theirs too; somehow she and they must dredge up whatever remained of courage and resilience and find the means to face it. The old days were over. Sad at heart, she gave the horse a final pat and reluctantly quit the stall.

As she left the stables, she became aware of other people all moving in solemn procession towards the burying ground. For a moment her heart misgave her and she wondered who else was dead. Then she remembered. Wulfrum had promised that the Saxon graves might be blessed. Fear was overlaid by relief and a measure of surprise. He had kept his word. Though his men were everywhere in evidence, they made no attempt to interfere. She noticed Sweyn in the background. He gave her a sardonic smile. Elgiva ignored it and looked away, focusing her mind instead on the priest and the words of the blessing.

Standing in the midst of the crowd, she became aware of the man next to her. He seemed familiar, but it was hard to see his face for he wore a hood that concealed his features in its shadow. Then he turned just for a moment and she started. Brekka!

She stared at him aghast. 'What are you doing here?'

'I had to speak with you, my lady.'

'Why?'

'Lord Aylwin sent me.'

Elgiva paled and for a moment thought she might faint. With a severe effort she regained her self-control.

'Aylwin lives?'

'Aye, he lives.'

'Where is he?'

'In the forest with those of our warriors who survived the battle.'

'Is he well?'

'Well enough, though his wounds are not completely healed.' Brekka paused. 'He bade me tell you to be of good cheer and to say that he will come for you.'

Elgiva drew in a sharp breath. 'Brekka, he must not. The Vikings will kill him if they catch him.'

'They will not catch him. When he is recovered, he will gather a force to retake Ravenswood.'

She stared at him in consternation. 'It is madness. It will but lead to more bloodshed.'

'That is unavoidable, my lady.'

'Tell him he must not do this thing. Tell him to get away, far away—Wessex, perhaps. Anywhere the Vikings hold no sway.'

'I will tell him what you say, my lady, but I think he will not heed it.'

After that they spoke no more, being unwilling to draw the attention of the Viking guards. However, Elgiva's mind was in turmoil. Aylwin was alive. He had survived against all the odds. The news made her glad and at the same time much disquieted. He would not lightly relinquish what had been his, but this plan was madness. He had too few men. Surely he must see that. She prayed he would heed her message and go before Wulfrum found out. She shivered, not wanting to contemplate the thought. She was married to the Viking earl and he would keep her. He had made that plain enough. Plain too, what would happen if she disobeyed him again. If he thought for a moment that she plotted his overthrow with her former betrothed, his wrath would be terrible indeed. She had meant it when she said there had been enough bloodshed. Pray God Aylwin saw sense. She could not speak of this to Wulfrum—to do so would be to betray her own people. However, it sat ill with her to deceive him, though she could not have said precisely why.

Halfdan's war band left the next day and Sweyn with them. Elgiva watched him go with a certain sense of relief, for soon he would be far away and she would never see him more. Besides, there were other things on her mind quite apart from Aylwin—Wulfrum had let it be known that he would decide on the fate of the Saxon prisoners taken in the forest. Suddenly she wondered if her optimism had not been misplaced. Would he really kill them, or exact some other fearful penalty? There was no way of knowing.

At midday the prisoners were dragged in their chains to stand before him on the greensward outside the great hall. Having been chained in the open for several days, prey to the elements and fed on scraps, all were filthy and ragged and fearful now for their lives. Wulfrum had given them time to ponder their fate, time for their defiance to leach away. Now he had their full attention. He surveyed them keenly, flanked by two of his most trusted warriors, Ida and Ceolnoth. Behind him the rest of his men waited in silence, flanking the fearful Saxon villagers who had been rounded up to watch the punishment. Off to one side stood a brazier full of hot coals in which irons were heating. Beside it was a large wooden block where stood Olaf Ironfist, leaning on the handle of a great axe. From time to time the prisoners eyed him with distinct unease.

Elgiva slipped out of the bower and along the side of the hall unnoticed, coming to a halt on the leading fringe of the Danish group. She could see her husband quite clearly, but his face was impassive and it was impossible to tell what was in his mind. Then he turned and said something to Ida. As he did so, she saw him look beyond the man to the place where she was standing. Her heart beat faster. Would he command her to leave, tell her this was men's business, that she had no place or right here? However, Wulfrum said nothing, turning back to the prisoners. Elgiva moved closer. Then she heard him speak again, this time to Ironfist.

'These are all the men who were taken in the forest?'

'Aye, my lord. Cowardly dogs all that fled after the battle.'

'Indeed.' Wulfrum let his eyes rest on them. 'They will learn that there is no escape. This land and its people belong to me now and I will guard well what is mine.'

Elgiva shivered, recalling how he had used the words to her on another occasion. Their import was the same, but the tone was grimmer by far.

'The penalty is clear enough for slaves who run: the loss of a foot or the cutting of the hamstrings.'

The prisoners shifted in their chains, looking with horrified understanding at the brazier and the guards who flanked it, then at Ironfist. Elgiva drew in a sharp breath, shooting a fearful glance at Wulfrum as the implications sank in. Surely he could not really be going to do this. It was inconceivable. With thumping heart she moved forwards. For a moment his glance flicked towards her but the handsome face remained stern and he made no other acknowledgement of her presence.

'Bring forwards the first prisoner.'

Elgiva watched appalled as the guards moved to obey, seizing the nearest man, a serf called Drem, who, panic stricken, began to struggle. Several heavy cuffs about the head subdued him while they unfastened the length of chain that joined him to the others. Then he was dragged forwards and thrown at Wulfrum's feet. The earl glanced down a moment and then turned to Elgiva.

'Well, my lady, what is it to be? Shall we hack off a foot or have the varlet hamstrung?'

'Have mercy, lord, I beg you.' Elgiva fought back tears. 'Do not maim these men.'

'It is the standard punishment. They tried to escape.'

'Surely there can be no blame in that. The battle was lost, the place overrun. Who could think of aught at such a time beyond the need to survive?'

Wulfrum's face was expressionless as he looked down into hers. For the hundredth time, Elgiva found herself wishing she might know what he was thinking. Seeing he did not immediately brush her aside, she pressed her case.

'You said the slaughter was over, my lord. That you had need of every able-bodied man available. Does it make sense to cripple these? Spare them, and they will serve you well.'

At her feet Drem hung on her words, ashen faced. Then both of them turned to Wulfrum, though in truth he saw only one. Elgiva was trembling now, her beautiful eyes pleading.

'Show mercy, lord.'

'Leniency may encourage further transgressions. Would you have me show weakness to these people?'

'Mercy is not weakness. All here know you are the lord of this domain and its people and that your will is law. The matter is now beyond dispute. What purpose will be served by fuelling their hatred and their fear? Give them this chance, I beg you.'

Wulfrum appeared to meditate the matter. Beside him Elgiva bit her lip, heart pounding in her breast. Would he heed her at all? The wretch at her feet closed his eyes.

'Very well, then. Since it is your wish I show mercy, it shall be so.' He turned to the guards. 'Henceforth these prisoners shall wear the iron collar of the slave as a reminder of where their duty lies. In addition, each man will receive ten lashes. Carry out the punishment.'

Elgiva let out the breath she had been holding. All around her she heard a similar exhalation and the tension eased as the watching Saxons gave silent thanks for the deliverance of the prisoners. A flogging was a painful reminder of the new order, but Wulfrum had let them off lightly and everyone knew it. The first glimmer of hope awakened in their hearts that perhaps the worst was truly over. In silence they watched as each of the prisoners was forced to kneel by the wooden block while the iron collar was fastened around his neck and then closed with a hot rivet. Elgiva had no desire to witness their humiliation and would have quitted the scene then, but Wulfrum's hand closed round her arm.

'You will stay, my lady, and watch the sentence carried out.'

Swallowing hard, she looked up at him, but his expression

permitted no further parley and she knew she must obey. Her heart filled with pity for the men beneath the lash, but she also knew that Wulfrum had shown great forbearance in this punishment. Even so, as the strokes were counted, Elgiva had to bite her lip to fight down the nausea she felt. Only with an effort could she prevent herself from flinching at each blow. However, she knew it was nothing to the way she would have been feeling now if he had followed his first thought.

Eventually it was over and the gathered crowd began to disperse. Elgiva would have left then, but Wulfrum held her beside him, seemingly in no hurry to let her go, watching his men break off into smaller groups while the serfs returned to their allotted tasks. From the buzz of conversation it seemed that recent events were much under discussion. Elgiva turned to look at her husband.

'Thank you for sparing those men.'

'No thanks are necessary,' he replied. 'I have need of them and now they will all live to serve me well.'

Elgiva caught the gleam in his eye and a suspicion began to form in her mind.

'You never had any intention of doing anything other than flogging them, did you?'

'No.' Wulfrum smiled. 'But it was important that they believed otherwise.'

Elgiva stared at him as the extent of the plan became apparent. 'You knew I would plead for them too, didn't you?'

'I thought you would try to intercede,' he acknowledged, 'and you did. Most eloquently, I might add.'

For a moment she was speechless before the sheer brazen effrontery of the man. Then anger replaced disbelief and she hit him hard.

'You let me think you were really going to maim those men. You let me make a fool of myself.'

Wulfrum caught her wrist before she could deal a second blow.

'No, you didn't make a fool of yourself. Anything but.'

'I believed you back there.' Elgiva tried in vain to disengage herself from his hold. 'I really believed you.'

'Yes, I know. I needed you to believe it.'

'So you used me to make yourself look magnanimous.'

'No, I used you to resolve a dilemma. Believe me, I am grateful.'

'Oh, good.'

Wulfrum smiled down into the amber eyes, thinking how very attractive she was when she was angry. 'Come, now, admit that this was better than the alternative.'

Elgiva was silent, but under her ire she knew he was right. He was also detestably arrogant and high-handed and much too close for comfort. The silence stretched between them.

'Admit it.'

'All right, the way it worked out was better,' she conceded. 'Let's just say I don't approve the means.'

'Then for that I am sorry.'

Elgiva wondered if she had heard aright, but there was no trace of mockery in his face or his tone.

'I must govern these people, Elgiva, and they must learn to obey me. In that way only lies their peace. The sooner they learn it, the better.'

He let her go then and she watched him walk away, turning over his words in her mind. Knowledge of the stratagem still rankled, however, and she felt foolish to have been so easily deceived. In truth, she had played her part to perfection. He must have enjoyed it enormously. Elgiva kicked a loose stone at her feet. Men! They were devious and ruthless in the pursuit of their goals, and Wulfrum was no exception. In future, he would not find her so easy a dupe. She had to admit his apology had sounded sincere enough, but then so had everything else. It was impossible to tell whether he meant it or merely wished to placate her.

She began to walk back to the bower, her annoyance still

simmering. Part of it was directed at herself for having fallen so easily for a ruse. Surely she should be able to read him better. He was her husband, after all, and yet it seemed to her now that she knew nothing about him. On the other hand, he seemed able to read her with uncanny precision. He could read a situation too, and manipulate it for his own ends. The man was insufferable. Worse, he was right—on this occasion, at least. The matter had fallen out better than she or anyone else could have devised. Except that he had devised it, of course.

'Hateful brute!'

Elgiva sent another stone scudding out of her path. He was an arrant knave, a domineering, overbearing rogue. However, he was not cruel. Sweyn would have punished the prisoners with the utmost rigour and would have enjoyed doing it. She shivered. Wulfrum was the lesser of two evils, although bad enough. Glancing across the intervening space betwixt herself and the barn, she saw him there speaking with some of his men. By chance he glanced round and she saw him smile. Disconcerted, Elgiva returned him a cool look and kept on walking.

Chapter Eight

As Wulfrum's men began to set about the necessary repair work, Elgiva experienced mixed feelings. More than anything she wanted to see Ravenswood prosper again, but could never have foreseen the circumstances in which it might happen. That Wulfrum was a strong and capable leader was in no doubt. His word was obeyed without question and he supervised the work with a critical eye. Nor was he above getting involved when occasion demanded it. Gradually, life began to move into a routine as a sense of order and purpose were established.

Wulfrum too noted this with satisfaction. He determined that Ravenswood would be prosperous again and bent his energies to that end. Slackness and mediocrity had no place in his scheme of things and he oversaw the ongoing work with a keen and critical eye. The Saxon workforce might resent his presence, but they were quick to recognise a master who would not be trifled with and bent themselves to their tasks accordingly. They discovered also that he was fair. While he would not tolerate poor workmanship of any kind, he was ready to praise when praise was merited. Nor did he punish lightly. However, a culprit got only one warning. The message was not lost on the rest. Moreover, no one knew where he would be at any given time and he tended to appear when least expected.

One morning, having left Ida to supervise the serfs clearing a ditch, Wulfrum decided to see how the repairs on the root store were progressing. Heading that way, he had barely taken a dozen strides when a movement near the women's bower caught his eye and he saw a small child running from the doorway. He recognised Ulric. Wulfrum grinned, expecting to see an anxious Hilda appear in pursuit at any moment. Even so, he kept his eye on the boy, following his erratic progress, only to see him stumble on a stone a moment later and fall hard. For a second there was silence. Then the air was rent by howling.

Wulfrum sprinted across the intervening space and picked the child up. A swift inspection revealed little actual damage. The tears were more about fright than pain. Lifting Ulric into his arms, he held him close and spoke as he might to soothe a timid horse, letting him understand he had nothing to fear. Eventually the tears abated and the sobs quieted to shuddering breaths. Wulfrum ruffled the child's hair and smiled. Very shyly Ulric smiled back.

Elgiva watched in silence from the doorway. She had seen her nephew run from the nursery and, as Hilda had been busy changing Pybba's soiled underclout, she had offered to go in pursuit. Her surprise could not have been greater to discover Wulfrum there first. The readiness and ease with which he comforted the child moved her to no small degree. She could never have believed a man so physically powerful could be capable of such gentleness. It was an altogether different side to him and one which drew her in spite of herself.

Sensing a presence nearby, Wulfrum turned and she saw him smile. 'Were you looking for the boy by any chance?'

'Yes.' She drew closer, looking the child over, but he seemed none the worse for his mishap.

Wulfrum noted her expression. 'He's not hurt, are you, lad?'

Ulric burbled a reply and smiled.

His large mentor grinned. 'I'll take that as a no.'

Elgiva found herself smiling too. 'Hilda will be relieved. Ulric ran off when her back was turned.' She paused. 'Thank you for taking care of him.'

For a moment Wulfrum was thrown by the warmth of that smile. To cover it he looked away and surveyed the child instead.

'How old is he?'

'Three.'

'A fine boy. Like his brother. A man would be proud of such strong healthy sons.'

'And yet my brother showed little enough interest in them.' Elgiva bit her lip. 'Do you think me disloyal for saying it?'

'No. But you are not as your brother, I think. These little ones mean a great deal to you.'

'Yes, of course. I am their aunt, after all.'

'It is more than that,' he replied. 'You like children.'

'Yes.'

'That's good.'

The tone was light enough, but Elgiva sensed more beneath, and a suggestion that brought sudden warmth to her neck and face. Just then, however, Hilda appeared on the scene, holding Pybba in her arms. Seeing Ulric's present situation, she checked uncertainly. Wulfrum glanced at her and then handed the child to Elgiva.

'I'll leave him in your capable hands.'

With that Wulfrum took his leave. Elgiva watched him go. The man continued to surprise. Just when she thought she understood his character, some new facet was revealed. Clearly he liked children and would not suffer them to be hurt or abused. Had he not saved her nephews from Sweyn? And now he had shown unlooked-for kindness to Ulric. Then she recalled the latter part of the conversation and was jarred by the unspoken implication. Once she had wanted children. Had she married Aylwin she would have borne his sons without complaint. Wulfrum was another matter—he was her husband, but how could she bear his seed without compromising everything she held dear? Elgiva took a last look at his retreating figure before turning abruptly away.

Having spent some time at the root store and found everything progressing as he would wish, Wulfrum returned to the hall. There he found the two healers embarked on their morning round of the injured. His glance slid over Osgifu and came to rest on Elgiva. She was changing a dressing, her whole attention on the task as her hands moving surely and gently about their work. Occasionally she spoke quiet words to her patient. It was Harald, one of his own men. A youth of seventeen, Harald had received an arrow in the shoulder in the battle for Ravenswood and then contracted a fever afterwards. For some days his life had swayed in the balance and it was only thanks to the skilled care he received that he survived at all. Now it seemed he was recovering, for he was able to speak to his nurse. Wulfrum saw her smile. He could not hear the words she spoke in reply, but, from the expression on the young man's face, they were having a most powerful effect. Wulfrum's eyes narrowed.

Before he had time for further thought, Ironfist appeared. One look at the giant's expression was sufficient indication of bad news.

'What is it, Olaf?'

'Half the work party for the barn roof failed to turn up this morning. Their companions said they'd gone down with the flux.'

'And have they?'

'It's true, my lord. I've just come from the village. They're sick, all right.'

Wulfrum frowned. 'Is it known what caused this? Tainted meat, perhaps?'

'No, lord. It seems only a few had eaten meat. The rest had bread and pottage.'

'We must find out. I've seen what the flux can do to entire armies. Somehow this must be checked—I can't afford to lose the better part of the work force.'

'I know not how it may be done,' replied Ironfist, 'but we have with us those who may.'

Wulfrum followed the other man's gaze to the other side of the hall. Elgiva was still with Harald. The young man never took his eyes off her. It occurred to Wulfrum for the first time that Harald was a good-looking youngster and well made withal. He had, besides, a most winning smile. It drew the like from Elgiva. The earl frowned. Leaving Ironfist, he crossed the intervening space until he stood by the pallet bed. His wife glanced up in surprise.

'My lord?'

'I would speak with you and Osgifu when you have finished here.'

The tone, though quiet, was distinctly cool and two women exchanged glances.

'As you will, my lord,' replied Osgifu.

Elgiva's hands continued with their task on the bandage. Wulfrum looked down at Harald.

'You are recovering well, I see.'

'Indeed I am, my lord. Thanks to this lady.' Harald's eyes spoke his admiration louder than words. Wulfrum saw Elgiva smile again in response and his jaw tightened.

'I hope it will not be long before you're on your feet again.'

'I hope so too, my lord.' Harald threw another fond look at Elgiva. As she fastened the cloth strip into place, her hands rested a moment on his breast.

'I'm glad to hear it,' replied Wulfrum.

At last Elgiva got to her feet and he took her arm, leading her aside. Osgifu followed them. As Wulfrum explained the situation they listened in silence, though Elgiva exchanged a troubled glance with her companion. It was Osgifu who spoke.

'I would need to see the sick for myself, lord.'

'You may go into the village. Ironfist will accompany you.'

Elgiva looked up at him. 'May I go with her?'

'No. You will remain here and prepare whatever medicines are necessary.'

'But I may be able to help.'

'Even so.'

'But—.'

'I have said.'

She bit her lip, but remained silent, watching the other two depart. Then she turned away.

'Stay!'

Elgiva paused. 'Lord?'

For a moment the amber eyes met his and he caught a glimpse of anger there and something else besides that said more plainly than words what she thought of his decision. Wulfrum concealed the smile that would otherwise have risen to his lips.

'You will tend to your duties here.'

'Whatever you say, lord.' The tone was cool and level, but it carried a nuance of criticism that did not escape him.

'Osgifu will assess what needs to be done.'

'Indeed she will, and right well too. But if this is an epidemic, it will require more than one pair of hands to deal with it.'

'If it is an epidemic.'

For a moment she was silent before the amber eyes met his own. 'You still think I might run away, don't you?'

'The thought had occurred to me.'

'Do you think I would leave my people when they are sick and dying?'

'It did not stop you before.'

He saw the colour rush to her cheeks, but she held his gaze. 'That was a moment of madness I regret. Besides, I had a much better chance to run afterwards, but I did not take it.'

'Because you knew I would find you eventually.'

'Because I would not leave my people to the tender mercies of the Vikings.'

'But they are at my mercy, are they not? You included.' Wulfrum watched the colour deepen in her face to a most attractive shade of pink.

'Then let me help them.'

'You are helping them.' Wulfrum gestured to the men she had just left. 'Saxon and Dane alike have much to thank you for.'

'That is not what I meant and you know it.'

'Nevertheless, it is where your duty lies at present and where it will remain.'

The tone was casual enough, but Elgiva could not miss the note of iron beneath. With an effort she forced back the protest that sprang to her lips and held on to her temper, aware of his eyes on her the while.

'Then I shall return to my duties, lord.'

'When I give you leave,' he replied.

Elgiva stopped, every line of her body rigid. Wulfrum waited, wondering if she would yield to the impulse to hit him, for he correctly divined it was in her mind. The provocation had been great—and deliberate. Would she rise to the bait? In a part of his mind he hoped she might.

The silence stretched out, but Elgiva said nothing, forcing herself to remain still under that penetrating blue gaze. The bastard was enjoying this. He would enjoy it even more if she tried to defy him now, but she wasn't about to give him an excuse to touch her. She saw his smile widen. The urge to hit him grew stronger, but she controlled it.

'You may return to your work, Elgiva.'

Her chin lifted. Throwing him a most expressive look, she turned on her heel and strode away. Wulfrum watched her go.

He wasn't sure his decision to keep her here was the right one, but time would tell. Meanwhile, she would remain where he could see her.

Elgiva initially headed for the women's bower where she paced the floor for some minutes in impotent ire, her pride in complete revolt. It seemed his arrogance knew no bounds. After a while, though, when her temper cooled a little, her thoughts went next to Osgifu. If the problem in the village was the flux, then they would need something to reduce fever, a soothing tea to calm the stomach and a tincture of white clay to bind the gut. She might as well get on with the preparations now. Even if the Viking would not let her go outside the pale, she could still do something useful. Thus she went to the still room where she and Osgifu kept their herbs and dried them for their potions and salves. After making up the fire and setting some water to heat, she selected a jar of willow bark. Then she began to prepare an infusion.

After three hours' work she had prepared a goodly supply of medicines for Osgifu. It was a satisfying job in many ways and a soothing one; she could forget about everything else and concentrate only on what she was doing. She was so absorbed that she didn't hear the door open.

Wulfrum paused on the threshold, looking round. It was the first time he had been in this place, but his eye took in the neat arrangements of pots and jars and the bundles of herbs hanging from the beams. The scent of the herbs was pleasant and filled the room with their fragrance. He identified mint and thyme and sweet lavender, perfumes he had come to associate with Elgiva. She was standing by her work bench across the room, for a moment or two unaware of his presence. He smiled and stepped into the room.

Elgiva heard the movement and looked up.

'My lord?'

He glanced at the jars of cooling liquid. 'You have been busy.'

'Yes, Osgifu will need these medicines tomorrow.'

Elgiva strove to keep her tone level, but for all her outward air of calm her heart was beating faster. Suddenly the room seemed much smaller too.

'Your skills have already proved most useful,' he said.

'I'm glad you think so, my lord.'

'What other hidden talents do you possess, Elgiva?'

For a moment she met his gaze, but as always his expression was hard to read. Even so it was disturbing. She bit her lip and turned away, busying herself again with her task. Wulfrum watched. Under that dark gaze Elgiva grew warm. Although he had remained quite still, he seemed to emanate dangerous strength. The air was charged with it, charged too with the memory of their earlier disagreement. Unwilling to provoke his anger by alluding to it, Elgiva remained silent.

Wulfrum had a shrewd idea as to her thoughts and knew he couldn't entirely blame her. When he refused her permission to go to the village, it wasn't because he feared she might attempt to escape—it had been an excuse. Just as this visit to the still room was an excuse. Looking at her now, he knew why he had come. Advancing with slow deliberation, he came to stand beside her. To cover her confusion, she turned away, but his arms slid round her waist and prevented it. She felt him nuzzle her hair and then the warmth of his lips on her neck. Elgiva's blood raced even as her mind rebelled. Then, without warning, she was tipped back into the crook of his arm and his mouth was on hers. Intent initially on stealing a kiss, Wulfrum had not reckoned with the powerful effect of the scents on her clothes and skin. The kiss grew more passionate and all of Elgiva's resistance availed her nothing. Only when he eventually drew back and looked into her face did he seem to recollect himself.

'Was that another demonstration of power?' she demanded then.

'You know it wasn't.'

The words were quietly spoken and she knew them for truth—if he had really chosen to demonstrate his power over her he would have pursued the matter to its conclusion. He surveyed her keenly.

'Whom do you fight, Elgiva? Me or yourself?'

'You flatter yourself.'

'Do I?'

Her cheeks burned as indignation mounted, but for the first time she was lost for words. Wulfrum returned a slow infuriating smile that only added to her discomfiture.

'*Do I?*' he repeated.

Though he held her but lightly now, she could feel his hands through the stuff of her gown. It seemed that where they touched her flesh burned.

'Believe what you like,' she retorted.

'I believe you want me as much as I want you.'

'You are mistaken.'

'Shall we put that to the test?'

'No!'

'Are you afraid I might be right?'

'I have no such fear. Now let me go.'

To her surprise and relief his hold slackened. His expression then was compounded of amusement and frustration and something more, something harder to define.

'All right, Elgiva, I'll let you go—for now.'

Watching him move away, she let out the breath she had been holding.

'Until later, my lady.'

Then he let himself out and she was alone. It was some time before she could compose herself sufficiently to finish her work.

Osgifu and Ironfist did not return until late afternoon. Elgiva had been watching for them from the door of the bower and hurried to the hall, anxious to hear what Osgifu had to say. When she arrived, Wulfrum was already there. After their earlier encounter she had wondered how to face him again, but he merely glanced round, inclining his head in acknowledgement of her presence, before turning his attention to Ironfist.

'How goes it, Olaf?'

'Not good. We've had the first fatality already: a child of six. Many more will die unless we can discover the cause.'

Elgiva listened in mounting concern. Catching Osgifu's eye, she saw her own sadness mirrored there. In any outbreak of sickness the old and the young were the most vulnerable. She thought of Ulric and Pybba and her sense of helplessness increased.

'There must be a common link somewhere,' she said. 'Something we're overlooking.'

As the others turned to look at her Elgiva reddened, realising she had been thinking out loud. She half-expected Wulfrum to be annoyed by her interruption, but he made no comment, merely giving her a searching look.

'Osgifu has suggested that latrines should be dug to take the waste,' Olaf went on. 'I think she's got a point. The place stinks.'

Wulfrum nodded. 'I'll get Ida to organise a work detail in the morning. This thing must be stopped somehow.'

Having expected him to reject the idea out of hand Elgiva was unable to conceal her surprise and with it pleasure that he should be willing to listen. If only he would let her accompany Osgifu on the morrow. However, after his previous reaction, she didn't dare raise the topic.

Osgifu had no such reservations. Meeting Wulfrum's eye squarely, she spoke up with calm assurance. 'My lord, there are more people sick now than I can tend. I need help.'

Beside her Ironfist nodded. 'She speaks the truth, lord.'

Wulfrum looked from one to the other and then at his wife.

'Very well, you may go with her tomorrow, but you will be accompanied at all times.' He gave Ironfist a meaningful look.

Elgiva inclined her head in token of acceptance. 'As you will, my lord.'

The dulcet tone didn't deceive him for a moment, any more than the lowered eyes and meek expression. The vixen had never done anything meekly in her life. She was enjoying this retraction and he knew it. If he'd been alone with her, he'd have…

Before that seductive thought could finish itself, Ida hove into view and Wulfrum's mind was recalled to present business. Summoning the newcomer, the earl took him aside along with Ironfist and soon the three were deep in conversation.

Osgifu turned to Elgiva and smiled. 'It will be a happiness to have you with me again, child.'

'It will be a happiness for me too,' returned Elgiva. 'In the meantime, I have prepared some medicines.'

'In good time. We're going to need them.'

The words were prophetic—half an hour later Ceolnoth appeared with the news that two of the Danes had fallen ill. It struck a sombre note with the rest and the meal that night was taken in an unwontedly quiet atmosphere.

Elgiva slipped away as soon as she could and went to check on her nephews. They were asleep and, according to Hilda, both had been quite well before she put them to bed. Reassured, Elgiva returned to the chamber she shared with Wulfrum. It was her habit to retire first and often she was asleep before he returned. This evening, therefore, she was surprised and not a little dismayed to see him there already and clearly preparing to retire. He had stripped off his tunic and shirt and her startled gaze fell on the silver arm rings and the muscles beneath, muscles whose strength she already knew.

'Are the children well?' he asked.

Elgiva stared at him in surprise, wondering how he could have known her errand.

'Quite well, my lord.'

'I'm glad to hear it. I would not have them succumb.'

He sounded sincere and she was touched in spite of herself. It behoved her to make an effort in turn.

'Thank you for allowing me to go with Osgifu tomorrow.'

Wulfrum unfastened his breeches. 'It was what you wanted, wasn't it?'

'Yes. I know I can be of help.' Elgiva turned away, removing her girdle and laying it aside, keenly aware of the naked form just feet away.

'So I think.'

Her hands paused on the laces of her gown and she looked up, half-expecting to see mockery in his expression, but it was conspicuous by its absence. For the second time she was taken aback. If he knew it, Wulfrum gave no sign, but merely climbed into bed.

'If we could just discover the cause, it would be something,' he said.

Elgiva unlaced her gown and drew it off, laying it with the girdle. 'I was thinking about that. If food is not the common link among the sick, could it be the water?'

She unfastened her hair and shook it loose. It fell in shining waves across her shoulders as she reached for the comb. Wulfrum propped himself on one elbow, watching. With an effort he dragged his thoughts back to the question.

'How so?' he replied. 'The villagers draw their water from the stream, my men from the well by the hall.'

'Is it possible your men might have drunk from the stream too?'

'It's a thought. I shall question them tomorrow.'

Elgiva nodded. 'It might be a good idea, my lord.'

She resumed her task, taking her time over it, aware the while of Wulfrum's gaze. His face gave no clue as to the thoughts behind but the memory of the afternoon was still keen, his parting words in particular: *I'll let you go—for now.*

Eventually she could delay no longer and, with reluctance, laid aside the comb. Then she blew out the lamp and joined him, hurriedly drawing the pelts up under her chin. With thumping heart she felt his weight shift and her body tensed. Then she realised he had but stretched out beside her; she could feel his warmth beneath the furs. She swallowed hard, waiting, every nerve alive to him, every fibre of her being keyed to fight. The outcome could be in no doubt, but there would be no tame submission.

For some time she remained thus, straining to catch the least sound or movement that might signal danger, but none came. Wulfrum made no attempt to touch her. She could detect no trace of his earlier behaviour in his manner this evening. It was almost as if the incident had never happened, except that memory would not be denied. Almost she could still feel the searing passion of that embrace and with it resurgent anger. No man, even her betrothed, had ever dared to kiss her like that. Her fingers brushed her lips. Would Aylwin *ever* have kissed her thus? Somehow she doubted it. That thought led to others that were infinitely more disturbing and with them the mocking echo of another voice: *Whom do you fight? Me or yourself?*

The two women set out early for the village. Wulfrum watched them leave, noting with some interest that it was Ironfist who carried the heavy basket of potions. His gaze followed them until they were out of sight. Then his mind began to turn over what Elgiva had said earlier about the water supply. He went to find the two Danes who had fallen sick. Both were feverish and stricken with cramps, but had sense enough to be able to answer his questions. After hearing their replies, he went to saddle his horse.

Wulfrum rode slowly, skirting the village, and came to the stream from which the peasants drew their water. There was nothing in the clear flowing depths to indicate aught amiss. He knew it had its source in the hills some miles away and that it joined the river further on. Turning the horse's head, he rode upstream, as close to the bank as he could, keeping his eyes peeled. He had not gone a league before he saw it, the remains of a dead sheep lodged among boulders on the stream bed. It seemed Elgiva had been right. He dismounted and waded into the water. It wasn't deep, but it was cold and the rotting carcase was foul. Almost gagging on the stench, he dragged it out on to the bank and then staggered away, retching. It took him several minutes to get his breath; the stink of putrefaction seemed to lodge in his throat. No wonder people were sick. He thought it surprising more of them hadn't died. Reaching for the reins, he remounted his horse and headed back towards the village.

Elgiva emerged from the peasant hut into the pale sunshine, drawing in a welcome breath of fresh air. Ironfist straightened, pushing his shoulders away from the door frame he had been leaning on.

'Whither next, lady?' he enquired.

Elgiva was about to reply, but the words died in her throat as she recognised the approaching rider. Her mind raced to try to discover the reason for his presence. Had he come to drag her back to the hall? Was he angry about something? He didn't look angry, but that was no guarantee of anything. He reined in before the hut. Just then Osgifu emerged from a neighbouring dwelling and, seeing the others, came over to join them. Wulfrum glanced at her a moment before turning to his wife.

'It seems you were right, my lady,' he said.

'Lord?'

'The village water supply had become contaminated.'

'How, my lord?' asked Osgifu.

'A dead sheep further upstream. It was truly rotten. 'Tis no wonder so many here fell ill.'

'You went to check,' said Elgiva, regarding him with open curiosity.

'Yes. After what you said, it seemed the logical thing to do. You were right about my men too; they told me that the last time they were in the village they also drank from the stream.'

Osgifu shook her head. 'Well, I'm blessed! At least we know now. I'll pass the word that all water is to be drawn fresh and the old discarded.'

Wulfrum dismounted and came to stand by his wife.

'I think the epidemic is as good as over.'

'I think so too.' She paused. 'Thanks to your timely discovery, lord.'

'It was you made me think of it,' he returned.

'At least no one else will fall sick, though some are in poor enough case.'

'If anyone can help them, I think it will be you.'

She looked up in surprise, but there was no trace of a smile on his face now.

'I will do my best.'

'I know.'

The intensity of his gaze was disconcerting and Elgiva felt her pulse quicken. He extended a hand towards her.

'Will you return with me now, Elgiva?'

She hesitated and it was Osgifu who spoke. 'You go, my lady. There is little left to do here. I can finish off. Besides, you look tired.'

Wulfrum seized his opportunity. 'She is right. You have done everything possible. Come.'

The tone was gentle, but firm. He intended to be obeyed and Elgiva knew it would be pointless to argue. She watched him remount and then nod to Ironfist. With no more effort than if she had been made of thistledown the giant lifted her on to the crupper. Then he looked at Wulfrum.

'Have no fear, my lord, I'll see Osgifu safe home.'

Wulfrum nodded and then turned the horse's head. For a while they rode in silence, he holding his mount to a walk. Having achieved her company, he had no intention of losing it again too soon. Almost he could feel the tension in the figure at his back, though her hands rode but lightly on his waist, just enough to steady herself. If he had been composed of burning coals she could not have touched him with greater caution. Thinking of his earlier suspicions, he was conscious of a twinge of guilt. It had been churlish when, clearly, her desire had only been to help. Mentally he strove to find the right words but, being unused to baring his thoughts to a woman, found they did not come easily.

'Where did you learn such skill in healing?' he asked.

'From my mother while she lived, and then from Osgifu.'

'They taught you well.' He paused. Then, 'I owe you much, Elgiva, and I thank you.'

Caught off balance by the remark, Elgiva stared for a moment at the broad shoulders in front of her. 'You owe me nothing,' she replied. 'These are my people and their welfare is my concern.'

'They are fortunate then.'

Again she listened for a note of mockery, but heard none. Like his actions this morning, it took her aback. She would not have expected him to take so close an interest in the matter. He could have sent one of his men to investigate the water supply, but he had not. In spite of his earlier opposition, he had listened and acted on her words. It was, she acknowledged, quite an admission and one she could not have envisaged him making even yesterday. Who could have expected so proud a man to unbend so far? It seemed to call for a reciprocal gesture.

'You did your part too, my lord.'

Wulfrum could detect no irony in her voice and was surprised, being well aware how cutting her tongue could be. And yet perversely the same tongue could disarm him in a moment.

It had never occurred to him before that a woman might be an ally, much less a friend. Yet these last few days had shown how valuable a woman's allegiance might be. A man might achieve much with such a one at his side. The idea was disturbing and welcome at once. Yet how to tell her his thought? Again, such words did not come readily; if he said the wrong thing, the fragile truce would be broken. Worse, she might laugh in his face. If she did, he could hardly blame her, given their brief history together. It was probably better to say nothing.

Elgiva had no clue as to his thought, but sensed a change. The tension between them had lightened, at least for now. Uncertain how it had come about, she was unwilling to do anything to change it and kept her own counsel. Thus they returned home in what she might, under other circumstances, have described as companionable silence.

Over the next few days the condition of many of the villagers improved and Osgifu was sufficiently encouraged to voice the opinion that they had turned a corner. Responding to treatment, their patients began to shake off the ill effects they had suffered. More were able to leave their beds and get about again. The fever left them weaker than before, but they were out of danger at least.

In the hall the number of patients had diminished also, until only a dozen or so of the worst cases were left. For all that young Harald would have left his bed, Osgifu refused to allow it.

'If you want to tear that shoulder anew, by all means get up.'

'I have lain here three weeks already.'

'If you know what is good for you, lad, you'll remain a week more.'

He threw her a belligerent look that left her quite unmoved. She turned to Elgiva.

'You speak to him. See if you cannot talk some sense into that hot head.'

Elgiva regarded the young man with an understanding smile, but her tone was firm. 'Osgifu is right. You must remain abed a little longer.'

He sighed then and acquiesced. 'Your wish is my command, lady.'

'Have a care what you promise.'

Harald's expression grew earnest and he carried her hand to his lips. 'I would perform whatever you asked of me, my lady.'

Elgiva laughed. 'I will remember that, Harald. You may have cause to regret your words.'

'Never.'

She extricated her hand and gathered up her things, preparing to move on. As she did so, she looked up and saw Wulfrum watching them from the other side of the hall, his expression flinty. Elgiva noted it with some surprise. Surely a young man's infatuation for his nurse would not make the noble earl jealous? Yet he seemed much out of humour. She ought not to have been amused. Forcing back a smile, she continued with her round.

Across the room Wulfrum's gaze followed his wife's movements among her remaining patients. He saw their expressions as they looked at her, saw their eyes light, saw them smile. A few exchanged pleasantries with her. He saw her smile and reply with a kind word for all. His gaze went back to Harald. Quite clearly the young man was besotted. Wulfrum sighed. Who wasn't? It seemed half his men were in love with his wife. In that moment he felt ashamed of his ill humour. How was it with him that he should respond thus because a callow youth made eyes at her? Elgiva was his. None would dispute it. Harald was young and brave and had ever served his overlord with commitment and loyalty. He might imagine himself head over heels in love, but his was not a treacherous nature. Wulfrum had no reason to suspect him, or Elgiva, either. What she did now she did at his command, and, thanks to her and Osgifu, many lived who might otherwise have died. He had much to thank her for, not look for offence where there was none. In truth, no woman had ever caused the sensation he had felt a few moments ago when he saw Harald take her hand. Wulfrum shook his head. He had thought himself the conqueror here. Now he wasn't so sure. With a final glance across the room he turned and quit the hall, seeking fresh air to cool his head.

Chapter Nine

Elgiva looked round the still room with mounting concern. Tending the sick and injured in such numbers had severely depleted the current stock of medicines and used up most of the dried herbs that she and Osgifu needed for their salves and potions. If they did not replenish supplies very soon, there would be none left at all. The older woman had been thinking on similar lines.

'You must speak to Wulfrum,' she said.

'To what end? He will not let us go into the forest to gather plants.'

'He said he wouldn't let you go to the village too, didn't he?' replied Osgifu. 'But you went in the end.'

'That was different. People were sick.'

'People will be sick again and when it happens we must be prepared.'

Elgiva knew Osgifu was right. With some trepidation she decided to approach her husband on the matter, though she was doubtful of the outcome. Now she deeply regretted her previous attempt to escape. It had been madness, a moment of folly born of desperation and fear, but he would remember it and perhaps count her words suspect now. On the other hand, he had indeed let her go to the village. Besides which, the atmosphere had been less tense of late. Would he listen? With some reluctance she left Osgifu and went to seek him out.

She found him in the yard, supervising repairs to the gate where the carpenter and his team were already busy. Elgiva hesitated; she could see Olaf Ironfist there, as well, along with Ida and Ceolnoth and some of the others. They looked up as she approached and the conversation stopped. Under their speculative regard Elgiva's self-consciousness increased. Had the need been less urgent, her courage might have failed. As it was she waited, wondering if Wulfrum would be angry that she interrupted them. However, when he turned and saw her, he smiled.

'What would you, my lady?'

'A word, my lord, if the moment is convenient.' She looked round at his companions. 'I can come back later if…'

'No. There is nothing pressing. Come.'

He left them and took her arm.

'What is it, Elgiva?'

She explained, searching his face for clues as to his likely response. He heard her in silence and then nodded.

'Go and gather what you need. Osgifu may go with you.'

For a moment she wondered if she had misheard, then managed to stammer out her thanks.

'There is no need to thank me,' he replied. 'Rather I should thank you. The injured made good progress under your care. Now I have seen your skill I would be the last to do anything to hinder it.'

Elgiva felt herself redden under his praise. 'The plants should be picked with the dew on them, close to dawn.' She paused. 'We would go tomorrow, if you have no objection. The matter is urgent now.'

'As you will.'

She smiled, unable to think of anything else to say, all too aware of his closeness. She felt sure that he would return to his men now, being bored with women's affairs, but to her surprise he did not. Retaining his hold on her arm, he drew her away.

'The repairs on the gate will be finished in a day or two,' he said. 'After that the men will restore the doors to the mead hall.'

Thinking of the shattered timbers, Elgiva knew there was a goodly amount of work involved. Already men were busy in the saw pit, while in the village the serfs had begun the necessary rebuilding of the houses that had been destroyed by Halfdan's war band. Others had returned to tend the fields under the watchful eyes of their Viking masters.

As Wulfrum talked, they strolled on and came presently to the stables. It was quiet within and fragrant with hay and horses. Aside from the beasts it was deserted. Recalling the last time they had been alone in a place like this, Elgiva began to doubt the wisdom of remaining. Wulfrum glanced down at her.

'Why are you afraid?'

'I'm not.'

'Then why are you trembling?'

She bit her lip, unable to think of anything to say.

'Do you think I might throw you down on a pile of hay?' He let his gaze travel the length of her. 'Not such a bad idea, now I think of it.'

Her chin came up at once. 'Try it and I'll spit you with that pitchfork!'

'That's better,' he returned. 'But you needn't worry—I am too fearful of my life to do any such thing, although you do make it a tempting risk.'

He turned her to face him, his hands riding her waist. Elgiva caught her breath, suddenly aware of the quiet barn, the absence of people, the large pile of hay in the corner and his proximity. Over the sweet smell of hay and straw she could detect the musky scent of the man, sensual, alluring and dangerous. Would he kiss her again, and, if he did, what then? Appalled by the direction of her thoughts and in the cause of self-preservation, she stepped aside, out of his hold, into the stall where the bay mare was standing. Wulfrum smiled and followed her, moving to the horse's head, letting her breathe in his scent and accept him. Then he patted the glossy neck and ran an experienced hand over her shoulder and back.

'A beautiful animal,' he said, 'but finely made. Not up to a man's weight. A lady's mount, I think.'

Elgiva said nothing.

'Yours?'

'Yes. She was a present from my father.'

'A generous gift.'

'Yes.'

'She will breed fine foals,' he observed.

Elgiva's jaw tightened, but she remained silent. What was there to say? The mare belonged to him now, just like everything else around here. He could do with her as he liked. He could do with them both as he liked. Had he not shown her as much in the still room? A wave of resentment welled up and she turned away. Wulfrum frowned, sensing the change in her mood.

'Elgiva?'

He reached out a hand towards her, but she ducked under the horse's neck and thence out of the stall, running for the door. She heard Wulfrum call after her, but she did not stop. He stared in surprise after her departing figure and shook his head, unable to account for the sudden dramatic change in her mood.

'Now what in Odin's name was that about?' he wondered aloud.

The mare snorted and stamped a hoof. Wulfrum shook his head, bemused. Women were unpredictable creatures at the best of times, like horses. They needed careful handling, but they needed to know their master. Perhaps he should have taken Elgiva that first night, should have demanded her submission. It had been a novel experience for a woman to resist him tooth and nail. Initially he had found it exciting, until he had seen the look on her face, a look of fear and revulsion. It had stopped him in his tracks. He had never forced a woman and would not force this one, although he wanted her more than any woman he had ever met. Thus he had played a waiting game. Now he wasn't sure how much longer he could endure it. Night after night he lay beside her, listening in the darkness to the sound of her soft breathing or in the dawn light watching her sleep. It took all his will power not to touch her, to lay claim to what was his by right. So many times he had been on the point of using force, but each time he rejected it. She must come to him. Only then would she be truly his. So many times he had imagined that moment, tried to visualise the circumstances when she would give herself to him, willingly and without reserve. Wulfrum permitted himself a wry smile. He was not naïve enough to think it would be easy or soon, but it was a challenge and he had ever enjoyed those. A wild spirit was more worth the winning. Giving the mare a last affectionate slap on the rump, he made his way out of the stable.

Elgiva hurried back to the hall, angry with herself for having let him upset her. What was the use? Ravenswood belonged to him now and everything in it, and the sooner she accepted it the better. All the same, the knowledge rankled. Worse, because of her foolish behaviour, he might rethink his permission to let her gather herbs on the morrow.

That evening, as he spoke and laughed with his men, she watched him to see whether he seemed angry, but could detect no sign of it. On the contrary, the atmosphere seemed good numoured with the conversation turning on weapons and hunting. The forest abounded with game and the Vikings were wont to take advantage of it to supplement the food at table. Now it seemed there were plans afoot for a boar hunt. Elgiva, who had been standing in the background overseeing the serving of the food, listened and felt sad, thinking of all the times she had accompanied her father and brother on the hunt, recalling the thrill and speed of the chase. She could ride as well as any man and, for all the little mare was finely made, she was swift and had stamina enough to hold her own against the larger mounts. However, all that was of no import now. She would never be allowed to ride the horse again and Mara would be used to breed fine foals.

'Elgiva, what are you doing there?' Wulfrum's voice broke into her thoughts.

Drawn from her reverie with a guilty start, she threw a swift glance over the table to see what he lacked.

'Come, my lady, that is work for the servants. You will sit beside me.'

'My lord, it is my place to serve you with food and drink.'

'Your place is where I say it is.'

The tone brooked no argument and, with reluctance, she left off what she had been doing and seated herself in the chair beside him. Wulfrum nodded his approval while beside him Olaf Ironfist watched impassively. The other men exchanged glances before addressing themselves again to their meat and the conversation resumed. Elgiva assumed a manner of outward composure, aware the while of Wulfrum's eyes on her.

'From now on you will sit with me at table.'

'As you wish, my lord.'

'I do wish it, and my name is Wulfrum.'

'As you wish, Wulfrum.'

He nodded and, taking up a platter, served her meat and bread himself. For a while they ate in silence, Elgiva paying close attention to the food and trying to appear unconcerned by her husband's scrutiny. Then he called for more ale, waiting while a serf hastened to fill his cup.

'About your proposed excursion tomorrow,' he said.

'Yes?' She felt her heart leap. Was he about to change his mind?

'Olaf will accompany you.' He threw his companion a meaningful look.

Although relieved that he had not reneged on his promise, she couldn't hide an ironic smile.

'I will make no attempt to escape.'

'No, for I would find you soon enough and you know it,' he replied. 'But the forest may hold unseen dangers, for the times are uncertain. It is like to be so until the Danes have consolidated their rule in Northumbria.'

Elgiva said nothing, feeling a familiar surge of resentment. He spoke as if it was but a foregone conclusion. The trouble was, she suspected he was right. The Danes wanted this land, so much better than their own, and, having won it, intended to keep it. Looking round the hall at the assembled men, she knew it for truth. All of them were warriors, armed and trained, living for the thrill of battle and the taking of plunder. These owed their allegiance to Wulfrum as he owed his to Halfdan, and they would serve him well. Already she could see the respect in which they held him. Wulfrum wore his power lightly, but his word was law with them. They would give short shrift to any man who crossed that line, or any woman if it came to it. They treated her with due deference because she was his wife, but they watched her too, as Olaf Ironfist would watch her tomorrow. What Wulfrum had said about possible danger was true, but he was taking no chances on her slipping away into the forest, either. Not that she had intended to. To run would be to leave her people to the mercy of the Vikings.

Her thoughts were distracted by a shriek of protest and she looked up to see Hilda struggling in the hold of one of Wulfrum's men. It was Ceolnoth. The young man seemed intent she should sit on his knee and she equally intent that she should not. A loud slap rang out as her hand met his cheek, a gesture greeted by a roar of laughter from his companions. Elgiva looked at Wulfrum, but he did not seem minded to interfere. Ceolnoth got up with a glint in his eye and, before Hilda could flee, swung her into his arms and strode to the door with her. Her yells and protests were drowned in laughter.

Elgiva turned to her husband. 'Will you do nothing?'

'What would you have me do?'

'Stop your men molesting helpless women.'

'Helpless? Now that is not how I would describe you.'

'You know what I mean. Hilda is not a whore. Nor does she deserve to be treated as one.'

'She is comely and it is plain that Ceolnoth warms to her. Shall I forbid him what I mean to enjoy with my own wife?' He noted with satisfaction the hot colour that flooded her face, the spark of anger in her eyes, and knew she read the message aright.

Elgiva refused the bait. 'She is not his wife,' she retorted.

'No, but she soon will be. Evidently his passion for the wench has grown. He spoke to me this morning, seeking my permission to take her to wife, and I have nothing to say against it. He will wed her as soon as may be.'

'And what of Hilda's views on the matter? Did you seek to discover those too?'

He raised an eyebrow, for her tone was hot though the words were quietly spoken.

'I do not consult the wishes of servants,' he replied. 'Hilda will wed Ceolnoth and there's an end. He is a good man and will make her a fine husband.' He cast a comprehensive glance around the hall. 'Would that matters might be so simply arranged for all my men. However, there are not enough women to go around.'

That was undeniably true. Ceolnoth had made his interest in Hilda plain from the first. It seemed his desire had not abated and now the girl's fate was sealed, like her own. Sensing something of her mood, Wulfrum eyed her shrewdly.

'Is it not better for a woman to be a wife and hold a respected position thus?' he demanded. 'Would you prefer that I handed her over to my men to have her in common?'

'I would not wish that on any woman,' she replied. 'Nor would I wish any woman to be compelled to wed a man she does not—'

Elgiva broke off, blushing and inwardly cursed her hot temper. Again, Wulfrum raised an eyebrow.

'Does not love?' he finished.

'Care for, I was going to say.'

'You did not care for me, but you are my wife.'

'I had no choice.'

'True. But tell me, Elgiva, have you not grown to love me since?' The tone was mocking and her cheeks coloured a deeper shade.

'No.'

Wulfrum laughed out loud, causing several interested looks to come their way.

'You will.'

'You delude yourself, lord.'

'Do I?'

He let his gaze dwell on the lovely profile now turned towards him, drinking in every flawless line, and then move on to her neck and the swelling bosom beneath her gown. Mentally he stripped the cloth away. Aware of that penetrating gaze, Elgiva felt her face grow warm. Wulfrum saw it and grinned, enjoying her discomfiture. Presently she turned towards him, the amber eyes bright with anger.

'Must you stare at me like that?'

'What man would not stare?' He traced a hand down her sleeve. Elgiva forced herself to sit still, though it seemed that her skin burned beneath the cloth.

'Besides,' he continued, 'I think it does not displease you as much as you pretend.'

She fought the urge to hit him, as much for the accuracy of the comment as for its confounded self-assurance.

'Belief is free, my lord. If you choose to delude yourself, I cannot prevent it.'

'I think it is you who delude yourself, Elgiva.' The blue eyes were no longer smiling, and before she could think up a fitting retort he had leaned across his chair and kissed her full on the mouth. Taken thus by surprise and unable to move, she was forced to endure it, incensed alike by the treatment and the dawning knowledge that he was right. Wulfrum released her then, meeting her gaze with an expression that revealed not a shred of remorse. Crimson with embarrassment, Elgiva strove to regain her composure, keenly aware of the sudden heat in her blood and the amused stares they were receiving from all quarters of the room. She kept her voice low, though the tone throbbed with anger and indignation.

'This is mere sport to you, isn't it?'

His brow creased. 'Is that what you think?'

'I don't know what to think.'

'Then know that I do not sport with you, nor ever have.'

'Then what was that?'

'Don't you know? Didn't Aylwin kiss you like that?'

Elgiva stared at him, wondering what Aylwin had to do with it.

'Well, didn't he?' he demanded.

Her blush deepened. 'Certainly not. He always showed respect.'

Wulfrum let out a guffaw of delighted laughter. More heads turned their way. Elgiva rose from her seat and surveyed her husband with rage.

'You're impossible!'

Far from being grieved by the accusation, he only laughed the louder and made no move to stop her as she flung away from him and marched off towards the stairs.

* * *

Elgiva woke with the early light next morning and eased herself from the bed, throwing a baleful glare at Wulfrum as she did so. However, he slumbered on unaware. He must have retired very late for she had not heard him at all. Unwilling to disturb him in case it provoked another conversation like the last, she gathered up her clothes and dressed in haste before slipping away. Osgifu was waiting for her with a basket and with few words the two of them made their way to the gate where stood Ironfist, armed with sword and axe. Instructing the guard to let them through, he followed the two women to the forest.

The sun was high when they returned with laden baskets. The rest of the morning was devoted to tying bundles of herbs for drying, or steeping them in hot water, or grinding them to mix with goose grease to make salves. The room was filled with the smell of their potions, a scent that Elgiva associated with healing and well-being. Part of a woman's role in the household was to know what nostrums to use in the treatment of all ailments from a fever to a cut, from a boil to the toothache. It was a role that Elgiva enjoyed. Each season brought its own flowers for harvest. She knew them all and the places where they grew.

As she worked, it occurred to her that she wielded considerable power—not all plants possessed solely healing properties. Three or four grains of digitalis would provide relief from heart pain; eleven grains would kill. A few nightshade berries mixed in a stew would achieve the same end, as would the leaf or pounded root of monk's hood. She banished the thought, smiling in self-mockery. The chances of killing all the invaders were remote and those who survived would soon discover what had befallen their comrades and would exact a terrible revenge. If Halfdan thought one of his favoured earls had been a prey to treachery, he would be merciless. Besides, she knew it was one thing to think about taking life and quite another to do it. The Danes might hold life cheap, but she could not. Poison was a coward's weapon in any case. She might detest the invaders, but she could not murder in cold blood. Her part was to save life, not destroy it.

She was interrupted in these thoughts by Hilda, who burst through the door, wild-eyed and breathless.

'Help me, my lady! I beg you.'

'What is it?' Elgiva turned, and wiping her hands on her apron, went to comfort the girl. Hilda threw herself into her mistress's arms and clung to her, sobbing. Osgifu frowned, lowering the pestle she had been using.

'What ails thee, child? Are you hurt?'

Hilda shook her head, but before she could say any more half a dozen men appeared in the doorway, led by Ceolnoth. He spied Hilda and grinned.

'Come, my bird.'

He stepped forwards and took hold of Hilda's wrist, drawing her away from Elgiva. Hilda shrieked and struggled, but he held her without effort.

'What is the meaning of this?' demanded Elgiva. 'You have no right to hurt one of my servants.'

''Tis not hurt I intend, my lady,' replied Ceolnoth. 'I would have her to wife.'

Osgifu glared at him. 'You cannot wed without Lord Wulfrum's permission.'

'He has given it. The girl is mine.'

'Yours, Viking?'

Brandishing the pestle again, she took a step closer, but Elgiva laid a restraining hand on her arm.

'He speaks true, Gifu. Lord Wulfrum has given his consent.'

Osgifu stared as outrage gave way to shock. 'Is this so?'

'Yes.'

'My lady speaks the truth,' said Ceolnoth with a grin.

Hilda burst into tears.

'Can you do nothing, my lady?' demanded Osgifu.

'I tried, Gifu, but Wulfrum's mind is made up. If there were women enough to go around, he would marry them all to his warriors.' Elgiva turned to Ceolnoth. 'Go, wait outside. Hilda will be out directly, but first I would speak with her.'

He frowned and, for a moment, she thought he would refuse. However, one glance round the room assured him that the girl wasn't going anywhere since there was but one door and a small window.

'Very well, my lady. But don't keep her too long. I grow impatient for my bride.'

With loud laughter the warriors left the room and Osgifu closed the door behind them. Elgiva turned to Hilda.

'You know there is nought I can do to change this, Hilda.'

'I do not wish to wed him.'

Elgiva looked to Osgifu and the older woman stepped forwards.

'Hilda, listen to me. You have no choice but to wed Ceolnoth, unless to become the plaything of all the rest.'

Hilda drew in a ragged breath and stared at her in horror.

'Gifu is right,' said Elgiva. 'We are none of us free to choose, unless it is to take the lesser of two evils. As the wife of Ceolnoth, his companions will not touch you.'

'He has already forced the girl,' replied Osgifu. ''Tis no wonder she is not minded to have him.'

Hilda drew a deep breath, and dashed away her tears with the back of her hand. 'He has taken me against my will and mayhap I already carry his child in my belly. Must I breed a bastard too, and let it suffer the world's scorn?' She paused. 'I know you can do nothing, my lady, for you are in as sore case yourself. 'Tis just that I am so afraid.'

She began to cry again and Elgiva held her close to comfort her.

'I was too, Hilda.'

'You were never afraid, my lady. I was watching the day you wed Lord Wulfrum, the way you looked about with such calm, facing down all those men. All their eyes could not make you quail.'

'Not so, Hilda. I wanted to run away so far and so fast they would never find me. If I did not, it was because I knew I would never succeed, and I would not give them the satisfaction of seeing my fear. And so I am Earl Wulfrum's wife for good or for ill. There is naught to be done but make the best of it.'

Hilda heard her in wondering silence and then took another ragged breath. 'As I must do with Ceolnoth.'

At that moment a heavy fist pounded on the door.

'Will you come out, wench, or must I come in?'

Osgifu strode across the room, pestle in hand, and put her face close to the wood. 'She'll come when she's ready, Viking.'

'She'll come out now, old woman, or I'll know the reason why.'

'You come in here and I'll brain you, you charmless oaf!'

Further heavy pounding shook the door. Osgifu started back. Elgiva bade Hilda bathe her eyes in cool water from the bowl on the table and then went to the door and opened it. Ceolnoth, startled, lowered a clenched fist.

'Lady?'

'Hilda is coming. Be patient a few moments more.'

The quiet tone was courteous enough, but it bore a command too, and Ceolnoth hesitated. Though he would have liked to push her aside and drag Hilda out by main force, he dared not; he knew well that Lord Wulfrum would not take kindly to any man laying violent hands on his wife. Therefore he swallowed his anger and let his hands fall to his sides. Elgiva remained in the doorway, blocking his path. A few moments later Hilda joined her on the threshold.

'I am ready,' she said.

Elgiva stood aside and let her pass. The girl had regained her composure now, though her eyes bore signs of weeping still. For a moment she and Ceolnoth faced each other in silence. Then he smiled and offered his arm. After a brief hesitation Hilda took it and they walked together through the gathered group of warriors to the waiting priest. Elgiva removed her apron and tossed it aside and then, with Osgifu beside her, followed on.

The ceremony was brief enough and through it she recalled her own wedding day and the terror in her heart. For all she might have fooled the onlookers, she knew it would have taken only a small thing to make her run. Suddenly she became aware of someone beside her, and she looked up to see Wulfrum. He put an arm round her shoulders and drew her close. Still smarting, Elgiva tensed and tried to pull away. The arm tightened. Together they stood thus in uneasy proximity until the brief ceremony was over. Ceolnoth's friends clapped him on the back and gathered round the pair. However, seeing Wulfrum, they fell back a little. He moved among them, his arm still round his wife, drawing her with him to congratulate the newly-wed couple.

'Live long, Ceolnoth. Live long, Hilda.' He took off one of his silver arm rings and gave it to Ceolnoth. 'Wear this in recognition of your service to me. In addition, I will give you one hide of good land. There you may build a home and raise fine sons.'

A rousing cheer greeted his words.

'You are generous, lord,' replied Ceolnoth. 'My wife and I thank you.'

A shocked Hilda stammered out her thanks. Clearly she had not been expecting anything like this. Neither had Elgiva and she looked at her husband in surprise.

'This night we shall feast to celebrate your union,' said Wulfrum. 'Mayhap in future we shall celebrate many more.'

Another cheer followed this and then conversation broke out in different groups. Elgiva looked at Ceolnoth and Hilda and then threw a quizzical glance at Wulfrum.

'Thank you,' she said. 'It was a generous gift.'

'It is fitting I should reward those who serve me well,' he replied. 'Besides, land gives a man a stake in the place and ties him to it, ensuring his loyalty and that of his kin.'

'And providing for his wife.'

'Yes, that too. One day many of these men will have wives and when they wed they shall have land to farm. There is plenty for all and it is good land, rich and fertile.'

Saxon land, thought Elgiva, but she kept the thought to herself. With this gift he had ensured a good future for Hilda, as well as for her husband. It might yet turn out well. Certainly the matter had been settled more advantageously than she could have hoped yesterday.

Wulfrum sensed a slight softening of her mood. Her body no longer tensed against his arm and, though they regarded him appraisingly, the angry spark was missing from the amber eyes. Now that he was close he could detect the sweet smell of herbs and beneath it the warm scent of her flesh, subtle and arousing. He bent his head and let his lips brush hers. Taken by surprise, Elgiva did not fight. The kiss grew more insistent and her heartbeat quickened as pleasurable warmth swept through her. When he straightened she was pink-cheeked with confusion. Casting a swift glance around her, she could see their embrace had not gone unnoticed.

'My lord, your men…'

'Let them watch.'

He kissed her again, slowly, felt her lips yield to the pressure of his and tasted the sweetness of her mouth. Gods, how he wanted her, wanted to throw her down and make love to her till she begged for mercy, but he knew he couldn't. The damned place was a little too public for that and Elgiva far too shy of him anyway. Reluctantly he drew back, his gaze searching her face. There was a strange expression in those amber eyes, one that he couldn't quite fathom. What was she thinking? He would have given gold to know. Controlling himself with an effort, Wulfrum slackened his hold.

Elgiva turned away in confusion, shocked by her own reaction to his kiss. The first had been stolen, the second had not. She should have felt disgust, but she had not. On the contrary, what she had felt was stealthy and growing warmth. Almost she had wanted him to kiss her again. The realisation burned as his former words returned to haunt her: *You will come.* Humiliated by the memory and by her weakness, she detached herself from his arm and turned away.

'What are you afraid of, Elgiva?'

'Nothing.' The assertion was belied by the rosy blush on her neck and cheeks.

'Liar.'

'It is the truth.'

'Is it?' He drew closer and she saw him smile.

'I…it's the herbs. I was but part way through my work when Hilda came in. I must go and finish it. I don't want the plants to spoil.'

The smile widened, telling more than words of his scepticism and his enjoyment of her evident confusion. However, he made no further move to hold her and she turned and walked away, trying to gather her scattered wits, determined to put as much distance between them as possible and aware the whole time that Wulfrum watched her retreat. And it was a retreat. She acknowledged it to herself. Another few minutes and he would have kissed her again and she would have let him. Recalling the dangerous power of his kisses, Elgiva shivered. She would not allow him to manipulate her again. He wanted her surrender and meant to have it, to conquer her as finally as he had conquered Ravenswood. It was a challenge to him, nothing more, and she would not yield herself up as a prize. Women meant nothing to Wulfrum other than as a pleasing diversion, a distraction, and it seemed she was his latest amusement. To her horror Elgiva felt hot tears prick her eyelids and she hastened into the storeroom before anyone could notice.

Later, when she had calmed down, she cursed herself for her stupidity in seeming to give the incident too much significance. Certainly Wulfrum made no mention of it when they met that evening in the hall, and, if he was angry, he gave no sign. He greeted her with courtesy as she took her place beside him and to her eye appeared quite unruffled by an experience that had shaken her to the core. It seemed to her that it was the practised ease of a man completely familiar with women who took what he wanted and moved on. He might be her husband, but it was foolish to think she could ever mean more to him than any other woman. The only difference was that she belonged to him. He could take her whenever he chose. When she returned his kiss, he must surely have scented victory. Her own weakness appalled her. Had she so little resolution after all, that a man could conquer with a kiss? Elgiva bit her lip. She could still feel the warmth of his mouth on hers. What a fool she was. He would never regard her as anything other than a trophy.

Chapter Ten

As the days passed the brooding atmosphere lightened in the warm sunshine and, as the threat of death and destruction receded, the people in the village began to go more freely about their business again. Now the work was in full swing, for, apart from all the necessary repairs, there were crops and livestock to be tended and the work had to be supervised. Since the steward had been one of those killed in the fighting when the war band struck, Wulfrum needed to find another and soon. He decided to consult Elgiva.

'Whom shall I appoint?' he asked. 'Who seems to you to be the best candidate?'

Recovering from her surprise she gave her answer without hesitation. 'Gurth. He's got a good head on his shoulders and he's hard-working. I know my father always considered him to be reliable and honest too.'

Accordingly Gurth was summoned to appear before Wulfrum in the great hall. A short, stocky individual of middle years, with grey in his hair and beard, Gurth was, nevertheless, an impressive figure, for he had about him an air of quiet assurance. He stood calmly enough before Wulfrum, though he eyed his men with some inner unease, clearly wondering what he could have done to draw such unwelcome attention. He glanced once at Elgiva, though her face gave no clue as to the reason for his presence here, and then listened carefully as Wulfrum spoke. As he heard the words, Gurth could ill conceal his surprise and pleasure.

'I need a man I can trust,' said Wulfrum. 'My wife seems to think you are that man.'

'The lady honours me,' replied Gurth.

'Will you serve me in the office of steward?'

All eyes were on Gurth and, in the brief silence that followed, he was aware of the intentness of their gaze. It was possibly coincidence that several of Wulfrum's men rested their hands on their sword hilts. However, Gurth was no fool and this was a considerable promotion. It didn't take him long to make up his mind.

'I will, my lord.'

Wulfrum smiled. 'It is well. You will commence your duties immediately and you will answer directly to me. Tomorrow early we will ride out. I want to know every detail of this estate down to the last cow and chicken, the last sack of oats and sheaf of hay.'

'It shall be as you wish, my lord.'

There being little else to say, Gurth was dismissed shortly afterwards. He made his bow and left the hall.

'I think he is a good choice,' said Wulfrum as the man disappeared from view.

'Well, if he isn't, I'll spill his tripes for him,' replied Ironfist.

Seeing Elgiva's startled look, Wulfrum concealed a grin. 'You need have no fear, my lady. If he serves me well, Gurth will thrive.'

'He will serve you well,' she replied.

'Good, for I would have this estate restored to order.'

'I also. As it used to be when my father was alive.'

'I promise you it will be so again.'

Elgiva believed him. Already the signs of his rule were

everywhere in building and repair work. It gladdened her heart to see it. More than that, it pleased her to know he had asked for her advice and acted on it.

'Gurth will be a real asset,' she said. Then, throwing her husband a sideways glance, 'Would you really have Olaf kill if him if he were not?'

'Of course. I will have no truck with treachery or incompetence. Olaf here will keep an eye on the man, and he does not suffer fools gladly.'

'Gurth is no fool.'

'I'm glad to hear it. In that case he may live.'

Wulfrum caught Ironfist's eye and the two of them laughed out loud. Realising too late they had been teasing her, Elgiva glared at them.

'Why, you…' Words failed her.

Wulfrum's amusement increased. Elgiva shook her head, annoyed with herself for falling into the trap, and annoyed with him too. Then the funny side of it struck her and she began to laugh, albeit unwillingly. Wulfrum stared at her in surprise and his own laughter faded a little—he had not thought her beauty could be improved. Seeing her now, he knew he had been wrong. Feeling the intensity of that look, Elgiva felt suddenly self-conscious and her own amusement ebbed. It was definitely time to leave.

'My lord, I fear I am no match for you today. With your leave, I have matters to attend to.'

Disappointed, he nodded. 'As you will, my lady.'

She nodded to Ironfist and then crossed the hall and made her escape, knowing as she did so that every step was observed.

In fact, Elgiva had not lied when she said there was work to be done and she determined to turn her attention to it now, returning with swift steps to the bower. She entered and heard the door shut behind her. A man, garbed in the manner of a serf, stood in the shadow behind. Elgiva caught her breath.

'Who are you? What do you want?'

'Do you not know me, Elgiva?' He lowered his hood and she found herself staring at Aylwin.

'You.'

'Did I not promise I would come?'

Elgiva swallowed hard. 'My lord, you must not be found here. The Vikings would show no mercy.'

'Brekka keeps watch. He will warn if any approach.' Aylwin smiled. 'But danger or no, I had to see you.' He surveyed her critically. 'You look well, Elgiva.'

'I am well enough,' she replied. 'And you, my lord? Are your wounds healed?'

'Aye, for the most part.'

'Then I beg you to go. Leave this place while still you may.'

'And abandon you?'

'You must. I am Wulfrum's wife now.'

His brows drew together. 'The Viking may have forced you to wed him, but your captivity will be over very soon.'

'What do you mean?'

'I shall not tamely give up what belongs to me.'

She shook her head. 'I do not belong to you any more, Aylwin.' Even as she said it, she knew she never had.

'You will be mine again, Elgiva. I swear it. I will free you from the accursed Viking's yoke.' He took her by the shoulders and looked into her face. 'I have dreamed of this moment for so long and yet now I am here with you I can scarce believe it.'

Appalled by the tenderness in his voice and the almost fanatical light in his eye, Elgiva trembled. As Aylwin drew her to him, she turned her head aside so his lips only grazed her cheek.

'My lord, you must not.' She took a step back.

His hands dropped to his sides and he frowned. 'What is it, Elgiva? What is wrong?'

'Don't you see? I can never be yours. Wulfrum will never let me go. Even if you were to steal me away, he would find us, no matter how long it took, and his vengeance would be terrible.'

'I will find a way.'

In desperation, it was she who now gripped his arms. 'There is none. You must believe that.'

For a moment he was silent. 'No way?' he asked. 'Or is it rather that you do not wish to leave the handsome earl?'

'That isn't fair, Aylwin. I did not choose my fate. It was forced on me and I cannot change it.'

'You mean, you would not.'

'Ravenswood is my home. I will not abandon it or its people.'

'A noble sentiment and a convenient one.' His gaze bored into her. 'You hide behind it to avoid the truth.'

'No.'

'Aye. How long did it take the Viking to win your heart? Or is it the pleasures of his bed that draw you?'

Elgiva's cheeks grew hot, but she kept a hold on her temper.

'Insulting me will not change anything, my lord. For good or ill Wulfrum is my husband now and my first loyalty is to him.'

His lip curled. 'I had not thought you so faithless, Elgiva, or so treacherous.'

The words stung and brought tears to her eyes. To conceal her hurt, she turned away from him. Aylwin moved towards the door. As he reached it, he paused.

'I see it was a mistake to come here.'

'Just go, my lord, while you may.'

'I'll go.' His voice was soft and bitter. 'But I'll be back. And with an army to rout these Danish scum once and for all. Then I will slay your husband with my own hands.'

Elgiva heard the door open and close. Then she was alone. Heart pounding, she leaned against the wooden planks in trembling relief. For some minutes she remained thus as the enormity of the situation was borne upon her. Then, unable to bear the close confinement of the room any longer, she quit the place and went out into the fresh air. She needed space to think. Without conscious choice her feet turned towards the burying ground.

How long she remained there she had no idea. All she could see was Aylwin's face as he turned from her in disgust. She had betrayed him and sided with the enemy. Yet what else could she have done? Made him false promises? She did not love him and never would, but she wanted him safe all the same. If he continued on his present course, it could only end in disaster for all concerned.

A footfall behind roused her from the reverie with a start and she looked round to see Wulfrum approaching. Did he know? Had he seen? Her heart thundered in her breast. Only with an effort did she force an outward semblance of calm. If he had seen anything at all, or even suspected, then Aylwin and Brekka would be prisoners now.

Wulfrum halted a few feet away, his gaze taking in her evident agitation.

'Your pardon, I have startled you,' he said. 'You looked so rapt in your thoughts I did not wish to intrude.'

She took a deep breath. 'Was there something you wished to speak of, my lord?'

The tone was courteous enough, but there was a tension beneath that Wulfrum caught immediately. He excused it. Given the place, it was perhaps only natural under the circumstances.

'Nothing of importance,' he replied.

By tacit consent they walked back to the hall together, but he was aware that she had withdrawn from him somehow.

'What is it, Elgiva?'

'Nothing,' she replied. 'Or nothing that can be helped.'

'Grief is not soon healed,' he acknowledged. 'Nor can one set a time on it.'

Elgiva threw him a searching look, wondering what he might know of grief or loss. Surely that was what the Vikings inflicted on others. They walked on in silence for a little way.

'But life goes on,' he continued, 'and the living must learn to deal with their loss.'

'I cannot forget.'

'No, but you can move on. Besides, what is the alternative— to brood continually over the past until we grow old and withered?'

'You are an optimist.'

'No, I am a realist.'

'The Danes have made the reality we live in now,' replied Elgiva.

There was an unaccustomed bitterness in her tone and he eyed her shrewdly.

'You still feel anger in your heart, do you not?'

'Yes.'

'So would I, but destiny is a strange thing.'

'It was not destiny brought the Norsemen here,' she replied. 'It was a thirst for revenge, revenge and greed.' She turned to face him. 'That's all the Danes know, isn't it? Killing and destruction and the use of force.'

Wulfrum's gaze met and held her own. 'That is past.'

'Is it? I think that memory is not so soon erased.'

'No, it is not.'

'How would you know?'

His expression altered and for a moment she saw both pain and anger in the blue eyes. 'I discovered it early.'

'How so?'

'As a result of a blood feud. One night his enemies came to my father's hall and surrounded it. Then they set it alight and waited for those inside to come out. When they did, they were cut down. None escaped.'

'But you—'

'I wasn't there. I had gone with one of the men to a neighbour's farm to deliver some things for my father. It being winter, the days were short and we remained overnight. When we returned next day, we found the hall a smoking ruin and my family slain.'

Elgiva had heard of such things, though never till now from one who had experienced them, and she felt pity in her heart for the frightened and bewildered boy he must have been on that terrible day.

'How old were you?'

'Ten.'

'That is young to be cast adrift on the world.'

'Aye, but I was fortunate.'

Suddenly she remembered the words he had spoken that fateful morning when she had examined the sword, Dragon Tooth.

'It was Ragnar who took you in, wasn't it?'

'Yes, my father was one of his closest friends. He sheltered me, brought me up. From him I learned the warrior code—in fact, just about everything I know. When I grew to manhood, I avenged my family and slew those responsible for their deaths, all still living anyway. I slew them with the sword Ragnar gave me. Then I took back the title that was mine.'

'And when Ragnar was killed, you came to avenge his death.'

'That's right. As I told you, it was a matter of honour.'

As she listened it seemed to Elgiva that many things had become clear. In her mind's eye she could see the small boy standing alone amid the ruins of his home and the bodies of the slain. She could imagine him growing up, passing from childhood to manhood, learning the skills of the warrior, his rage becoming a cold, implacable thing, biding his time until his family should be avenged. It was not hard to see why he should have felt such love and loyalty for a man who was the sworn enemy of her people.

Wulfrum watched her closely, wondering why he had told her. It hadn't been his intention, but somehow it had come out anyway. Perhaps it had needed to. At least now she knew who he was, knew something of the events that had shaped his life.

'I'm sick of bloodshed and fighting, Elgiva.'

'What do you want, then?'

'To build something worthwhile.'

'Out of the ashes?'

'Aye, why not?' He paused. 'You and I together.'

'I? Am I not your chattel?'

'You are far more than that and you know it.' He drew her closer. 'Let there be no more secrets between us.'

There was no trace of mockery in his face or his voice. Bending his head, he kissed her very gently. Elgiva closed her eyes. No more secrets. How she wished it were true. But how could she make such a promise and keep it? Could she tell him that she was consorting with rebels? If he ever discovered the truth, his goodwill would evaporate on the spot. Worse, there would be a dire retribution. Even if he let her live, his trust would be gone for good. Then what would remain? She shivered.

Wulfrum glanced down at her.

'Don't be afraid, Elgiva. All will be well.'

Sick at heart, she wished she could believe it.

Later she told Osgifu about Aylwin. The older woman heard her in appalled silence.

'Aylwin should never have come. God send the Danes do not find out.'

'God send Aylwin has more sense than to lead a revolt. He and his followers would be slaughtered to a man.'

'True enough.' She paused. 'What will you do now?'

'Nothing.'

Elgiva sighed. If she spoke, she betrayed her people. If she kept silence, she betrayed her husband. Torn between two loyalties, she dreaded the time when she must be with Wulfrum again, acting a part now, pretending that all was well, knowing it was a lie. He was perceptive and intuitive, and, if the act was not convincing, would know immediately that something was amiss. He was her husband and he had in some measure given her his trust. The knowledge that she betrayed it was like a knife in her heart. She could never have imagined it would cut so deeply.

If Wulfrum noted aught amiss in her manner, he said nothing. Indeed, with the warm weather his days were busy anyway. Under his governance Ravenswood began once again to show signs of its former prosperity. The buildings were restored to a proper state of repair, the fences mended, the land well tended. The crops ripened in the fields and the first hay crop was cut. Under proper tending young lambs grew strong and new calves grazed beside their mothers in the pastures. Even the fruit crop would be good, for the branches of the orchard trees were laden. The air was filled with the drone of bees moving among the flowers and the hives. Beyond it all, the forest stretched in a rolling canopy of unbroken green.

The fine weather drew Elgiva out of doors and she and Osgifu did much of their work in the sunshine before the open door of the women's bower. Several times they went out to gather plants. Wulfrum made no objection to these small excursions, though each time one of his men was never far behind. To Elgiva it was a salutary reminder of the order of things, yet she gave no sign that she found the presence of the guards irksome, and it would have been futile to protest. Instead, she gave her full attention to the task, returning at length with Osgifu to prepare the balms and potions for which they were renowned. Never by word or look did she give any indication that the forest held more significance than its healing flowers and plants.

However, the knowledge of deceit weighed heavy on her and

Elgiva found it harder to sleep. She would lie awake in the sultry darkness, her mind racing, listening to the sound of Wulfrum's breathing, her skin damp with perspiration from his nearness, part of her wanting him to reach out for her and part of her fearing that he might, every nerve alive to his presence. For all manner of reasons the bed was too hot and eventually, after tossing and turning, she would doze for an hour or two and then waken unrefreshed.

Invariably Elgiva woke early with the sun and, one morning, unable to stay any longer in the stifling heat of the room, she left Wulfrum sleeping and dressed quietly. Then she slipped from the chamber and left the hall, heading for the unguarded postern gate. It was always barred, but that presented little obstacle. Thence the way was clear to the forest. The place she sought was not far off, but it was secluded and there the river flowed over a rocky outcrop into a wide pool beneath. The thought of the cool clear water was more than ever appealing and, at this hour, she could be certain of being undisturbed.

The early morning air was fresh and clear, smelling of damp earth for the dew was yet on the grass. It wet the hem of her gown as she passed and soaked into her shoes. Elgiva smiled, making her way unerringly through the trees to the river. It was narrow and swift flowing, and she followed it a little way before coming at length to the pool. Looking cautiously around to ensure she was alone, she slipped off her clothes and waded into the clear water. It was cold enough at first to make her gasp, but its freshness was delightful after the heat within doors, and, taking a deep breath, she plunged in.

Wulfrum woke early and stretched, yawning prodigiously. For all it was early, the heat in the room was already mounting. He rolled over and reached out a hand for Elgiva. The bed was empty. The knowledge brought him to instant wakefulness. A swift glance around the room revealed that her clothes were missing and the door unbarred. In moments he was out of bed and dressing swiftly before making his way down to the hall. Men sprawled on benches and floor, oblivious to his presence. Of his wife there was no sign. Wulfrum strode to the door and looked about, but found no sign of life or movement. Then he noted the unbarred postern and his jaw tightened. He ran to the stable to saddle Firedrake.

A few minutes later he was mounted and heading out on the track that led to the forest. He had guessed immediately which way Elgiva would go and, sure enough, as he left the hall behind and came into open ground, he found her trail in the wet grass. She had said nothing about wishing to collect plants and none of his men was in attendance. It was a matter he fully intended to take up with the vixen when he found her. Holding the horse to a walk, he followed the trail to the river. There he reined in and, studying the ground, found the print of a shoe in the soft earth, a small foot, undoubtedly a woman's. Certain now that Elgiva had come this way, he frowned, wondering what she was up to. Even after all these weeks she still had the power to surprise and unsettle. Unpredictability was, he reflected, all part of her considerable charm. He let the horse follow at a gentle pace until the dense growth made riding impractical and he was forced to dismount and continue on foot. The narrow path continued on a little way beyond and presently he saw a rocky outcrop and a waterfall with a pool below where a woman was swimming. Wulfrum grinned and moved forwards to a vantage point where he could watch unseen.

It was some time before Elgiva turned for the bank. However, the sun was getting higher and she knew she should return to the hall before her absence was discovered. Wulfrum might take it amiss that she had gone out without one of his men in attendance but, with luck, she would be back before he woke.

She waded ashore and was reaching for her kirtle when some sixth sense warned her of another presence. Her head jerked up and with a gasp of outrage she found herself staring at Wulfrum.

'You!'

He grinned, unrepentant. 'I.'

'What are you doing here?'

'Looking for you.'

'How long have you been there?'

'Long enough.' Long enough, he thought, to look his fill at that wonderful body. Despite the kirtle she was holding so close, an agreeable amount was still on view and he was un-ashamedly making the most if it.

A dark suspicion began to form in her mind. 'You've been watching me?'

'Yes.'

Unable to think of any immediate or suitable reply, she eyed him warily, only too aware of her present state of undress and that his eyes missed nothing. He surveyed her thus for some moments before getting to his feet. Before he had taken two paces Elgiva was struggling hastily into her kirtle, throwing her wet hair back over her shoulders. Wulfrum grinned. He drew closer, making her aware again of the remoteness of the place and that they were quite alone.

'I missed you when I woke.'

'It was hot. I couldn't sleep.'

'And you managed to get past my guards once more.'

'I…I thought there could be no danger here.'

'You will not do it again, Elgiva.' The words were quietly spoken, but there was no mistaking the implacable tone.

'Did you think I had fled, my lord?'

'No. I trust you more than that. But the times are uncertain and the place remote and I would not have you in danger.'

Elgiva was caught unawares, as much by the sincerity in his

voice as by the words themselves. The knowledge of her deceit returned with force. However, there was no time for deeper reflection, for his arms were round her and then his mouth closed over hers. As he kissed her, the familiar stealthy flame flickered into being deep within her. She shivered a *frisson* that was partly the residual chill of the water and partly fear—not of him, but of herself.

Wulfrum felt her shiver and looked down into her face. However, he could not fathom the expression he saw there. Did she fear him still? He wanted her now, wanted her with every fibre of his being, but he sensed a deep-seated unease behind her reluctance. Drawing back, he bent to retrieve her gown. Elgiva put it on quickly but her wet hair became entangled with the lacing and her cold fingers fumbled the task. Wulfrum's disquieting smile didn't help in the least. He watched her struggle for a while. Then she felt his hands on her shoulders turning her gently round. He untangled her hair and laced the gown himself. Then he held out his hand.

'Come, my lady.'

For a fraction of a second he saw her hesitate before placing her fingers in his. Then, together, they retraced their steps along the path to where his horse was tethered. Wulfrum turned her to face him.

'Ride with me.'

'There's no need. I can walk back.'

'It wasn't a request.'

The expression in those blue eyes admitted of no argument. He laced his hands and bent to receive her foot, sending her lightly into the saddle. Then he mounted behind her. For some time neither one spoke and the only sounds were the faint footfalls of the hooves on the turf and the creak of saddle leather. Elgiva's face was much warmer now, partly because the sun was higher in the sky, but chiefly because Wulfrum's arm was round her, holding her close, and she was annoyed to find that she liked it. Liked the warmth and the strength of him and the scent of musk and leather she had come to associate with him. Now they evoked other more disturbing thoughts: thoughts of his kiss, thoughts of fear and desire. She had tried so hard to hate him, but knew now that she did not.

Once he glanced down at her and she saw him smile. Her colour deepened, but still she said nothing. To be close to him thus and know she gave succour to those who intended his death turned the knife in her breast. If she had thought there was the remotest chance of escaping the high saddle, she would have taken it, but the arm that held her was as unyielding as oak. His face was dangerously close to hers now and the blue eyes alight with amusement.

'You're enjoying this, aren't you?' she demanded, striving for the bantering tone that would lull suspicion.

'Yes, very much,' was the unruffled reply. 'Aren't you?'

Elgiva remained silent. Wulfrum did not press her for a reply, but his smile widened. It had not escaped her either that his horse was being held to a slow walk and it was taking a mighty long time to get home.

It was a good half an hour later when he reined in by the stables. Elgiva breathed more easily and some of her self-command returned, for now he would lower her to the ground and she could make good her escape. She was quite wrong; he dismounted first, lifting her down after him and, retaining his hold on her waist, drew her into a more intimate embrace, a long, lingering kiss that set every nerve alight.

Wulfrum felt her response, felt her melt against him, and his passion woke in reply. He crushed her to him, hungry for her. The warmth of her flesh beneath her gown recalled the sight of her naked, pressed beneath him on the furs of their bed. He wanted her so badly it hurt. In that moment he would have sworn she wanted him, but then, just as soon, he felt her body tense and she turned her head aside. He looked into her face, saw the anguish there.

'What is it, Elgiva? What's wrong?'

'Nothing. I…'

'There is. Tell me.'

His lips nuzzled her hair, her neck, her throat. Elgiva closed her eyes, every part of her alive to his touch, every part of her wanting it to go on and knowing it must not. It took every ounce of her will to step away.

'Please, Wulfrum. Let me go.'

He wanted to deny her, to test her resistance, to carry her to their chamber and continue where they had left off, but he underestimated the power of the amber eyes that spoke more eloquently than words of some inner distress.

'Why, Elgiva? What are you afraid of?'

She shook her head, unable to frame the words to explain. He saw only her reluctance and his heart sank. In any other woman he would have suspected caprice, some game to whet his appetite, but he sensed this was something more. How he wished she would tell him, but he would not force her confidence any more than he would force her compliance. He let his hands fall from her waist.

'Go, then, if you must.'

The look of relief on her face was quite apparent and once he might have found it amusing. His hand tightened over the rein as he watched her walk away. Then he led the stallion into the stable. He unsaddled the horse and brushed it down himself, for in truth he required some space from his men and the public life of the hall. The mechanical task of grooming was soothing and busied his hands, though his mind was elsewhere. The early morning encounter with his wife had unsettled him more than he would ever have thought possible. When he had married Elgiva, he had taken a bride of good family and much wealth. That he had found her most desirable was an added bonus. The advantages of the match were obvious, at least for himself. He had never considered her feelings in the matter. He had forced her compliance in almost every way. It had never occurred to him then that he might find himself in the position he was in now, that what had begun as physical desire would turn into something much stronger and infinitely more disturbing. He did not deceive himself as to the feelings Elgiva had for him; she was physically attracted to him, but she continued to fight it—he was still the enemy. Once he had desired only her physical surrender. Now he wanted far more than that. The irony was not lost on him.

Having seen to the needs of his horse, Wulfrum left the stable, thinking to make his way back to the hall. However, a glimpse of blue gown caught his eye and he saw Elgiva standing by the gate to the paddock where Mara was turned out to graze. Since the coming of the war band she had not been permitted to ride, but still lost no opportunity to spend a few moments with the horse. Evidently the feeling was reciprocated for the mare had walked across to greet her, standing close to the fence while Elgiva stroked her nose. He heard her speak to the animal, but did not catch the words because the distance was too great. She remained there for several minutes more before moving with evident reluctance towards the women's bower. The mare watched her go and whinnied softly. Elgiva gave her a fleeting smile and turned to look over her shoulder once before continuing on her way. She did not see Wulfrum, being evidently preoccupied with her own thoughts, but he could see her clearly. The mask of poise and serenity that she wore in public had slipped for the moment and all he could see now was the deep unhappiness that lay beneath. It hit him with the force of a blow.

Chapter Eleven

Elgiva was rudely awakened the following morning by a lusty whack delivered by a strong hand across her bare buttocks. With a yelp of protest, she started up to see Wulfrum standing over her. He was already dressed in leather leggings and tunic, belted at the waist where a wicked-looking knife was sheathed.

'Get up, wench. 'Tis broad daylight already and I would hunt.'

'Your pardon, my lord. I had not realised it was so late.'

Elgiva scrambled from bed under his appraising gaze. Then she pulled on a kirtle and raked her nails through her hair, trying to bring about some semblance of order. Wulfrum grinned and strolled to the door.

'Make ready, Elgiva. I am not intending to wait.'

Abandoning the failed attempt to tame her hair into a braid, she slid her feet into shoes and reached for her gown.

'Shall I fetch you some food, my lord?'

'One of the servants can do that. Ready yourself.'

'My lord?'

'For the hunt. You are coming with me.'

Elgiva stared at him in stunned amazement and then her face was lit by a dazzling smile. 'Do you mean it?'

'I have said. Besides, that puny mare in the stable needs exercise and she is not up to a man's weight. Make haste now.'

Elgiva needed no second bidding. Summoning Osgifu, she went to the chest where her clothes were stored and drew out leggings, shirt and leather tunic, the clothes she had worn when she hunted with her father. She had not thought to wear them again and her heart beat faster at the thought of a long ride in the fresh air. It was with difficulty that she could sit still long enough for Osgifu to comb and braid her hair. When it was done, she hurried down to the courtyard where Wulfrum waited with his men. Her mare was saddled and ready. Seeing his wife, Wulfrum smiled faintly, running his eye over her costume, but he made no comment, swinging himself into Firedrake's saddle. The black tossed its head and sidled, eager to be off, but Wulfrum held him in while Elgiva mounted. The little mare seemed tiny among the larger mounts of the men, but she knew the horse would hold her own. Sensing her rider's excitement, Mara gave a half-rear for she too scented open country and freedom. Elgiva laughed and patted the glossy neck.

Once beyond the gate the riders set off a steady pace, holding their horses in, not wishing to tire them before the chase. The mare pranced and bucked to feel turf under her hooves. Wulfrum said nothing, but watched as Elgiva brought her under control, her hand gentle on the rein. He knew the animal was fresh for she had not been ridden these last weeks, but her antics seemed not to worry her rider in the least. He heard Elgiva speak softly and saw the spirited little horse drop her head and settle into her stride. He smiled to himself. His wife could ride, no question.

They rode further into the forest, following a well-worn path wide enough for two horses to walk abreast. Beside them walked serfs with Wulfrum's boarhounds, huge and powerful beasts hungry for the chase. It was early yet, but the sunlight dappled the ground with shade and the grassy verges were

bright with wild flowers. All around them the trees were full
of birdsong and every branch alive with new green leaves.
Elgiva breathed deeply and smiled, feeling the tension flow
from her, enjoying the clean air and the movement of the horse
beneath her. Beside her Wulfrum rode in silence, seemingly
wrapped in private thought, but Elgiva did not mind. From
time to time she cast a covert glance at him, noting well how
easily he controlled the powerful horse, how his body moved
with the animal's rhythm as though he were part of it. She
wondered where he had learned to ride, who had taught him.
It occurred to her there were still many things she did not know
about the man who was her husband.

Presently they came to a place where the spoor was clear
and the hounds were loosed. The riders followed, turning into
the trees. It was ancient woodland, where the branches of oaks
and beech met overhead in a green vault that shut out most of
the sun save for occasional dappled patches of light. Then the
hounds found the scent and the hunters were away. Elgiva
touched Mara with her heels and felt the mare shift from a
standing start to a canter. Leaning forwards, she guided their
course through the trees, ducking low boughs and weaving to
avoid the branches that slashed at them. The horse stayed for
nothing, leaping the fallen logs in her path, the flying hooves
thudding over the carpet of leaf mould beneath the great trees.
Once Elgiva thought she glimpsed the hounds, running swift
and silent ahead of her. Around her she could hear the voices
of the men calling, urging their horses on to greater speed.

The boar had been following a direct line, but now veered
away down a steep, open slope. This last was largely covered
by dense blackthorn. The pig plunged into the thicket where it
was much harder for the riders to follow. Elgiva drew rein,
thinking fast. If they followed into the thicket, she and Mara
would be scratched to ribbons, for she knew the place of old.
Her father's men had once brought down a boar nearby. The

slope ended in a stream with more woodland beyond, and she guessed the quarry would make for it, trying to throw the hounds off the scent. She knew a path that skirted the slope and came out by the stream further on. Turning Mara's head, she touched the horse with her heels once more, cantering off on a tangent. Out of the corner of her eye she saw Wulfrum's stallion and grinned. Thus far he had not let her out of his sight. They would see now whether his mount was the equal of hers for speed and stamina. Elgiva held to her course, hoping her guess had been right. Off to her right she could hear the men shouting and picked up curses on the wind. It seemed they had found the blackthorn. As the path curved, she glimpsed the stream and then the dogs. She was right. Her grin widened triumphantly. As she neared the place she saw other riders breaking from the thicket, urging their mounts across the stream. Elgiva slowed Mara a little and splashed through after them. The hounds were milling round, trying to pick up the scent again. A few moments later Wulfrum drew up beside her, grinning broadly.

'You know the land well, my lady.'

'I have ridden over it many times. My father hunted here very often and I with him.'

'So I see.' Wulfrum couched the great boar spear and sat back in his saddle, observing her. 'You follow your own path.'

'Where it is a better path, lord.'

He glanced at his men and the scratches they sported on face and hand, even on the tough leather hunting clothes, and he laughed.

'In this case it was a better path. I have no love for blackthorn.'

'Nor I.'

Just then the hounds picked up the trail again and the hunters pressed on. Elgiva urged the mare on and felt the little horse leap forwards to a gallop, hurtling down the narrow path, twisting and turning through the trees. Elgiva bent low over her neck to avoid the branches that clawed at her, thankful for the protection of her stout clothing. As they raced through the green gloom beneath the tree canopy, she thought she could see a pool of light up ahead and headed towards it. Before her lay a clearing, a grassy glade, edged by great trees and, between, dense thickets. Somewhere to her right she could hear the sounds of the other horses but she could no longer see them. Glancing left, she could see nothing there, either. That look was a mistake for she failed to see the low bough until she was almost on it. Swift reflexes saved her and she ducked, throwing herself low along the near side of her mount, and the branch that would otherwise have smashed into her body caught her right knee instead. It lifted her out of the saddle, pitching her clear off the horse. She landed hard and for a few dazed seconds lay still, fighting to regain her breath while the branches spun crazily overhead. Eventually, when her breathing steadied, she sat up cautiously to ascertain that there was no serious damage. All seemed well enough. However, when she managed to get back on her feet, she was immediately aware of the protest from her knee. She glanced at it ruefully. No doubt it would sport a magnificent bruise on the morrow. Still, it could have been much worse and there was naught to do but thank fortune for a lucky escape.

Her horse was grazing some yards away and Elgiva began to hobble in that direction. She was only feet away when Mara suddenly threw up her head and snorted. Elgiva spoke quietly to calm her, but the mare did not respond, staring instead across the clearing to the edge of the thicket. Following the horse's gaze, Elgiva looked to see what was spooking her. Then she froze. There, part shadowed by undergrowth, stood a huge boar. The red eyes glinted with menace and its tusks gouged out great chunks of turf as it tossed its head this way and that. With trembling hand she reached for the trailing reins, but

Mara bolted, shouldering her violently aside. Elgiva lost her balance and fell backwards. Attracted by the movement of the fleeing horse, the boar made a short charge in that direction. Elgiva screamed. The boar stopped short, sensing another quarry. Then it turned towards her, sniffing the air. She screamed again, edging away, an icy knot of fear in her gut. If it reached her, the creature would rend her limb from limb. She had no spear, no weapon save one small belt knife, worse than useless against such a foe. She was dry-throated with terror as her eyes scanned the nearest tree, but even if she could have got that far the branches were too high to reach. The boar moved forwards a few paces and pawed the ground, sending dirt flying. Elgiva swallowed hard.

Then there came another sound, the thud of galloping hooves, and a great black horse hurtled into her line of vision. It came to a sliding stop on its haunches just a few yards away. Then she heard a familiar voice.

'Don't move, Elgiva. As you value your life.'

With leaping heart she saw Wulfrum dismount, the great spear already in his hand. Then he moved across the clearing, all his attention on the animal in front of him. The boar discovered a new enemy and turned in his direction. Without warning it charged. Elgiva's hand flew to her mouth, stifling a cry of terror as in slow motion she saw Wulfrum drop into a crouch to brace the end of the spear in the turf, but the pig was upon him. She saw him throw himself to one side and watched in horror as the animal hurtled past, one of its tusks tearing a great rent in the sleeve of his hunting tunic. He rolled up on to one knee in an instant, bracing the spear fast as the boar spun round like lightning, coming at him again, squealing with rage. Ashen faced, Elgiva watched the great beast hurl itself on to the spear point, hearing its fury and pain as it charged full to the cross piece, burying the barb deep in its breast. Hot blood sprayed over Wulfrum's arms and chest, dyeing his leather gauntlets and tunic as he wrestled with the enraged creature, vicious and deadly even in its final moments. The squealing and the struggle went on for what seemed a horribly long time until at length the brute rolled over in its death throes. Almost rigid with fright, Elgiva watched the struggle between man and beast, hardly daring to breathe until the great boar lay still. Wulfrum got to his feet, breathing hard.

'Are you all right?'

Elgiva nodded, fighting faintness, unable to speak. He drew her to her feet and then his arms were around her and he was holding her. He could feel her shaking.

'It's over. The beast is dead.'

Weak with relief, Elgiva took refuge in that close embrace and closed her eyes, feeling the fierce pounding of her heart and the sickness in her stomach from her brush with death. She was aware that he was speaking to her softly, as he might to a child, quieting her fear. It was his gentleness that brought the water welling into her eyes and then caused it to spill over as all the tension of the past weeks found its outlet. Wulfrum realised then that he had never seen her cry. Through every trial her courage had borne her triumphant, but even courage has its limits. He heard in her sobs the stresses she never spoke of, the fear and the hurt that she kept hidden, and his arms tightened about her. For some moments they remained thus until, gradually, as the terror subsided and the sobbing ceased, some of her colour returned. Wulfrum smiled.

'It's all right,' he said. 'You're safe now.'

Elgiva looked into his face. 'Oh, Wulfrum. If you hadn't come…'

'I would never let harm come to you.'

He spoke as if it were an everyday occurrence to slay a boar single-handed, but she knew he had put his life on the line for her.

'Thank you,' she said. It sounded so inadequate to her ears but he heard the sincerity in those simple words.

For a moment neither one moved. Then, very gently, her hands reached up and drew his face down to hers and she kissed him full on the lips. In stunned surprise he stared into the amber eyes, not quite daring to believe what he saw there. Elgiva kissed him again. Then his arms closed around her, crushing her to him, his mouth seeking hers in a lingering passionate embrace that encountered no resistance. Rather he felt her arms around his neck, her soft mouth yielding to his as she pressed closer. He had dreamed of this so often that even now he was unsure whether he woke or slept.

Just then he heard voices and several horsemen appeared through the trees. With a rueful smile Wulfrum slackened his hold on Elgiva. She returned the smile and reluctantly let her hands slide from his shoulders. As they did so they encountered torn leather and the stickiness of blood. She glanced down, frowning.

'Wulfrum, you're hurt!'

'It is slight. The beast caught me with his tusk on that first rush.'

'Let me see.'

He extended the arm to reveal a ragged gash. It wasn't deep, but it had bled copiously, staining the shirt and the leather tunic.

'That must be cleaned and bound when we return,' she said, 'lest it should fester.'

Wulfrum didn't argue, for in truth the wound was beginning to ache. Looking at it, Elgiva was reminded again of how much he had risked for her sake and what she might have lost.

Further reflection was denied her by the approach of the oncoming riders. The huntsmen halted a few feet away, led by Olaf Ironfist. He looked at the waiting pair and then at the dead beast.

'By Odin's beard, a fine boar,' he observed. 'He must have put up a worthy struggle.'

'Worthy enough,' acknowledged Wulfrum with a wry grin. The two men exchanged a few words about the transportation of the dead pig, then, having seen the instructions carried out, Ironfist went to retrieve the horses now grazing quietly a few yards off. Wulfrum turned to Elgiva.

'Come, my lady, it grows late. We should return.'

It was a considerable relief when Ravenswood came into view half an hour later. As soon as they had dismounted Elgiva drew Wulfrum aside and led him indoors, calling to the servants to fetch hot water and cloths. Once in their chamber, she helped him unfasten his belt and remove the leather tunic. The shirt sleeve beneath was soaked in blood. With great care she removed that garment too, her practised gaze assessing the damage.

'You were lucky, my lord,' she said then. 'It isn't deep, but it does need cleaning.'

Wulfrum vouchsafed no comment, but seated himself as she prepared the things she would need. He had seen her tend others so many times but had little thought he would one day be the subject of her ministrations. He watched as she worked, her expression intent on the task, her small, deft hands cleaning the blood away from the wound, moving gently across his skin. The ride had brought the fresh colour to her cheeks and loosened tendrils of hair from her braid to form a halo round her face, a face whose contours were so familiar to him now he could summon them with his eyes shut. He could remember all too clearly the touch of those lips on his, the taste of her mouth, the subtle erotic scent of her flesh.

Elgiva broke into his thoughts. 'A boar's tusks are dirty, my lord. This cut must be washed with wine, but...I'm afraid it will hurt.'

'I'll live.'

The level tone suggested indifference, but the sudden sharp intake of breath as wine met torn flesh told a different tale.

'I'm sorry,' she said.

Wulfrum set his jaw against the pain and made no reply, but

the sudden pallor of his cheek spoke louder than words. Unwilling to prolong the agony, she worked fast and, having sluiced the wound clean, prepared a poultice of herbs. These too would help prevent infection. Having slathered the mixture over the gash, she bound it firmly.

'That should stay on for three days. Then I'll change it.'

'As you will.' Wulfrum flexed his hand. 'It eases already.'

Seeing some of his natural colour returning, she smiled. 'I'm glad.'

He looked up and met her gaze. 'Thank you.'

'It was the least I could do.'

He rose from his chair and took her hand in his, pressing it to his lips. Every fibre of her being thrilled to that touch, for the memory of the earlier scene in the forest was etched on her consciousness. Supremely aware of his nearness, of his warmth, of his scent, she knew only that she wanted him. If he kissed her now… Closing her eyes a moment to steady herself, she felt him release her hand. Then he moved past her to the door. Elgiva bit her lip. She heard the door close and then the soft thud as the bar dropped into place. For a second its significance escaped her. Then she was very still, hardly able to breathe, hardly daring to hope—until she felt his hands on her shoulders.

'I would thank you properly, Elgiva.'

Very gently he turned her to face him and then his arms slid around her waist and shoulders. For a brief moment he looked into the face tilted up to his before his mouth closed on hers. He felt her quiver, felt her mouth open beneath his, tasting again its honey sweetness on his tongue. Elgiva shivered, but not with fear, her body surrendering to the embrace, relaxing against him, answering his kiss with her own. She felt his hands move to her waist, felt him unbuckle her belt and heard it fall before he turned his attention to her tunic, unlacing the fastenings and sliding the garment down over her shoulders. The shirt followed a moment later. Then he loosened her hair from its braid, running his fingers through its silky length, twisting a hank around his hand to draw her head back. A longer, deeper kiss ensued. He bent and slid an arm under her knees, carrying her to the bed. There he drew off the rest of her clothing before removing his own.

His love-making was tender and passionate, he controlling his desire in order to increase hers. He had waited too long to spoil this with haste. So he prolonged the exploration of her body, whose beauty he already knew, and, paradoxically, knew not, relearning the curves of breast and waist and hip, stroking, caressing and arousing, by turns both tender and insistent. Elgiva's pulse leapt, her flesh burning beneath that knowing touch, every sense alive to the lithe power of the body pressed so close against her own. Wulfrum moved lower, exploring the warm hollows of throat and collarbone and thence to her breast, lingering there, teasing the nipple to tautness, sending a thrill of pleasure along her flesh. She felt his knee move between her thighs, felt the answering slick warmth. Deep within, the sensation intensified, growing, mounting until it seemed that blood became fire. Every last defence overcome, she knew only that she wanted him. Her breathing quickened. She felt his weight shift and then the hardness of him as he entered her. The pressure increased and there was a moment of exquisite pain. Then it was past and he moved deeper in a slow rhythm that stoked the fire laid down before. Elgiva gasped, closing her legs round him, drawing him into her, yielding all of herself, moving with him as the rhythm became stronger, building to its shuddering climax. She heard Wulfrum cry out, felt the surge of energy between them in a moment of heart-stopping delight.

For a while afterwards neither one spoke, too shaken by the intensity of the experience to find the words. She felt his arm draw her close, holding her in the hollow of his shoulder. Beneath her hand she could feel his heartbeat and the sheen of sweat along his skin. He glanced down and smiled.

'I've wanted to do that from the first, but I never imagined it would be so perfect.'

She looked into his face but saw only truth there.

'I was afraid,' she replied. 'First of you, and then of myself.'

'You have no cause to be afraid, Elgiva. I would never hurt you.'

He propped himself on one elbow and looked into her face, tracing a finger lightly along her cheekbone to her lips and chin and throat as if he would memorise every part of her. Even now he could scarcely believe what had happened. While he knew her nature to be passionate, its depths had astonished and delighted him. Never in his wildest dreams had he imagined such a magnificent surrender, and he had dreamed of it often. Yet even as the knowledge sank in, he found other thoughts intruding, thoughts he could never have imagined before he met her. Elgiva had yielded her body, but what of her heart? It had never mattered before. Women had satisfied a need. While he had ever treated them with gentleness, their thoughts and feelings were of no interest. This was different.

Unable to fathom his thought, Elgiva had yet to own to surprise. She heard that men were brutal or indifferent after making love. Wulfrum was neither. He had been gentle too, more than she could have hoped or imagined. For all that, his handling of her spoke of a man experienced with women. They held no secrets for him. Was she just another woman to him? Even at the height of their passion he had not said he loved her. Why should he? She was his wife, married by force out of political necessity. He had not prosecuted his right before because he had no need to. As he had said, time was all on his side. A consummate strategist, he had intended to have her submission and he had won. And yet it had not seemed like defeat. What manner of man was he, this enemy who could make surrender taste so sweet? More than that he had shown her what lay in her own heart. Wulfrum might have died today in the forest. A few short months ago the notion would have been most pleasing, but somehow a shift had taken place—there was no trace left of the hatred she had once felt. It had been replaced by something far worse. She could no longer evade the awful truth that she did care for him. It was bad enough that he was the enemy of her people, a conqueror, who had taken her as a prize of war. Now, in spite of her best efforts, he was stealing her heart, as well, and her case was perilous indeed, for who knew what was in Wulfrum's mind, or in his heart?

Chapter Twelve

'He saved your life?' Osgifu stared at her. 'How so?'

The two women had taken their sewing outside and were enjoying the sunshine by the door of the bower. It was peaceful there and private too; a place conducive to confidential conversation. As Elgiva summarised the events that had taken place on the hunt, the older woman listened with rapt attention.

'It would seem we owe him much,' she observed when the tale was concluded.

'He took the matter so lightly, Gifu, as though it was a perfectly normal thing to do, and yet he risked his life for me.'

Osgifu smiled. 'Men always make light of such things.'

'Do they?'

'Of course. They prefer to say little and hide their feelings for fear of showing too much.'

Before Elgiva had time to ponder the words, she heard a footstep and looked round, thinking to see Hilda or one of the other servants. Her heart missed a beat to discover Wulfrum in the doorway. For a moment he said nothing, taking in the quiet domestic scene. Then he smiled.

'I thought I might find you here.'

Elgiva laid aside her sewing and rose from her stool. 'Was there something you needed, my lord?'

'Will you bear me company awhile?' He glanced at her companion. 'I'm sure Osgifu can spare you.'

The servant inclined her head and hid a smile. Elgiva, knowing her well, was not deceived, though she could not see the occasion for this hidden amusement. She had no chance to dwell on it, though, with Wulfrum so close by. He offered her his good arm and, rather diffidently, she took it.

For a little while they walked in silence. Elgiva glanced up at him, wondering why he had sought her out. They seemed to be heading for the stables.

'I thought you might like to check on Mara,' he said.

Elgiva looked up in surprise. Any opportunity to visit her horse was welcome. How had he known? He did not enlighten her on the point, but stood aside to let her enter the building. Then together they made their way along the stalls until they came to Mara's. The horse turned her head and whinnied as Elgiva approached.

'Here. She might appreciate this.' Wulfrum produced a withered apple from inside his tunic. 'It is from last year's store, but I don't suppose she'll mind too much.'

He was right. The mare crunched the fruit with obvious enjoyment. As she stroked the glossy neck, Elgiva regarded her husband out of the corner of her eye. This was the hidden side of him once more, the one she had glimpsed when he was with Ulric. He liked children and he liked horses too. Glancing across the stable, she could see his stallion tethered nearby. At seventeen hands, the powerful horse took some riding, but with Wulfrum's hand on the rein the black was meek enough. She wondered at their partnership, for it was clear he had trained the animal himself.

'How long have you had Firedrake?'

'Two years.' He grinned. 'He was a handful at first, wild and mighty contrary.' He glanced down at Elgiva, thinking that, in some ways, the two were perhaps not so very different except, of course, that the stallion now obeyed his every command.

'He's a beautiful animal,' she acknowledged.

'So is the mare. Your father chose well.'

For a moment Elgiva remained silent, her eyes on the horse, stroking the velvety muzzle. Recalling the last time they had been in the stables and had spoken thus, Wulfrum could only wince. He seemed to recall his words then had been more than a little tactless.

'Do you still intend to breed her?' she asked at length.

'Not without your consent. After all, she is your horse.'

Her surprise was evident, for he saw warm colour rise in her cheeks, but the look in her eyes said more. It was a moment or two before she could speak.

'Thank you, Wulfrum. She means a great deal to me.'

'I know.'

Elgiva's heart was suddenly beating much faster, but her pleasure at his words was great. More, he had shown a true regard for her feelings. She laid a hand on his sleeve.

'Mara means a great deal, but it means even more to me to hear you say that.'

Wulfrum knew a deep inner glow, but, not knowing quite what to say, he smiled and remained silent.

Having left the horses, they walked a while and came to the orchard. It was a fine day and enjoyable to stroll in the dappled shade beneath the trees. For some time they did not speak, being content to share the quiet and the moment. Presently Wulfrum stopped and spread his cloak on the grass.

'Sit and rest a while, Elgiva. It is most pleasant out here.'

She sat down to join him, very aware of his nearness, of the lithe strength of the man. Her eyes drank in the powerful line of his jaw, the blades of his cheekbones, the sensual curve of his mouth, remembering its pressure against her own. Shocked by the direction of her thoughts, Elgiva looked away.

If he was aware of her confusion, he gave no sign. Indeed, Wulfrum's thoughts were on the scene around him, on the land, his land. Here in this rich earth was wealth indeed, a place where a man could set down roots and belong. He thought back to the country of his birth, of the farm where he had been a boy. Back then it had seemed very fine, but he had had nothing like this to compare it with. It seemed to him that in England a man could put a stick in the ground and it would grow and thrive. Back there the land yielded a living far more grudgingly. He thought of it as back there rather than home. This was his home now, the place he intended to stay, and the place where his sons would be raised—one day. He glanced at Elgiva. It was a strange fate that had brought him to this place, to her. The two were inextricably bound up. In some ways she was this place for him and always would be.

Unable to follow his thought, she surveyed him closely. 'Is there something on your mind, Wulfrum?'

'I was thinking of the strangeness of destiny and how it brought me here.'

Elgiva remembered the evening in the bower when she had asked Osgifu to cast the runes. It was but a few months since, but already it seemed a long time ago. In her mind she heard the voice saying, *The runes never lie.*

Wulfrum stretched out beside her, hands behind his head, looking up through the leafy branches to the sky beyond. Watching him, Elgiva felt the truth of his words: it was a strange destiny that brought him here, a destiny with its beginnings in an ancient feud. So many lives, yet all were strangely linked. Osgifu had long ago told her of the Nornir, the three old women who spun the threads of fate. It had seemed then like just another fabulous tale. Now she wasn't so sure. Wulfrum had told her something of his past. It was as if a corner of that mysterious web had been lifted, allowing her a tantalising glimpse of the man she had married. He had learned early to conceal his thoughts, to use his head and not his heart. Though he had not said so, she knew his life must have been hard, but he had survived and become strong, a man whom other men would follow. They trusted him, respected him, and obeyed him. It made her want to know more.

'Was it in Lord Ragnar's hall that you met Olaf Ironfist?'

'Aye. He and I go back a long way. He saved my life.'

'Tell me.'

There was a note in her voice he had not heard before, curiosity and something else that was harder to define. Withal there was an earnestness in those amber eyes that would not be resisted.

'We were hunting wolves and had a beast at bay. It was a fearsome creature, weighing full as much as a man, and savage with hunger. I came upon it first and, being young and foolish, thought to take it on armed merely with a belt knife.'

Elgiva laughed out loud. 'Never! What happened?'

'The beast attacked and I gashed it with the knife, which only made it madder. It went for my throat. I managed to hold it off for a little while, but my strength was waning and I knew I was going to die. Fortunately for me, Olaf appeared and grappled with the creature. He throttled it with his bare hands.'

'How old were you then?'

'Three and ten.'

'It is surprising you lived to manhood.'

'But for Olaf I might not have. He was five and twenty back then, and already well known for his feats of strength. I have seen him kill a bull with his bare hands. I can see him now, standing over the body of the dead wolf; how he laughed when he saw that belt knife. Then Ragnar arrived on the scene and of course he had to be let in on the joke. I swear, I thought the two of them would die laughing.' Wulfrum smiled, remembering it. 'It took me a while to live that one down.'

'And you and Olaf became friends.'

'Yes. He mistook my stupidity for courage, you see. But, like Ragnar, he taught me much, and we have stood together in the shield wall many times. He is a brave warrior and a good friend. There is no man I'd rather have at my back in a fight.'

'I believe it. Truly Olaf Ironfist is well named.'

'Indeed he is.'

They lapsed into companionable silence, Elgiva pondering the things he had told her and keen to hear more. Even so, she would not press him. Confidence could not be forced. If he wanted to tell her about the past, he would do it in his own time. Once, not so long ago, such a conversation would have been unthinkable. She could never have envisaged then that she would discover so much—or that she would wish to.

For a long time they stayed together beneath the tree, soaking up the afternoon warmth, neither one in any hurry to move, both knowing that something important had changed and fearing to do anything that might break the fragile balance that had been established. The sun was setting before they eventually started back to the hall.

Preparations for the evening meal were well underway and the hall already lively with talk and laughter when they entered. Many eyes turned in their direction and several knowing smiles appeared on the faces of the observers. Elgiva knew what they were thinking: two lovers returning from a cosy tryst. It wasn't altogether wide of the mark either. Somewhat embarrassed, she glanced up at her husband. However, he seemed not in the least discomposed and paused to exchange greetings with some of his men. She would have slipped away but his hand on her arm forbade it.

'Stay, Elgiva.'

'Whatever you say, Wulfrum.' The tone was demure enough, but he was undeceived. She saw him laugh.

'I'd like to think so, but I'm not so naïve.'

* * *

Later that evening, when they retired to their chamber, he made love to her again. Again he was gentle and patient, wanting her to enjoy the experience as much as he did. He found her willing, even eager now, responding to his passion with warmth and he lost himself in her, forgetting the past and all the brutality of the world. Nothing existed for him then but her. And afterwards, when they lay in drowsy slumber, he dreamed of the future they would carve out together. He had heard it said that behind every successful man was a strong woman. He had not believed it until now. With Elgiva at his side he felt invincible, that anything was possible. No other woman had ever made him feel that way, think that way. He couldn't even remember what those women looked like now, but it didn't matter. He knew he had found the one he sought, a woman to cherish and to trust.

As Wulfrum continued to familiarise himself with the land and its people, he found increasing pride in this rich and fertile domain with its warm, dark soil and fields of growing crops. Under his hand, Ravenswood had begun to resemble its former self. Elgiva watched too, and knew her husband a capable ruler of men. The Norsemen might be warriors and of fearsome appearance, but they also worked hard, and gradually the Saxons began to view their presence, if not with gladness, at least with a grudging acceptance.

From time to time they received news from further afield. Halfdan had established his rule in York and his war bands had roamed far and wide through Northumbria. Much more of the kingdom was now within their hold. It was not welcome news to Saxon ears, but there was naught to be done about it. They heard that the southern kingdom of Wessex stood out against the Danes, and some secretly hoped that the resistance would spread. Others prayed it would not, being tired of slaughter and destruction. From time to time pockets of rebellion flared up across Northumbria, but these were dealt with ruthlessly. The Danes would not tolerate any such infraction and the perpetrators were hunted down and killed.

Elgiva shivered when she heard these tales, praying that as she had heard nothing of Aylwin for a while he had abandoned his former plans and gone to safety. It seemed to her that she had seen enough bloodshed and killing to last a lifetime. War meant waste and destruction, a ravaged land that could not support the people. Peace meant a future for all. It came at a price, but there was nothing to be done about that, either. It was futile to try to live in the past. They must make the best of now. Accordingly she set her shoulder to the wheel and, when not accompanying Wulfrum, turned her skilled attention to the household affairs.

Wulfrum observed more than he ever said, but he found no fault with her management of domestic affairs. Food was well prepared and appeared on the table to order; the serfs knew their tasks and obeyed her; the hall was well kept. It was a comfortable place and one that men, hungry and tired, looked forward to returning to. He noticed how his men would greet her now when they returned from work, sometimes with a jest, but always within the bounds of decorum. They knew that if one of them got a cut or a splinter she would tend it, and came to have a respect for her skill with herbs and potions. It occurred to Wulfrum that his marriage to Elgiva had been more than a shrewd move: it was a decision that pleased him more with every passing day. More than ever he looked forward each night to the time when he would be alone with her and she would share his bed. He knew other men envied him his good fortune. He saw them follow her with their eyes. Elgiva never returned such looks or showed she was aware of them, never once gave him cause to doubt her. How should she? In her was only goodness and sincerity. He was proud that she was his wife and he trusted her.

* * *

Towards the end of July the watchman announced the approach of a group of horsemen. It was a warm day and Elgiva was sitting with Osgifu outside her bower, mending one of Wulfrum's shirts while Ulric played nearby. They heard the sentinel's warning shout and then, soon after, the arrival of the horses. Leaving Ulric in Osgifu's care, Elgiva went to see who the newcomers were. When she entered the hall, she saw a dozen men, all Danes, and all with the dust and sweat of travel upon them. They were already being received by Wulfrum. Elgiva, standing apart, listened as he welcomed them and, catching his eye, gave quiet instructions to the serfs to fetch ale and food. When she turned back to the guests, she realised that one of their number was watching her with interest. With a feeling of dismay she found herself looking straight at Sweyn. He smiled and bowed. Elgiva acknowledged him with the barest inclination of the head and then turned her attention back to the rest, for the man called Torvald was speaking to Wulfrum.

'We carry messages from Lord Halfdan to his brothers, and also for you, my lord.'

Wulfrum nodded. 'I thank you. But first wash off the dust of travel, and then sit and eat. You've had a long ride.'

The men were only too glad to obey and, having sluiced their faces and necks with cool water, disposed themselves around the table. As they ate they spoke of matters in York and elsewhere. Elgiva listened with close interest. It was as she had suspected. The Danes increased their hold on their new kingdom daily. They put down rebellion with ruthless efficiency and brought Northumbria under their yoke.

'There are still pockets of resistance,' Torvald continued, 'and bands of rebels who hide out in the forest. We have reason to believe one of them may be Aylwin.'

Elgiva froze at the mention of that name, but the men paid no heed.

'Since the forest is hard by, my lord, it might be as well to double your guard around the place until such time as the troublemakers can be flushed out.'

'I shall do so, Torvald, and I thank you for the warning.'

'It is but a matter of time before they are caught and destroyed.'

'I think so too. I will have my men search the area immediately. If any rebels are in hiding hereabouts, they will be found.' Wulfrum exchanged glances with Olaf Ironfist and missed his wife's expression. 'Take some men out tomorrow and see what you can discover.'

'I will, my lord. And if we find any renegades?'

'Then you will either kill or capture them.'

Ironfist nodded and looked at Ida, who grinned in obvious anticipation.

'What news more?' demanded Wulfrum.

'Lord Halfdan holds a council in the autumn,' said Torvald. 'It is his will that all his earls should attend.'

Wulfrum regarded the speaker and nodded. 'I will do so.'

Elgiva caught the look that passed between him and Olaf Ironfist, though the latter said nothing, only listened attentively to the conversation. She noted he also looked once at Sweyn, though it was but a fleeting glance and probably not significant. The man's presence caused her deep uneasiness and she longed to see him ride on. Having thought never to see him again, it was a disagreeable surprise to find him here in the flesh.

She said as much to Osgifu a little later.

'Disagreeable indeed,' replied Osgifu. 'Worse, he is alive and well. The gods have not heard my prayers on that score.'

'Fortunately they ride on tomorrow.'

'Good riddance.' Then, 'What news did the riders bring from York?'

She listened with close attention while Elgiva summarised what she had heard.

'I must get a message to Aylwin, warn him.'

'You cannot risk venturing out there.'

'Not personally, but it should still be possible to get a message through.'

'How?'

'Through Leofwine. Can you let him know what is afoot and bid him find Brekka if he can? I know the rebels move their camp often.' She paused. 'It is the last thing I can do for Aylwin. Let us pray that he heeds the warning.'

'Let us hope so. Let us hope also that Wulfrum never finds out that his plan has been betrayed.'

'This is not done to betray Wulfrum, but to prevent more blood from being shed.'

'He would not see it that way.'

'I know it,' replied Elgiva, 'but I cannot just let Aylwin and the others be slaughtered.'

After Osgifu departed for the village, Elgiva paced the floor in an agony of suspense and inner turmoil. It seemed to her then that every turn of events mired her deeper in deception. She needed something to do to take her mind off it all and keep her away from their visitors. It was politic to keep her distance until the men should have gone. As always there was spinning to do, enough to last until the evening meal when she would have the safety of numbers about her.

She occupied herself thus until the late afternoon. Then, feeling the need of fresh air, Elgiva went out, heading away from the bower and the hall towards the paddock. The day was fine and warm and scented with flowers and cut grass. Glossy horses grazed beyond the fence, cropping the lush turf. However, being preoccupied, she devoted little attention to them. Had the message reached the rebel group? It was all she could do and little enough. Recalling their last meeting, Elgiva sighed. Aylwin's words still stung. What made it worse was that much of what he had said had the ring of truth. She would not undo her marriage to Wulfrum, would not be Aylwin's bride instead. He was a good and respected man, but she knew that she had never felt for him what she felt for Wulfrum. Aylwin's look did not send a pleasurable shiver along her spine, nor did his touch burn. His kiss would never set her heart aflame. She could never return the feeling he had for her. She wondered why it should be that one man could inspire passion and another not, no matter how worthy. Wulfrum was her lord and there could be no other.

Elgiva walked slowly from the paddock towards the orchard and sat down in a pool of dappled shade. It was pleasant out of doors and for the time she began to relax, to let the sweet air and the sunshine soothe her. She did not hear the man's approach, for the turf silenced his steps, and was not aware of his presence until his shadow fell across her face.

'Aylwin!' For a moment she was numb with shock. 'Are you insane?'

'I had to see you again, Elgiva.'

'In heaven's name, why?' She looked round, scanning the place with anxious eyes. 'If you are found here…'

'I had to thank you.'

'For what?'

'For the warning and the information…' he paused, searching for the words '…and to say how much I regret what occurred at our last meeting. I can see now that the words were harsh. You don't know how often I have wished them unsaid.'

Elgiva shook her head. 'Let's not quarrel about the past.'

'You are generous.' He gave her a wry smile. 'And brave too. You took a risk to send that message.'

'All the more reason for you to heed it and take your men away from here before it is too late.' The amber eyes were earnest as they met and held his gaze. 'Ravenswood is of strategic importance to the Vikings. They will not suffer a Saxon challenge.'

'There are many kinds of challenge, Elgiva. I am not so foolish as to think we could meet them in open battle yet. They are too numerous, but more men will join us. Our intelligence improves apace. We are in communication with other rebel groups. In the meantime, we shall use what means we have to harry the foe and then melt back into the forest.'

'Give it up, I beg you. It can only end in more deaths.'

'I told you, Elgiva, I will not give up what is mine.' He bent a meaningful look upon her. 'But I was wrong to doubt you. Come away with me now. The forest has many secret places. The Viking will never find you.'

'Wulfrum would find me,' she replied. 'I am his wife.'

'You were mine before you were his.' His hand closed round her wrist. 'I know you fear his wrath and rightly so, but I will never let him harm you.'

'His wrath would not fall on me alone, Aylwin, but on others too.'

'That is a price I am willing to pay.'

'But I am not.' She tried to disengage her hold, but his grip tightened. 'You must understand that.'

His gaze hardened. 'Still you make excuses to remain with him.'

'Aylwin, please! This is a futile argument. You must go before someone sees you here.'

He let out a ragged breath and she saw some of the tension leave him. The grip on her wrist slackened a little.

'I'm sorry, Elgiva. I did not come here to quarrel with you. I shall go—for now. But know this: one day soon I shall kill the Viking and free you.'

'You cannot.'

'Lord Halfdan has shown me the way, Elgiva.'

'What do you mean?'

'Be ignorant of the knowledge until you can applaud the deed. Suffice it to say that Wulfrum must ride for York in the autumn. The waiting is almost over.' Aylwin smiled and released his hold. 'Meanwhile I must go.'

'Stay. Will you not tell me what you intend?'

He shook his head. 'Farewell, Elgiva.'

'Aylwin, wait!'

But he was gone, running swiftly through the trees. Elgiva watched until he was out of sight, her heart thumping with fear and horror at his words. Automatically she massaged her wrist, feeling yet the imprint of those strong fingers. She was left in no doubt now that he had meant every word. He would not go. Anxiously her gaze scanned the quiet orchard, but she was alone. The nearest men were raking hay two fields away, too far to have seen or heard anything. She drew in a deep breath. Aylwin had taken a foolish risk to come here. His words had disturbed her much and she understood now how far she had underestimated the strength of his feeling for her. Ironically her warning had had the opposite effect from the one she had intended.

She was so preoccupied in thought that she failed to see the man at the orchard's edge until she was almost upon him. Then her heart missed a beat. Sweyn! He smiled at her, the cool grey eyes missing no detail of her appearance.

'Well met, Elgiva. It seems married life agrees with you.'

'As you say, Sweyn.' She tried to step around him, but he blocked her path.

'I have missed you, my lady.'

'Really?'

'I can't get you out of my mind.'

'Try harder.'

'You are still cold, Elgiva.'

'I am not like to be different.'

'Not toward me, perhaps,' he agreed, 'but what of the man you were with just now? He didn't look much like Wulfrum to me.'

Elgiva forced herself to meet that mocking gaze. 'Hardly,' she replied. 'It was one of the serfs.'

'Indeed?'

'I do not think I need explain myself to you.'

'But would your husband feel the same if he knew?'

'Why don't you ask him and find out?' The words were uttered with far more confidence than she felt. 'Though, of course, he might wonder then how it was that *you* sought out his wife for a private conversation.'

He frowned and she saw the shot go home. 'It is nothing to me if you lower yourself to converse with peasants.'

'It was ever the custom to treat our people well,' she replied. 'You should try it some time.'

She would have swept on, but he seized her arm, detaining her.

'I would treat you well, Elgiva, if you gave me the chance.'

Incredulous, she could only stare at him. Then, recovering herself, 'Let go of me, Sweyn. I am Wulfrum's wife and he would not take kindly to having another man lay hands on me.'

'Do you think I fear Wulfrum?'

'No,' she replied, 'but I have seen enough bloodshed to last me a lifetime. Even the sight of yours has no appeal. Now let me go.'

For an instant she saw something like admiration in his eyes. Then he loosed his hold. With intense relief Elgiva walked away, conscious of his gaze at every step.

She returned to the chamber she shared with Wulfrum, and lay down on the bed, trying to order her scattered thoughts. The experience had left her feeling shaken and she needed to be calm when Wulfrum returned, lest he suspect something untoward. She had no wish to see Sweyn again before he left, and no wish to play the hostess to his companions, either. Somehow she must avoid the evening meal without arousing suspicion. Elgiva closed her eyes and tried to think.

Some time later she awoke with a start to see Wulfrum looking down at her in concern.

'Are you well, Elgiva?'

She struggled up on to one elbow, feeling groggy and disorientated.

'A headache, that is all.'

Her pallor was genuine enough and Wulfrum frowned, sitting down on the edge of the bed to scrutinise her better. His hand felt her forehead for fever, but if anything it felt cooler than usual. He pushed her gently back and covered her with a pelt.

'Stay here and rest,' he said. 'I will send Osgifu to you.'

'There is no need. I am sure a little sleep will serve.'

Wulfrum frowned, but did not press the point. 'As you wish.'

He bent over her and brushed her cheek with his lips, a caress that was both gentle and caring. Elgiva wanted to put her arms around his neck, wanted to feel his arms around her, but she was afraid that he would suspect something. Unhappily she watched him move to the door, saw him pause and look back with concern in his eyes. Then he smiled.

'Rest, my lady.'

With that he was gone. Elgiva felt tears pricking her eyelids and forced them back, feeling both relief that he had suspected nothing and guilt that she had lied to him, if only by omission. If Wulfrum ever found out about her meetings with Aylwin, his anger would know no bounds. As for Sweyn, she could only pray he would not attach any real significance to what he had seen. Aylwin had been garbed as a peasant and from a distance the disguise protected him well. Her story was credible. Elgiva sighed. She felt as though she were caught in a web of deceit. Yet what else could she do? To speak would betray Aylwin—not to speak betrayed Wulfrum. For that was how he would interpret her silence. Once she would not have cared, but now she knew his good opinion of her was important. More than that, he was important. He never spoke of his innermost feelings, but his behaviour towards her spoke of regard and warmth. She wanted to think that she had his heart as he had hers. It was the reason she had not wanted to see him fight Sweyn. Though she knew well his prowess in battle, what if, in defeating his enemy, he were to be fatally injured? Or what if, through some evil trick, Sweyn were to emerge the victor? The idea was chilling. She would rather be dead than fall into his clutches again. Better to remain silent and let the matter rest. Sweyn would be gone on the morrow.

Elgiva unfastened her gown and slipped out of it, laying it aside over a chair. Then she bathed her face and hands and unfastened her hair to comb it out. The familiar rituals were soothing and some of her former mood began to lift. From the hall below she could hear the muted sounds of men's voices, their laughter. Wulfrum would play the host well. In her mind's eye she could see him there among his men and for the first time was thankful for their presence. The thought of Olaf Ironfist was a distinct comfort tonight. With him at his back Wulfrum would be safe from treachery. Elgiva smiled to herself and, finishing her grooming, slipped off her kirtle and returned to bed drawing the coverlet over her.

She did not hear Wulfrum return or see him bend over her. Her face was peaceful, untroubled, and he noted with relief that some of the healthy colour had returned. Golden hair spilled across her shoulders, taking on a soft, resinous sheen in the lamplight. He lifted a stray tress and his fingers brushed her naked shoulder. His eyes followed it along the curve of her arm to her wrists. There they stopped. Wulfrum frowned, looking closer. His frown deepened as he looked at the dark bruises encircling its slenderness. Five prints left on her skin, the prints of a man's fingers.

He straightened, looking at the sleeping figure of his wife, tempted to rouse her now and demand to know how they came there. He controlled himself. It was late. There would be time enough to speak to her on the morrow. He undressed and blew out the lamp before climbing into bed beside her. Elgiva stirred in her sleep, but did not wake; for a long time he lay there in the darkness pondering what he had seen. Someone had left those marks on her, someone with a strong hand. Grim faced, he turned over the possibilities. His men wouldn't touch her. He had seen their growing respect for her; besides, he trusted them. They would not lay hands on his woman. He thought of the Saxon serfs and knew it wasn't one of them. Elgiva was their lady. In any case, it was more than their lives were worth and they knew it. Well, come what may, he would know the truth on the morrow.

Elgiva woke with the light and stretched lazily, pushing her hair out of her eyes. She felt Wulfrum's warmth beside her and smiled. She had not heard him come to bed. It wasn't until she turned her head that she saw he too was awake, propped on one elbow and regarding her intently. His expression was grim and her heart beat just a little faster as she tried to remember what day it was. Had he wished to rise early to hunt? Should she have risen and brought food? She started up in concern.

'Wulfrum, I…'

A strong hand pushed her back on to the bed and held her there.

'There is no matter pressing, Elgiva. Save one.'

She looked at him in confusion. 'What is it?'

'These.' He slid his hand down her arm to her wrist.

Elgiva stared in dismay at the dark bruises there and the memory of their creator returned.

'I…I must have hit my wrist yesterday, though I cannot say I recall doing it.'

Wulfrum's blue gaze burned. 'You play me for a fool, Elgiva. Do you think I don't know the difference between an ordinary bruise and those left by fingers? A man left those marks and I would know his name.'

Elgiva swallowed and tied to rise, but his hand forbade it.

'You are mistaken—'

'Don't lie to me, Elgiva.' His voice was harsh now. 'Who was it?'

'Wulfrum, it is of no consequence.'

'I will decide that.'

'It was a foolish matter, not worth the mentioning.'

Her reluctance to speak caused Wulfrum's frown to deepen as another thought occurred to him.

'Whom do you protect, Elgiva? A lover?'

'What!' Elgiva's heart thumped unpleasantly hard. Did he really think she would be capable of it? Did he trust her so little after all? 'You cannot seriously think so, for you have had me well guarded, my lord. Would I carry on an illicit affair for the amusement of your men? Were it so, you would know of it by now, I think.'

Wulfrum saw the anger in her eyes and knew she spoke the truth. However, it still did not explain those marks and he was determined to discover their cause.

'Then tell me truth, or, by all the gods, I will beat it out of you.'

Elgiva pushed his hand away and struggled to her knees, eyes blazing.

'I will not be cowed by a Viking bully! You are no better than Sweyn, for I see you learned your manners in the same sty!'

'Sweyn! Was it he who did this?'

'Aye. It seems he has not forgotten how you kept me from him.'

Wulfrum's brow darkened further. 'Did he force himself on you?'

'No, he only grabbed hold of me for a moment.' It was a partial truth only, but Elgiva knew it could not be helped.

'Why didn't you tell me, Elgiva?'

'Because I didn't want you to fight him.'

'Have you so little faith in my prowess as a swordsman?'

'No, but Sweyn is treacherous, and I was afraid you

would—' Her voice quavered and she broke off, turning away. Wulfrum took her shoulders and turned her back.

'Afraid I would what?' he demanded.

Tears started in her eyes. 'That you would be hurt or killed, even.'

'Not likely. Sweyn isn't that good.' He paused as the import of her words sank in. 'Would it matter to you then if I had been?'

'Of course it would.'

'Why?'

When she remained silent, he took her chin in his hand and tilted her face to his. 'Look at me, Elgiva.' Reluctantly, she met his gaze, but he persisted. 'Why?'

Elgiva felt herself blushing. Wulfrum grinned.

'Come, my lady, I await your answer.'

'Because you are my husband and I owe my loyalty to you.'

'Don't prevaricate.'

She saw his grin widen and grew hotter. 'Because if you were dead, I might fall into Sweyn's clutches.'

He chuckled. 'He would get more than he bargained for, then. However, our guests left early, at first light. Sweyn is gone.'

'Gone?'

'Aye, but he will pay for his insults in good time. Meanwhile, you have nothing to fear from him.'

The tone was mild and threw Elgiva off her guard. A powerful arm tipped her backwards and she found herself pinned beneath him.

'Wulfrum?'

'You still haven't answered my question, Elgiva.'

'I have. At least all the answer you're going to get.'

'Is that right?'

'Wulfrum, let me go.'

'No.'

She tried to push him away, but her efforts left him unmoved, except perhaps to deepen his amusement. Then he took a kiss.

'Answer the question.'

'I will not.'

He kissed her again and for longer this time and there was a dangerous glint in his eye.

'What did you call me just now? A Viking bully, was it not?'

Elgiva struggled in vain. 'If the cap fits…'

'Oh, it does, my lady, as you are going to discover.'

Chapter Thirteen

Mindful of what he had been told by Torvald, Wulfrum sent out various patrols to test the truth of the rumours about raiders and outlaws. Having established peace at Ravenswood, he had no intention of having it destroyed by neglect. Therefore, Ironfist and his companions rode out into the forest and made a thorough search of the surrounding area, but found no sign of the rebel band Torvald had spoken of. He reported back to Wulfrum.

'We found evidence of an old camp, but the rebels were long gone.'

'All the same, we will increase the patrols on the boundaries and post extra guards until we know more.'

'You fear a surprise attack?'

'I fear nothing, but I will not be caught napping. See to it, Olaf.'

Ironfist nodded and went off to deal with the matter.

Elgiva, who had been listening carefully to the exchange, felt both guilt and relief. Aylwin *had* thought better of it and heeded the warning after all. Surely now the rebels would not attack Ravenswood. It was a question she put to Wulfrum.

'If they do, it will be the last mistake they ever make,' he replied. Then, seeing her worried look, he smiled. 'Have no fear, Elgiva. No harm shall befall Ravenswood while I have breath.'

'You guard well what is yours,' she replied.

Wulfrum laughed then. 'Just so, my lady. Therefore, no harm shall befall you, either.'

Elgiva regarded him quizzically. Was he merely guarding her along with the rest of the property? Somehow she did not think so; his behaviour to her of late had been more markedly gentle, or mostly anyway. Recalling that recent scene in their chamber and the confession he had extracted, she felt her face grow rather warmer.

'Meanwhile,' he went on, 'you and Osgifu will not go out to collect herbs again until we know more.'

She did not argue for she could see the reason behind the words. Besides, thanks to their former efforts she and Osgifu had replenished many of the plant supplies they needed. The forest was no longer the sanctuary it had seemed. Once she had thought that, being a Saxon, she would never come to harm at the hands of her fellows. Now she wasn't so sure. Would they consider her to be treacherous, a turncoat? It was not a pleasant thought.

Wulfrum was as good as his word and posted men at strategic points around Ravenswood to forestall any attempt to attack his holding. However, as the days passed, there was no sign of the raiders.

'It is most like they have moved on,' said Ida when a week had gone by with no trace of the enemy.

'Perhaps,' replied Wulfrum. 'However, we shall maintain our vigilance until we can be certain.'

Elgiva hoped that Ida was right. However, two days later one of the men reported the loss of two sheep from the flock. Tracks were found leading into the forest but a thorough search again revealed nothing. The guards were increased and men took it in turns to patrol the boundaries, but still no trace was found either of the livestock or the thieves. Shortly after that a steer was taken.

'How are they getting through our defences?' demanded Wulfrum when the news was brought to him. 'This place is so tightly guarded now that even a mouse would find difficulty in stealing anything.'

'Maybe they aren't,' said Ironfist.

'You think someone in Ravenswood is giving them aid?'

'It is a possibility.'

'As you say. It is strange how the raiders know the exact moment and place to strike.' Wulfrum's expression grew hard. 'If you are right and there is a traitor in our midst, we shall discover him soon enough and he will rue the day.'

Elgiva heard the words with misgivings, her mind running through the names of all the people she knew, but she could not think that one of them had been responsible. And yet she had to acknowledge that there were many who only tolerated the new order because they had to. After all, someone had helped Aylwin to escape in the first place. Would they join in secret confederacy with the outlaws to strike back at the Danes? She realised that she did not know the answer. The woodland was large and there were many hiding places in its heart, places hard to find unless you knew them. There were caves too, some big enough to shelter a considerable number of men. However, it was all surmise on her part. She had no real proof.

Meanwhile the summer days grew sultry with a sticky heat that made every exertion uncomfortable. Elgiva thought longingly of the forest pool, but she would not disobey Wulfrum and venture out there. The brooding air foretold a coming storm, although some rain would be welcome now for the land lay listless beneath a metallic sky. Elgiva laid aside her sewing and rose from her stool, unable to bear the confinement within doors. Her head ached and her clothes stuck to her and every movement seemed to bring beads of perspiration to her face. She walked towards the orchard, thinking to find some respite from the heat.

Indeed, it was a little cooler there and she sank gratefully on the grass beneath the leafy canopy. All around the ripening fruit was swelling on the branches, sure sign that the coming harvest would be plentiful. Soon the corn harvest would begin and the barns and granaries would fill. The first hay crop was already gathered in. In a few more weeks the first leaves would begin to change colour. The year turned and all their lives with it. Who could have foreseen in the previous winter what would befall them in the spring? Already it seemed like a past life.

At the evening meal Elgiva found herself watching Wulfrum, listening as he spoke and laughed with his men. He was relaxed, leaning back in his chair, his hand toying with his ale horn. From time to time he glanced her way and smiled and her heart would leap. She knew that later they would retire to their chamber and he would make love to her once more and she would yield. *You'll come*. He had said that long ago. Had his knowledge of other women fuelled his confidence? She knew there had been others; his skill as a lover could only have been born of practice. What had they been like, his other women, the ones before her? Had he loved any of them? Was there one he remembered with more fondness than the others? He never spoke of them. Did it mean he had forgotten? Elgiva forced the thoughts to the back of her mind, angry with herself for even entertaining them. What did it matter? It was in the past. She was his wife now, a relationship made real every night they retired to bed.

On this evening Elgiva excused herself early from the table and went before him to their chamber. She undressed to the thin kirtle and went to stand by the window to find relief from the heat. A breeze had sprung up and in the west the clouds had begun to mass like the vanguard of a great celestial host labouring up. Distant flashes of lightning preceded its arrival and the air was pungent with promised rain. Elgiva leaned back against the wooden frame, watching the storm approach, feeling the wind lift strands of hair from her neck as it cooled her skin. She had not bothered to light a lamp, for although it grew late some light yet lingered in the sky.

She stood for some time, watching the display in the heavens, fascinated by its power. The storm rolled nearer. Soon it would be overhead, for the thunderclaps followed each other in quick succession. A brilliant flash of light illuminated the whole area around the hall and with it a dark figure running towards the stables. Elgiva frowned, staring into the twilight shadows. Perhaps it had been one of Wulfrum's men hastening to take shelter before the rain came. The man paused and looked round. The next lightning flash lit him plainly for a split second. Drem! Elgiva started. It couldn't have been. He had no business there, wasn't even a groom. Another flash of lightning lit the scene, but this time she saw no one. Even so an uneasy feeling prickled between her shoulder blades like an itch she couldn't reach. She remained by the window a few moments more, her eyes scanning the area, but she could see no sign of the man again. It wouldn't have been Drem, only someone who looked a bit like him. After all, she had only seen him for an instant. Most likely it *had* been one of the guards seeking temporary shelter, for in truth the storm would be fearsome when it really hit them.

She closed her eyes, suddenly aware that her earlier headache had gone as if somehow the release of tension in the skies had found its parallel in her. Just then the breeze brought with it a whiff of smoke and she heard a horse neigh. Elgiva opened her eyes, scanning the ground in her view. Her gaze was arrested by flickering light in the thatch of the stable roof. For a moment she froze before her mind grasped the significance. Suspicion became certainty. Grabbing her mantle from the top of the clothes chest, she threw it about her shoulders and ran from the room, heading for the hall. At the head of the stairs she paused.

'Fire! The stable is on fire! Make haste!'

All conversation stopped and fifty pairs of eyes looked up in astonishment to see the apparition on the staircase, a wild-eyed figure with golden hair tumbling across her shoulders and clad loosely in a cloak that revealed only a kirtle beneath. For perhaps the space of a few seconds they stared before the import of her words began to sink in. Elgiva had by then reached the bottom of the stairs and turned to Wulfrum.

'My lord, quickly! The stable is ablaze!'

Wulfrum leapt to his feet, but she was ahead of him, making for the door. Behind her she could hear shouting and running feet as men sprang into action. Elgiva raced for the stable, ignoring everything save the need to get Mara and the other horses out. She could hear restless hooves and whinnying now and the smell of smoke was stronger. In the darkness beyond the door flickering flames lit the far end where a pile of hay was already ablaze beneath the burning roof. Elgiva darted forwards, feeling smoke sting her eyes, coughing on the thick fumes. Mara's stall was towards the far end and already the little mare was snorting and rolling her eyes in fear. Elgiva went to the horse's head and unfastened the halter rope, speaking gently to try to calm the frightened animal. However, when she tried to back the horse out, it refused to budge. All around the smoke thickened and the sinister crackling of the flames grew louder. Fragments of burning thatch fell about them and she heard Firedrake scream with terror, his hooves drumming on the side of the stall as he fought the rope that held him. Then other horses took up his cry, their panic spreading. Shouting voices sounded from the entrance way and flaring torches showed men freeing the animals nearest the door. In desperation Elgiva pulled on Mara's halter rope, but still the horse wouldn't stir.

'Elgiva, give me your cloak.'

She heard Wulfrum's voice beside her. She tore off the cloak and watched him use it to cover the horse's eyes. Then, speaking softly, he coaxed the mare out of the stall and led her to the door with Elgiva stumbling after. Outside a line of men had formed a chain from the well to pass buckets of water in an attempt to douse the fire while the others tried to get the remaining animals out. Fortunately most of the horses had been turned out, the nights being fine and warm.

'Get the mare away from here.' Wulfrum removed the cloak from Mara's eyes and shoved the halter rope at a serf. Then he soaked the cloak in the trough before turning to Elgiva. 'Wait here.'

She saw him throw the wet cloak over his head before plunging back into the chaos of the stable. Elgiva watched through stinging eyes the smoke swirl through the thatch on the roof. The fire was louder now, the flames brighter. Smoke billowed from the open doorway as from the gateway to hell, while above them the storm rumbled on. Tight-throated with fear, she looked in horror as the moments passed and Wulfrum did not return. Visualising the stallion's panic and his flying hooves, Elgiva's heart pounded. What if Wulfrum were hurt and couldn't get out? What if he were overcome by smoke? He would die in there, a horrible lingering death. It couldn't happen. It must not happen. She began to run back towards the stable, but a strong arm caught and held her. She heard Ida's voice.

'You cannot go back in there, lady. It's too late now.'

'Wulfrum's in there. Let me go.'

Elgiva struggled hard, but the arm did not yield. Tears coursed down her face as she watched the thick smoke and the leaping flames. Surely nothing could live in there now. In her mind's eye she saw Wulfrum overcome by smoke, lying helpless on the floor as the blaze licked closer. Desperate now, she fought to free herself.

'I must go back. Wulfrum!'

Ida held on for grim death, ignoring her tears and pleas for he dared not let her go. He knew enough about her now to re-alise she would run straight back into the flames if he did. His gaze moved beyond her to the burning building, willing Wulfrum to come out. Seconds passed and the roar of the flames grew louder. Ida stared in horror at the smoke billowing through the open doorway.

Then, through the choking fog, came Wulfrum leading Fire-drake. He was coughing hard and his clothes were singed and blackened, but he was alive. The horse was frightened, but otherwise seemed none the worse for his brush with death. Elgiva slumped, weak with relief.

'He's alive! Oh, Wulfrum!'

Freed from Ida's hold, she ran to him, watching anxiously as he struggled for breath.

'Are you all right?'

He nodded, unable to speak for the bitter fumes in his throat. His gullet felt raw. It was some moments before he could draw breath again. Elgiva shut her eyes, trying to stop her tears. She thought she had really lost him. Then her arms were around him, holding him close. Wulfrum glanced down in surprise, but before he could say anything Ironfist appeared beside them.

'All the horses are out, my lord, but we can't save the stable.'

'Let it burn, then. We'll risk no more lives tonight.'

The heat was fierce now and they retreated to a safer distance, watching the flames lick into the night sky. The supporting roof timbers sagged at one end and then collapsed in a wave of heat and smoke. Elgiva shuddered, thinking of what might have happened if they had come too late to save the horses. A stable could always be rebuilt.

Suddenly a mighty clap of thunder shook the earth and the first drops of rain began to fall, and then more until, with a roar, the clouds opened and poured their stored burden on the earth beneath while jagged lightning streaked the sky, illuminating the human drama for a brief moment. Then it was absorbed again into the gathering gloom as the rain intensified to a deluge. Elgiva gasped, soaked in seconds, staring in disbelief at the curtain of rain sweeping across the land, a curtain so dense it shut out all view. Then she became aware of Wulfrum smiling down at her.

'Come.'

Together they staggered back towards the hall, heads down against the deluge. Elgiva stumbled and would have fallen but for the strong arm about her waist; at length they reached shelter. It seemed a haven of peace and light after the nightmare darkness outside. Gasping, Elgiva wiped the water from her eyes and face and wrung out her hair. Like herself, Wulfrum was drenched, his dark locks plastered to his head and shoulders, his clothing hanging in sodden folds. Then she became aware he was regarding her with a most keen interest, a broad grin splitting his face. Following his gaze down, Elgiva realised with a shock that her kirtle had become transparent with the water and clung tight, revealing every detail of her body. She felt her face grow warm.

'We had better get you upstairs, my lady, before my men return. Otherwise I couldn't answer for the consequences.'

She nodded, but already she could hear voices without and at any moment now men would be coming through the door. It was also some distance to the stairs. Appalled at the implications, Elgiva ran. In much amusement Wulfrum watched her go. She just reached the top of the staircase before Ironfist and Ida entered the hall, followed by the rest.

'Fenrir's fangs, what a night!' The giant shook water from his hair and beard. Water streamed from his clothing. A large pool formed on the floor at his feet.

'It might have been a lot worse if the fire had spread to the barn and the byre,' replied Ida. 'As it is, the rain will quench the flames. We'll probably have to rebuild the stable all the same.'

'How in the name of all the gods did the fire start anyway?'

'Could have been a lightning strike.'

'Not likely. We'd have heard it. It would have blown the roof apart. Although the thatch was burning, it was still more or less intact when we first got out there.'

Ida frowned. 'That's right, now you mention it. Belike the fire began within—an overset lamp, perhaps.'

'Perhaps. I'll question the grooms tomorrow. If any of them has been careless, I'll wear his guts for garters.'

Wulfrum called for ale. He knew he needed some and, after being choked by smoke and fumes, his men would need to rinse their throats too. As he suspected, it was a suggestion that found instant favour. He joined them in a horn or two and thanked them for their efforts in rescuing the horses. As Wulfrum thought of Firedrake and the others burning to death his anger revived, for he held the beasts in great affection. Had Elgiva not sounded the alarm when she did, they might have come too late to save them. He recalled her racing to the burning stable and how his heart had leapt almost into his mouth when he saw her plunge into the smoke. However, she would not leave her horse to die like that, or any of them, indeed. Her courage was keen and he was proud of her. Then he recalled the sight of her in the sodden kirtle and his mind turned in a new direction. He tossed off the rest of his ale and was about to bid his men goodnight when he overheard his wife's name being spoken across the room.

'It was thanks to the Lady Elgiva that we saved the horses at all,' Ironfist was saying. 'But for her the outcome could have been very different.'

'Did you see her go into that stable?' Ida shook his head in wonder. 'Didn't even hesitate. Courage of a lion, that one.'

'Aye, she has.'

'When she thought Wulfrum wasn't coming out that last time, she was all set to go back after him too. I only just managed to hold her. Struggled like a fury.'

'Oh?' Ironfist's ale horn paused in mid-air.

Wulfrum was listening intently now, though the pair seemed quite oblivious to the fact they were overheard.

'Almost beside herself, she was. Kept saying, "Wulfrum's in there", and begging me to let her go. She's crazy about him, obviously.'

'Only the gods know why,' replied the giant. 'I've never seen anything in the bastard.'

The two of them guffawed. Wulfrum reddened, feeling strangely pleased. Had Elgiva really been so anxious for his safety? She had once said he was more use to her alive, but her actions tonight suggested that she cared rather more than he could have hoped. He smiled to himself and made his way to the stairs.

When he entered the chamber, it was to see his wife drying her hair with a large linen cloth. Her sopping kirtle lay discarded nearby and she had wrapped a pelt around herself against the chill from the rain. For a moment he watched her, then shut and barred the door before crossing to join her. Elgiva watched him strip off his wet clothes and rub himself dry.

'I have you to thank for being in time to save the horses,' he said then. 'If you had not raised the alarm when you did, they would have been lost.'

Elgiva shuddered. 'Don't, Wulfrum. It doesn't bear thinking about.'

He reached out and caressed her face with his hand, then gently removed the towel from her and took over the business of drying her hair. Elgiva remained very still. In truth, the gentle movement of his hands was soothing and gradually she let herself relax.

'How did you know?'

'I was watching the storm approach and smelled smoke.' Then she froze, remembering. 'There was something else too.' She told him about the figure she had seen just before the fire broke out. Wulfrum's hands stopped what they were doing.

'Did you see his face?'

Elgiva hesitated. The evidence was circumstantial and she was reluctant to name Drem and put him in danger.

'No, and it is possible the two things are not connected anyway.'

'I think it was no coincidence.' For a moment his expression was grim. 'But I will find the man who was responsible, I swear it.'

She laid a hand on his arm. 'Do you think it is one of our own people?'

'I don't know—yet.'

For a moment there was no sound save for the rain, which had slackened from a torrent to a steady downpour.

'Do you think they will strike again?'

'Undoubtedly. It is why they must be found.' Then he smiled. 'However, that is for tomorrow. Tonight I would show my appreciation.'

He drew her to her feet and took her in his arms. The kiss was long and passionate and Elgiva shivered. Wulfrum looked down at her in concern.

'You are cold, my love. Come.'

He took her to bed and lay beside her, holding her close, sharing his warmth. Elgiva lay still in his arms, the heart thumping in her breast, wondering if she had heard him correctly. *My love.* He had never used the word before. Did he mean it? His hand brushed her skin gently and she turned towards him, her mouth meeting his in a long passionate kiss, her hands stroking him, rousing him, bringing him to an equal pitch of desire. This time she took the lead and Wulfrum knew all the sweetness of her willing compliance as they came together in fierce and urgent joy, meeting in a mutual climax of shuddering delight.

Later, lying in his arms, Elgiva pondered his words anew. He trusted her, she knew that. Was he beginning to love her too? She bit her lip, glad of the darkness that hid her face. Would he love a woman whose silence aided his enemy? Had it been part of Aylwin's plan to burn the stables tonight? Would there be an attempt on the barn next or the hall? Matters had taken a turn she would never have believed. Wulfrum would not let this go unanswered. She closed her eyes. What to do for the best? She was still considering the matter when the spreading warmth and the sound of the rain lulled her to sleep.

Chapter Fourteen

By sunrise the following morning the storm was long gone. The only sign of its passing was damp earth and a few puddles, for the sun shone again in a clear sky. However, the stable was a blackened ruin with half the roof burned away and the remaining timbers sagging under the weight of the thatch. The charred and sodden straw stank and everywhere dark ash stained the ground. Elgiva shuddered, hearing in her imagination the screams of the frightened horses once again.

'We'll have to rebuild it, all right,' said Ironfist, surveying the wreck with a critical eye. 'We couldn't put a hog in there, never mind a horse.'

Beside him Wulfrum concurred. 'It's fortunate the weather is warm. The horses will take no harm from being out at night. In the meantime, we'll organise a team of men to start clearing away the mess.'

'I'll see to it.'

Ironfist was about to depart when Ida appeared from inside the shell of the stable. His face was grim.

'My lord, I think you'd better take a look at this.' He paused, throwing a speaking glance at Wulfrum. 'It might be better if the lady remained here. It is not a sight for her eyes.'

Puzzled, Elgiva watched as the two of them drew closer to the ruin, to a place where part of the wall had crumbled, allowing ingress. She heard the sound of timbers being kicked aside and then the men's voices, too low to be overheard. After that was silence. When finally they emerged, her husband's expression was chilling. With a dreadful sense of foreboding, she summoned up the courage to ask.

'What is it, Wulfrum?'

'It's the body of one of the stable-boys. He must have been in the loft and he didn't get out. Unfortunately, no one knew he was there.'

Elgiva's eyes filled with tears and she could only stare at him in dumb horror. All around her she heard a buzz of angry voices as the news reached the others.

'The person responsible will pay dearly for this,' he went on. 'Had the boy any family?'

'Just his mother, I think,' replied Ironfist. 'I have seen her hereabouts on occasion.'

Before anyone else could volunteer information Ceolnoth approached, bringing one of the Saxon serfs with him. The latter looked fearfully about, but could not escape the firm hold on his arm.

'Now what have we here?'

Wulfrum looked round, following Ironfist's gaze.

'My lord, this man may be able to shed some light on what happened last night,' said Ceolnoth.

'Oh?'

'Yes, lord. It seems one of the other hands did not turn up for his work this morning.'

Wulfrum frowned. 'What has this man to do with it?'

The serf paled and began to tremble. 'Nothing, my lord, I swear it. 'Twas I that discovered Drem was missing this morning, that is all.'

Elgiva froze in stunned disbelief. Then her mind threw back

the memory of a man at the whipping post and she knew with sick certainty that it had been he whom she had seen.

'Drem?' demanded Wulfrum.

'One of the field hands, my lord,' said Ceolnoth.

'I know the man.' Wulfrum's gaze never left the serf's face. 'Go on.'

'That is all I know, lord. Drem was there last night and gone this morning.'

'Have you made a search for him?'

'Yes, lord. He is nowhere to be found.'

'What more?'

'Nothing more, lord.'

'Well, I think we can guess who fired the stables last night,' said Ironfist.

Ceolnoth nodded. 'Belike the rat has slipped away into the forest to join the rebels.'

'Is that so?' demanded Wulfrum.

The serf began to shake. 'It may be so, my lord, but he did not confide in me.'

'Then who were his friends?'

The man remained silent, crushed by the sombre looks cast upon him, a picture of abject terror.

'I'll get it out of him,' said Ironfist.

Elgiva laid a hand on his arm. 'Wait, Olaf.' She turned to the serf. 'How are you called?'

'Oswy, my lady.'

'Then, Oswy, I beg you to say what you know. Those who are innocent have nothing to fear. We must find out who did this. A boy is dead.'

He blinked rapidly. Clearly this was news to him too.

'A boy, my lady?'

'Yes, one of the stable lads. He must have been trapped by the flames for he did not get out.'

Oswy was shocked and his face went a shade paler. 'Elfric

and Leofwine knew Drem best, my lady, for he sometimes helped out at the forge. Even so, I think he would not have told them what he planned. They would never have agreed.'

Elgiva turned to Wulfrum. 'What he says is true, my lord. I know these men and they have ever served Ravenswood loyally.'

Even as she spoke, she knew he would recall the incident when they had tried to help Hunfirth and Brekka. Would he hold that against them now?

Wulfrum heard her out impassively. 'Nevertheless, I would speak with them.' He turned to Ceolnoth. 'Bring them here.'

The two men arrived a few minutes later, looking round uneasily at the assembled group of stony-faced warriors. However, they answered readily enough to the questions put to them. Wulfrum heard them without interruption. Beside him Elgiva watched his face, trying to glean any clue from his expression as to what he might do next but, as was usual in these affairs, he gave nothing away. Once, her gaze flicked to the smith and his son and thence to Oswy. They stood in silence, never moving a muscle, but the tension was almost palpable. Behind them stood half a dozen of Wulfrum's men, all armed to the teeth. If he gave the word, the three would be dead before they hit the ground. He deliberated a moment longer.

'Very well,' he said at last. 'You may go.'

The exhalation of breath was audible, but they needed no second bidding.

'You believed them?' said Ironfist, watching the retreating figures.

'Yes. If they knew anything at all, they would be with Drem in the forest,' replied Wulfrum, 'which is where we shall find him, I have no doubt.'

'How are we to do that, in the name of all the gods?'

The earl's smile was grim. 'Have the horses saddled, Olaf, and fetch the hounds. If Drem left this morning after the deluge ceased, there is a good chance of picking up his trail. Ceolnoth, find something that has the man's scent on it. Something from his sleeping place, maybe. 'Tis time to go a-hunting.'

Elgiva saw understanding dawn in the faces of the listening men, and they hastened to do his bidding. Wulfrum turned and strode back to the hall, heading for the stairs. Elgiva had almost to run to keep pace. Presently they reached their chamber and she watched anxiously as he donned chain mail and buckled on his sword belt, settling Dragon Tooth firmly in the scabbard. He checked the dagger in his belt and slid a smaller, slimmer blade into his sleeve before finally taking up the linden-wood shield embossed with iron.

'Wulfrum, take care, I beg you. These are desperate men and you know not how many there are.'

'True, but I know how many there will be by the time I return tonight.'

Elgiva shivered. Then she felt his hands on her shoulders drawing her closer.

'Have no fear, my lady. I will return. But I must smoke out this nest of rats or live in fear of them ever more.'

She nodded unhappily. There would be more killing before the day was done, but she knew he had no other choice. The raiders might have got away with the theft of a sheep or two, but the moment the stable was fired their fate was sealed. Wulfrum would find them, she was certain of it, and he would show no mercy this time.

'Wulfrum, I fear that Aylwin may be with them.'

He frowned, his expression suddenly intent. 'Aylwin?'

'Yes. After he fled Ravenswood, he went into the forest. You trailed him that far yourself. He could be with the rebels there.'

'Pray he is not.'

'You intend to slay him.'

'Can I do anything else?' He took her by the shoulders and looked down into her face. 'I know you have had ties of friendship with this man in the past, but you cannot have divided loyalties, Elgiva.'

'I know it.'

Her heart felt leaden in her breast but she knew he was right. An innocent child had died in the fire. Had Drem been taking his orders from Aylwin? It did not bear thinking about. Reluctantly, she followed her husband out to the waiting horses.

Olaf and Ida had returned with twenty mounted men. Beside them were four great hounds, leashed. Wulfrum swung into Firedrake's saddle and looked down at his wife. For a moment their eyes met.

'Until later, my lady.'

Then he turned the horse's head and rode away at the head of his force.

Elgiva watched until the column was out of sight and then recollected her own duties. Before anything else, she must speak with the mother of the murdered stable lad to offer what poor comfort she might. Accordingly she made her way to the village. She arrived to find that Father Willibald had anticipated her and he looked up thankfully as Elgiva entered the mean dwelling. As she expected, the wretched woman was distraught, for her son was the only surviving member of her family, her husband having died of fever the previous year. Now she wept inconsolably. Elgiva could well understand that terrible outpouring of grief and knew that no words of hers could possibly suffice. Instead she put her arms round the sobbing figure and held her close. It was a long time before the tears abated sufficiently for coherent speech.

'Why? Why, my lady?'

'To strike back at the Danes.'

'They have not hurt the Danes. They have murdered my boy.'

'He will be avenged,' replied Elgiva. 'Those responsible will pay a terrible price.'

'That will not bring him back.'

'No, but it will stop them from ever doing it again.'

Elgiva glanced at Father Willibald and saw the sadness in his kindly face. He too had suffered since the taking of Ravenswood, his church burned and his life threatened. Would there ever be an end to the violence, to the killing? Would this land ever know peace again?

Father Willibald cleared his throat. 'My lady, the boy should be given a proper Christian burial.'

'He shall be. I will speak to Lord Wulfrum.'

He regarded her in some surprise not unmixed with hope. 'Then perchance we shall say a mass for the child's soul.'

It was a small comfort, thought Elgiva when she left them some time later. Truly death was absolute. Her own powerlessness appalled her. If only she had given the alarm sooner, had realised the child was in the stable. It was her fervent prayer that he had been overcome with smoke very quickly and not suffered pain before he died, but in her heart she doubted it. Anger vied with sorrow as she relived the night of the fire. One stupid act by a vengeful man and an innocent child had lost his life. This day others would die too. She knew that Wulfrum had no choice but to follow his present course of action, The renegade Saxons were her own people, but her loyalty now was with her husband and she prayed that he would prevail and return safe to her.

All the rest of that day Elgiva looked for his return, though she knew it likely would not be till eventide. All day she tried to occupy herself with familiar tasks but could concentrate on none of them, her hands falling idle in her lap and her mind elsewhere. Beside her Osgifu worked on her mending, saying little, though her eyes went often to Elgiva's face.

In her mind's eye Elgiva saw the forest paths and the great

trees whose green domain held so many secret places. She saw the mounted men and the dogs. Would they pick up the trail? Would the hunters come upon the raiders' hideout? She closed her eyes, hearing in her imagination the clash of swords and the shouts of men, the blood and the screams. Her stomach heaved and she rushed from the bower just in time to vomit in the grass. With a shaking hand she pulled her kerchief from her sleeve and held it to her lips, waiting for the nausea to die down. The other rested lightly on her belly as she struggled to come to terms with the knowledge she could no longer ignore.

'How often has that happened?' asked Osgifu.

'Two or three times, perhaps.'

'Have you missed your monthly bleeding?'

Elgiva nodded.

'How many times?'

'Twice.'

Osgifu's hand covered her own against her belly. Its warmth was reassuring.

'Does he know?'

'Not yet.'

'When will you tell him?'

'I don't know. Soon. I needed to be sure.' Elgiva drew in a deep breath. She would indeed have to tell him soon. The matter could not be kept quiet for long in any case. 'I just haven't found the right moment yet, that's all.'

'I'd like to be a fly on the wall when you do.' Osgifu smiled. 'It would worth something, I think, to see the Viking's expression then.'

'Oh, Gifu, how do you think he will take it? Will he be pleased or angered?'

'What man is angered to learn his wife carries their first child?'

'Wulfrum is not like other men. I hardly ever know what he is thinking.'

'He is not so different from other men,' replied Osgifu, 'at least not in essentials anyway. And he is not so hard to read, either, not when he looks at you.'

She made Elgiva sit down then and fetched a cup of cool water. 'Sip this. It will make you feel better.'

Elgiva took the water, turning over their conversation in her mind. If only Osgifu was right. Then she thought about the grim hunt being enacted in the forest. If only it might be over soon. If only Wulfrum might come back safely.

It was sunset when the hunters returned, the cavalcade emerging from the trees in a slow, steady line. The men did not talk, but their sombre expressions spoke more than words. Elgiva watched from her chamber window as they rode in, her heart leaping as she saw Wulfrum at their head with Ironfist beside him. With a final glance at the preparations she had made, she hastened down to the hall, calling instructions to the servants to bring ale and food before going to the door.

From that vantage point she watched the riders approach, their tired horses dark with sweat and mud. Elgiva's eyes went to the men, noting well the sinister darkening stains on their armour and weapons. All looked weary. One or two nursed obvious injuries and one horse was led with its dead rider slung across the saddle. Then her gaze came to rest on Ironfist and she swallowed hard as she realised for the first time what it was he carried on the point of his spear. Drem would fire no more buildings.

'Put the traitor's head on a spike by the gate,' said Wulfrum. 'Let all see it and know that justice has been done.' He swung down from Firedrake's saddle and crossed the intervening space to the door of the hall.

'Osgifu, some of the men are hurt. Tend to them.'

Wulfrum turned to his wife. For a long moment neither spoke. Elgiva looked anxiously at the blood staining his chain-mail shirt. Seeing the direction of her gaze, he smiled.

'The blood isn't mine.' He paused, surveying her in his turn. 'You look pale, Elgiva. Are you well?'

'Quite well, my lord.'

He saw the tears start in her eyes. 'Never tell me you feared for my safe return, wife.'

'Oh, Wulfrum, I was afraid. All day I have been imagining terrible things.'

'No cause, my love.' He bent and kissed the top of her head. 'It would take more than a few thieves to take on a Viking war band and win.'

'You found all the raiders, then?'

'Yes. We found them.'

'Did you… Are they…'

'Yes. All are dead and the carrion birds feed on their remains.'

Elgiva shut her eyes, fighting faintness, but she had to know. 'And Aylwin?'

'He was not among them. There was nothing to connect him to the band we found.' He paused, regarding her with shrewd eyes. 'After we let the hounds learn the scent, we cast a wide circle round the hall until they found it. Drem's trail led us straight to them. An arrow could not have flown more true to its mark.'

The relief on learning that Aylwin had not been there was huge, but she strove to control it. 'How many were there?'

'About twenty, all told. We took them by surprise. Even so, they fought well; I lost one man and four are injured. They will require your help, I think.'

'Of course.'

'Meanwhile I would wash off the sweat and stink of battle.'

'There is a kettle of hot water prepared for you. Or, if you would prefer it, the meal is ready.'

'I will wash first and eat after.'

He put an arm through hers and they went in together. At the foot of the stairs Elgiva left him and went to help Osgifu, who was laying out her things in readiness to treat the injured. Fortunately the wounds were simple enough—sword slashes and bruises for the most part, though one or two of the wounds were deep and needed sewing. They dealt first with the most serious cases, the others waiting their turn with good humour, refreshing themselves with a horn or two of ale in the meantime. Others had sluiced themselves at the trough or the well, divesting themselves of their weapons before washing off the grime of battle. When the last of the wounds had been dressed and more ale drunk, it was time for the food.

Wulfrum rejoined them, changed now into a light tunic and leggings, all signs of battle gone. He took Elgiva's hand and led her to the table. The atmosphere was lively enough, for the raiders had been overcome and would not trouble Ravenswood again, and almost all of Wulfrum's men had returned without serious hurt. It was cause enough for celebration. She thought it did not need much cause for the Danes to celebrate.

'What is it, Elgiva?'

She turned to see Wulfrum's gaze on her. 'I am thinking about that stable-boy.'

'He shall be buried properly with the priest to perform the ceremony, if you wish.'

'I do wish it, Wulfrum.' She hesitated a moment. 'His mother... I visited her today.'

'She shall receive the wergild. Since Drem cannot pay it and has no kin, I shall do so. Nothing can bring the boy back, but the money may help his surviving family.'

'Thank you.'

'It was a bad business, Elgiva, but the traitor has paid; when the fate of the raiders is known, it will deter others from thinking Ravenswood a soft target.'

'I think no one could ever make such a mistake again.'

Wulfrum was silent a moment, then bent on her the familiar

easy smile that made her heart leap. 'And now we shall feast, and celebrate.'

'Because your enemies are slain?'

'No, because I can sit here and look at you.'

Elgiva blushed as a glow of happiness spread over her. Perhaps he would be pleased to hear the news she had to impart after all. However, this was not the time or the place. She glanced round surreptitiously and decided it must be later, when they retired to the privacy of their chamber.

For all he shared the sentiments of his men that evening, Wulfrum was not disposed to linger late and he and Elgiva left them carousing to seek their own room. Wulfrum undressed and climbed into bed. She heard him yawn and saw him settle back comfortably, watching her undress. She cast a swift look down her body, but the slight roundness of her belly showed no sign yet of the life within. Her breasts were bigger, but her waist was as slim as it had ever been. Slowly she unfastened her hair and began to comb it, teasing out the small tangles. It took her some time, but eventually she was finished. However, when she turned towards the bed it was to see that Wulfrum was watching no longer. He lay on his back, eyes closed, his breathing regular and deep.

'Wulfrum?' There was no sign that he heard her. 'My lord?'

For a moment she regarded him with strong indignation before her sense of humour got the better of her. Trust him to fall asleep now. Evidently her news would have to keep till morning. She crossed the room and blew out the lamp before climbing into bed beside him.

She had slept well, snuggled close to the familiar warmth of the man beside her. The sun was fingering its way through the shutters when she woke, aware suddenly that a gentle hand was stroking her back. Elgiva smiled and stretched, arching her body towards the hand, for its touch was sensual and exciting.

Wulfrum drew her backwards and pressed her down into the bed as he leaned across her, holding her there with an arm either side of her shoulders. He kissed her then, long and passionately. Elgiva felt the familiar glow inside her, then her arms were about his neck and she was kissing him back, moulding her body to his, feeling his arms tighten around her. With the familiar feeling of astonishment and delight, Wulfrum looked into her face and saw her smile. Then she was kissing him anew. He felt her mouth open to his tongue, felt her yield, felt her body press closer. Elgiva shivered as she felt his lips move on to her neck and throat, his hands brushing the peaks of her breasts, raising sensations that both thrilled and appalled. Yesterday he had shed Saxon blood, but he was no longer the enemy in her eye, for she loved him. To lose him would be like losing part of herself. Warming to his touch, she gave herself now unreservedly.

Wulfrum felt her shudder, sensed the desire rising through her blood. He entered her then, gently, but Elgiva wanted him now every bit as much as he wanted her. He felt her legs close around him, her hands on his shoulders, pulling him deeper inside her. Still Wulfrum held back, fanning the flame to a blaze that would eventually consume them both, reaching a peak of ecstasy so intense he thought he might die. Looking into the depths of the amber eyes beneath him, he knew it had been the same for her.

The intensity of the feeling took him by surprise. Nothing that had gone before compared to this. In his experience hitherto, women had been a means to an end. They satisfied a need and afterwards were quickly forgotten, but this Saxon wench had woven a spell that had him in its grip. He found himself thinking about her all the time, seeing her face, wanting her. He knew then that he would hold her till death.

Watching him closely, Elgiva saw his expression change as he looked at her and felt in her heart the stirrings of disquiet.

However, he reached out a hand and touched her cheek, brushing away stray wisps of her hair, his fingers tracing a line along her nose, across her lips and chin and thence down her throat to her breasts. Then he kissed her lightly. She could not fathom his mood, but it showed yet another side of him she had not seen before. It was new and disturbing and hinted at so much more to learn. Suddenly she wanted to know, all of it, for there could be no more pretence. She loved him, had loved him since that day in the forest glade when he had risked his life to save hers. If Ida had not prevented it on the night of the fire, she would have gone back into the flames, for the thought of a future without Wulfrum was inconceivable. He was as necessary to her as sunlight and breathing.

Seeing her preoccupation, he smiled down at her. 'I never know what you are thinking.'

'I was thinking about you.'

'Good. What about me?'

'I shall not tell you, for it would only make you conceited.'

He laughed. 'I think it would not be easy for a man to be conceited too long in your company. You have a way of cutting us down to size. One look at those amber eyes and we crumble.'

'You credit me with powers I do not possess, my lord.'

'Not so. I must speak as I find.'

'And what else do you find?'

'A Saxon wench beautiful enough to make a man forget all others.'

Her expression was suddenly serious. 'Have you forgotten them, Wulfrum?'

'You are the only woman in my life now and always will be.' He leaned over and kissed her very gently. 'You are my love, Elgiva.'

For a moment she stared at him in stunned surprise and then felt only intense happiness. His arms closed round her again and she laid her head against his shoulder, revelling in his nearness and warmth. They lay thus in silence for some time until Wulfrum smiled and glanced down at her.

'What?'

'I was thinking that I want our son to be like his father,' she replied.

For a moment he did not stir, but then the import of the words struck him.

'Elgiva?' He shifted his weight until he could see her face. 'You don't mean…'

'Yes, I do.'

'Oh, my love. When?'

'In the spring.'

'That's wonderful!' Then another thought occurred to him and his face registered concern. 'But you should have told me sooner. I might have hurt you.'

'You haven't hurt me, Wulfrum.'

'Are you sure?'

'Quite sure.'

He threw back the coverlet and looked at her, running a gentle hand down her body until he came to her belly. As yet he could detect no sign of the life within, but a fierce joy burned in his heart to think she carried his child, their child.

'It will be a while yet before you see any sign.'

'No matter. It is enough to know.'

He kissed her then, but too decorously for Elgiva's liking. Taking his face in her hands, she returned the kiss with passion.

'Have a care, wench,' he warned. 'You play with fire.'

'No, my lord, 'tis you who play with fire.'

'Were it not for your tender condition, I might have put that to the test.'

'Let's put it to the test anyway.'

He was about to reply in kind, but found he couldn't, for her tongue was subtly probing his ear, sending a delightful shiver through his entire body and temporarily robbing him of the power of speech. Then her lips moved to his chest, then lower and lower still. Wulfrum drew in a sharp breath.

'Elgiva?'

She made no reply, but glanced up, once, just long enough for him to glimpse a new and unfathomable expression in those amber eyes. Then she resumed. Wulfrum gasped as he began to experience other infinitely more exciting sensations.

'Elgiva?'

'Mmm?'

'Elgiva, I'm not sure we should…'

The sentence ended in a groan as the first shock wave of pleasure hit him.

Chapter Fifteen

The harvest that year was a good one and every man and woman who could lift a scythe or thresh grain was pressed into service. The granaries and barns filled rapidly. Wulfrum spent his days out in the fields or in the storehouses and saw it all with satisfaction. According to Gurth's careful accounting, there would be more than enough food for the winter. Besides, soon the apples and root crops would be laid down. Cheeses ripened in the storerooms. Game was abundant. With care, no one need go hungry. In the late autumn the cattle would be killed and the meat salted for, despite a good hay crop, the fodder would only be sufficient to see the breeding stock through the cold weather to come.

In the forest the first leaves began to turn and the time drew near for Wulfrum to leave Ravenswood for York. He was loath to go but knew he had no choice. Lord Halfdan required his presence and would take it much amiss if he were denied. Accordingly he chose a dozen men to accompany him on the ride, leaving a large contingent behind to look after matters in his absence.

'It is only for a week,' he told Elgiva. 'If there are any problems, you can consult Ida. However, I do not think there is cause for concern.'

She forced a wan smile. No cause for concern? With Aylwin and the dispossessed Saxons seeking his life? They would never have a better chance to act than now. Elgiva was racked by guilt, for the knowledge of her own complicity weighed heavily on her conscience. With it her fear grew apace. Time and again she had tried to summon the courage to tell Wulfrum, but the thought of his reaction stayed her. Already she could see the hurt in his eyes. How could she bear it? How could she bear to see his love turn to suspicion and hatred? Yet how could she remain silent while he was threatened by a danger that was, in part, of her making? She had to speak now, to warn him before he left. Yet how to find the words? How to tell him what she had done?

Unaware of her inner turmoil, Wulfrum finished dressing for the journey and then came to stand before her, drawing her to him.

'Take care of yourself, Elgiva, and look after my son.'

'Depend upon it.'

'I do.' He paused. 'Do you wish me to bring you anything from York?'

'Only yourself.'

They kissed, Elgiva holding him close. Then he buckled on his sword and slid his knife into his belt. The second, slimmer blade was slid into his sleeve.

'It never hurts to be prepared,' he said humorously, seeing the direction of her gaze.

Elgiva took a deep breath, her heart hammering. 'Wulfrum, I must tell you…'

He smiled. 'Tell me what?' Then he saw her unwonted pallor and the anguish in her eyes and his smile faded. 'My love, what is it?'

'Be vigilant on this journey. I think Aylwin is planning your death.'

For a moment or two there fell a silence so intense that

Elgiva could hear the blood pounding in her ears. Throughout, Wulfrum's gaze never left her face.

'How can you know this?'

'Because he…he as good as told me.'

His eyes narrowed. 'How could he have told you?'

'After he escaped from Ravenswood he took refuge in the forest but…' she licked dry lips '…he returned.'

'Returned? When?'

'After his escape. He came here twice, the last time when Halfdan's messengers were here.' She paused. 'He told me that he planned to unite the rebels and take back what was his.'

'Did he so?' Wulfrum was very still, his expression stony as the implications sank in. 'And all these months you have aided and abetted him behind my back.'

'No. I urged him to flee and prevent more bloodshed. I had to try. I had no choice.'

His brow darkened further. 'No choice?'

'I owed him that much, Wulfrum.'

'What did you owe me, your husband?'

'I wanted him to abandon all hope of revenge. I never meant to hurt you.'

'No? Yet knowing he wanted revenge, you still waited all this time to tell me.'

The tears started in her eyes. 'Forgive me. I did not tell you earlier because I could not.'

'Could not or would not?'

'Both, since you will have it.' She swallowed hard. 'There is more.'

Wulfrum remained silent, waiting.

'I warned him of the plan to seek out and destroy the rebel group. That was why the men you caught were not his.' Elgiva closed her eyes a moment, waiting for the explosion of rage. It never came, but the calm was infinitely more chilling.

'Why have you chosen to tell me these things now, Elgiva?'

'Because I don't want any more secrets between us.'

'And I am supposed to trust you from now on?' The coldness in his voice was worse than anything she had anticipated.

'I can only beg your forgiveness and ask you to try to understand.'

'I understand, all right. You love him.'

Elgiva's head jerked up. 'No. I have never loved him. I love you.'

He laughed then, a harsh sound as cold as the expression in his eyes. 'You speak of love! I trusted you and you betrayed me.' Taking a step closer, he seized her shoulders in an iron grip. 'How else have you betrayed me with him, Elgiva? What else have you not said?'

She stared at him in shocked disbelief. 'Nothing. You cannot think so.'

'Why not? How was it—a passionate woodland tryst with the fugitive lover? It would be a fitting revenge, would it not?'

Elgiva, at first appalled, felt her own anger rising at the injustice of this.

'That's not true.'

'Isn't it?'

'No, and you know it.'

Wulfrum's eyes glinted. 'I know only that I was a fool blinded by your beauty. A fool who believed you when you spoke to him of love.'

'The words were true, Wulfrum, I swear it.'

'If they were true, you could not have protected him. You could not have betrayed me.' He paused, his face white with anger. 'By rights I should kill you now, you faithless whore!'

'Do it, then!' Before he was aware of her intent, Elgiva had seized the dagger from his belt and held the point to her breast. 'If you really believe I have cuckolded you with Aylwin, then it is your right. All you have to do is lean upon the point.'

Her gaze met his, unflinching. In it she read anger and pain, a hurt far deeper than she could ever have guessed. His hand closed round hers and the blade touched her throat. He would kill her, then. Suddenly she didn't care. She had lost his love and the look in his eyes was more than she could bear. Unheeded, the tears flowed down her face as the silence stretched between them. Then, without warning, his grip changed, sliding to her wrist before tightening with brutal force. Elgiva gasped. The dagger fell to the floor. He flung away from her and retrieved it.

Elgiva lifted a hand towards him. 'Forgive me.'

Wulfrum made no answer. Casting her a last contemptuous look, he grabbed his cloak and strode to the door. He threw it open with a crash and marched out. In sick horror she heard his receding footsteps and then only silence. Gradually, from outside, the sound of horses' hooves impinged on her consciousness and she ran to the window. Through her tears she watched in hopeless longing as Wulfrum mounted and moved to the head of the column. Elgiva willed him to look her way as her hands clenched over the wooden sill. Almost as if he sensed the intensity of her gaze, he glanced up once and their eyes met. Her heart skipped a beat. Let him smile, she thought, let him give some sign that he forgave her. His expression was forbidding as he held her gaze for a moment, and then he looked away, touching his heels to his horse's sides. Elgiva felt her throat tighten. She watched until he was out of sight and then she wept.

Wulfrum rode fast and his men, seeing that flinty expression, left him alone with his thoughts. In truth he had only one: Elgiva. Their conversation had shaken him to the core and the knowledge of her deception turned like a knife in his guts. For a moment back there he had wanted to kill her. He had no idea what had stayed his hand or how he had governed his ire. It burned still and for some considerable time after until eventually fresh air and exercise tempered it a little. Even so, the memory of the scene was bitter. Her look as he left haunted him. His last words to her had been spoken in anger, anger born of pain the like of which he had known only twice before. He wanted to believe it was all baseless, but he had the evidence of her words. Why had she kept silent so long, only to tell him now? Who could understand the workings of a woman's mind? What traps did subtle beauty lay for the unwary? How could he have been so naïve as to fall for melting looks and tender words of love? And yet she had seemed so sincere. Had she meant *any* of the things she had said? Once he had thought so, but now…

For a long while he rode thus, his brain a ferment of tormented thought. Then, as his rage cooled and he grew calmer, his mind began to clear. In truth, he had been much to blame for allowing himself to grow too fond, to let beauty blind him. He had known from past experience that loving made a man vulnerable and in so doing he had broken a cardinal rule. His marriage to Elgiva had been made for political reasons by and large, something he had forgotten. Only a fool would think a woman could take an enemy to her bed and love him.

In the days that followed Wulfrum's departure, Elgiva kept herself busy about her household tasks, but she found herself thinking about him all the time, wondering what he was doing just at that moment. She had no doubt that he would receive a warm welcome from Halfdan and his mind would be filled with men's business, leaving no time to think of anything else. While their days would be filled with council matters, the nights would be left to carousing. There would be women too, young and attractive and only too pleased to be the object of attention to a handsome earl. And he was handsome, dangerously so. Elgiva bit her lip. So many times she had relived that last quarrel and seen again the hurt in his eyes. He had trusted her and she had betrayed that trust. It mattered not that her motives had been of the best. It was betrayal. Now he had gone with his heart full of anger. Would he seek his pleasure elsewhere? Out of sight, out of mind, the proverb said. For her part it had proven manifestly untrue. Now each day passed much the same as the one before it with nothing to break the monotony. Sometimes she would hear a footfall behind her and turn round, half-expecting to see him there, but it would be Ida or one of the other men. Most acutely she was aware of how big their bedchamber seemed without him. She could not but recall the scenes that had taken place there. Now all that remained was echoing emptiness.

'You miss him, don't you?' said Osgifu. They were sitting outside the women's bower, spinning. Elgiva's attention never left the yarn, but a telltale blush crept into her face.

'Yes.'

'Well, 'tis only a week he'll be gone and the time will pass swiftly enough. Then you might regret that it was not longer.'

Elgiva burst into tears. In a moment Osgifu was beside her.

'What is it, child? What's wrong?'

Between sobs she managed to glean an account of the events that had preceded Wulfrum's departure.

'I wanted things to be right between us, for there to be no more lies. Now I've made it a hundred times worse. I have never seen him so angry. He looked at me at though he hated me.'

'His pride has been hurt and he's jealous. It's a dangerous combination, but he'll get over it.'

'But he had no cause to be jealous. I love him, not Aylwin. I thought he knew that.' Elgiva sobbed harder. 'Now he has gone away. What if he never comes back?'

'He'll come back. He's too bloody minded not to.'

Sick with fear and doubt, Elgiva endured the long days of Wulfrum's absence with a heavy heart. She performed all that was required of her with regard to the household affairs, but could take no pleasure in any of it. When her duties were done she sought solace out of doors, for the chamber she had shared with Wulfrum was too full of bitter memories to allow of its being a sanctuary now. The quiet burying ground offered most tranquillity and the prospect of being undisturbed. Having told Osgifu of her intent, it was thither she bent her steps.

However, she found that she was not alone. A man was already standing there in the shade beneath one of the trees on the far side. With a start, she recognised Brekka. For a moment she regarded him with resentment. What did he want? Why couldn't he leave her alone? Did he not know the peril he put them both in if he were seen? She looked around, but there was no sign of anyone else. Taking a deep breath, she calmed herself, ashamed of such uncharitable thoughts. Then she made her way towards him.

'My lady.' He bowed. 'I have been waiting here in the hope of meeting you.'

'What is it, Brekka?'

'I bring word from Lord Aylwin.'

'From Aylwin?'

'Aye, my lady. He bade me say that he has reconsidered your advice. He said you would understand what that meant.'

Elgiva's heartbeat grew a little faster. Aylwin was going to leave after all. Wulfrum was safe. Her spirits lifted as they had not for days. Before she could question further, Brekka continued.

'He asks that he be permitted to see you once more.' He paused. 'If you refuse, he will understand.'

Elgiva looked over her shoulder. There were still no Danes in evidence. Of late, the watch on her person had been relaxed, proof of Wulfrum's growing regard and trust. Guilt stabbed. Then she thought of Aylwin, of his long and lonely exile in the forest, hunted by his enemies, never knowing if each day would be his last. He had been her betrothed. He had fought for Ravenswood, for her, and been wounded in their cause. Surely it was not too much to ask that he should be allowed to say farewell.

'Where is he, Brekka?'

'At the clearing where stand the old woodsmen's huts.'

She nodded. It wasn't far. She could be there and back before she was missed.

'Very well. I will come.'

As she had anticipated, it was but a short distance they had to walk and twenty minutes later they reached the clearing. As they did so, Elgiva could see the men and horses gathered there, perhaps twenty in all. Evidently they were on the point of departure. Elgiva stopped, looking around, relieved to think that sense had prevailed.

'He is within, my lady,' said Brekka, nodding towards the foremost of the huts.

Even as he spoke three men emerged and she saw the familiar figure of Aylwin. The others she did not know. They had been deep in conversation, but, seeing her and Brekka, they stopped. For a moment there was silence, then Aylwin hurried forwards to greet her. He took her hand and pressed it to his lips.

'I knew you would come.'

Elgiva glanced at the mounted men. 'I think my arrival is opportune.'

'Indeed, there is little time. We must be gone.'

'Where do you go, my lord?'

'To Wessex, to throw in our lot with Alfred and the free Saxons.'

Elgiva felt a surge of relief. He would be safe and now so would Wulfrum. 'I am glad. After our last conversation, I did not think you would leave.'

'Indeed, there is nothing now to stay for.' He smiled. 'Your arrival makes everything complete.'

'I don't understand.'

'You are coming with me, Elgiva.'

Apprehension prickled as she glanced around her. All the men on the far side of the clearing had mounted and were waiting. The two who had been with Aylwin before were now just a few yards off, flanking her. Brekka stood a pace behind.

'I apologise for the ruse used to get you here,' Aylwin went on, 'but it seemed the safest way, all things considered. Besides, according to my intelligence, Earl Wulfrum is in York and not due back for days. By the time you are missed this evening, we shall be long gone.'

'I cannot go with you, you know that.'

'Did you think I would leave you behind, Elgiva?'

'You must. Wulfrum will follow. He'll kill every last one of you.'

'No. The noble earl will not follow.'

Apprehension turned to real alarm now. 'What do you mean?'

'Our Saxon allies have undertaken to prevent it. An ambush has been laid for him on his return from York.'

'What?' She was aghast. 'You can't mean it.'

'I was never more serious in my life,' he returned. 'And with your husband dead, I take back what is mine.'

Elgiva shook her head, feeling sick with dread. 'I cannot let you do this, Aylwin.'

'You cannot prevent it,' he replied. He nodded to his companions. 'Take the lady to her horse.'

'No!' Elgiva confronted him in anger. 'I will not go with you.'

'You're coming with me, Elgiva, whether you will or not.'

Aylwin nodded to his companions. In a moment she was held and her wrists bound securely in front of her. Then, despite all protest, she was carried to the horses and lifted into the saddle. Someone took hold of her reins and the whole cavalcade set off.

Frightened and shocked, Elgiva concentrated first and foremost of staying in the saddle, for the pace was swift. With every stride all she could think of was Wulfrum riding into an ambush. And if by some miracle he survived it and returned to Ravenswood to find her gone, he would think her complicit, that she had gone with the Saxon rebels of her own free will. It would be for him the ultimate proof of her guilt. Heartsick, Elgiva saw in her mind her husband's face and the hurt in his eyes, the silent accusation and the killing rage. He would never forgive her.

Chapter Sixteen

The council had been a notable success so far as Wulfrum was concerned; it had finished ahead of time and Halfdan had acceded to his request for reinforcements to crush the Saxon rebels in Ravenswood, offering twenty-five men. It wasn't as many as Wulfrum had initially hoped, but Halfdan had his own problems with local uprisings and could spare no more. Even so Wulfrum knew it would give him the advantage. With skilful deployment he could achieve his goal. The only negative was that Sweyn was among their number, but Wulfrum would not let personal matters cloud his judgement here. For all his faults Sweyn was a good man in a fight, being both experienced and ruthless. Once the rebels had been crushed, then there would be time to consider past grievances, but not until.

Having turned their backs on York, they made good progress with Wulfrum calling a halt at noon to rest the horses and let the men refresh themselves. Then they rode on. The mood was buoyant; as they reached the edge of the forest, they knew they were within ten miles of Ravenswood. Wulfrum breathed in the subtle evocative scent of the woodland and smiled, for he associated it with home and with Elgiva.

Elgiva! Despite all his efforts not to, he had missed her more than he had ever dreamed possible. Yet their last words had been filled with anger. How much he had regretted it since. While his days had been busy enough, the nights had afforded leisure to think; it had occurred to him then that she could have kept silent and he would never have known of those meetings with Aylwin. She could have kept silent and let him ride un-suspecting into possible danger. That way she would have been free of him, free to join her Saxon lover—if, indeed, he was her lover. She had told him long ago that she respected Aylwin, but had denied ever loving him. A marriage of convenience, she said. It had sounded like the truth, but was it? If not, why had she chosen to speak at last, to risk his wrath and worse? He had been so close to killing her. The truth hurt, as she had known it must but, as she said, what was the alternative—to build a future on secrets and lies? He knew it was not a future he wanted. She had begged for his forgiveness and he had spurned her, too angry to realise that she was asking for a completely different relationship with him. A prize of war, forced to marry the victor, she had had no say in the events that would shape the future. Her world had been turned upside down. Torn be-tween two loyalties and put, by him, into an impossible po-sition, Elgiva had only done what she thought she must. Should he blame her after?

Wulfrum sighed, calling himself all kinds of fool. He had regarded his marriage with complacency and then, at the first real test, he had allowed rage and jealousy to impair his judgement. While he was familiar with the former, he had never known jealousy before. No woman had ever mattered enough—until now. He had told Elgiva he loved her, but he had not taken her part or even given her the benefit of the doubt. Could she ever forgive him? Could they make a life together after this? He prayed it might be so for the idea of any future without her was meaningless. When he had taken her to wife he had little thought he would come to love her to the point where only she could do him hurt.

Wulfrum was given little more leisure to indulge these thoughts for the road narrowed among the trees, forcing the party to slow the pace. The forest around them grew denser and the landscape more rugged. Presently the way passed between two steep banks, compelling the horsemen to ride in single file. Firedrake slowed and snorted. Wulfrum frowned, snapping out of his reverie instantly, reining in while he scanned the path ahead and the trees around.

'What is it?' Ironfist drew rein behind him.

'I don't know. Listen.'

At his signal the men ceased all conversation. Apart from the occasional stamp of a hoof and the creak of saddle leather, there was silence.

'I don't hear anything,' said Ironfist at length.

'Exactly.'

The giant's eyes narrowed as he looked at the defile ahead. 'A good place for an ambush.'

'Aye, but our way lies through it all the same. Have the men keep their wits about them.'

Wulfrum heard the word passed back, heard swords loosened in scabbards. Then he urged his mount forwards. The stallion's ears flicked back and forth and he snorted anew, placing his hooves with neat precision on the path, his steps more reluctant. It confirmed Wulfrum's suspicions, but still he could detect no sign of life. The skin prickled on the back of his neck. He guessed if there was an attack, it would be when his men were deep in the defile. Closing his legs around the horse's sides, he urged him on. From out of nowhere an arrow hissed past and a man behind him cried out. More arrows followed, thudding into shields amid warning shouts from his escort. He saw a man fall, pierced through the throat. Then came whoops and yells and suddenly the trees were alive with armed men hurtling down the steep banks towards their quarry. He had an impression of woodsmen's garb and rough bearded faces, but the attackers were not without courage or skill and laid on right willingly.

Wulfrum drew Dragon Tooth from the scabbard. Moments later the sword became a deadly arc of light, cutting down the first two attackers before they knew what had hit them. Then the third was upon him. Wulfrum parried the blow aimed at his head, but the blade slid off his own and left a bloody gash along his arm. Gritting his teeth, he fought grimly on, knowing there could be no quarter. He dispatched his opponent with a wicked slash to the throat. The man dropped where he stood, his life blood gushing from the wound. As he fell, another took his place. The outlaws were violent men, who preyed on travellers and would sell their lives dear. Wulfrum knew it was unusual for them to attack such a large group, but desperate fugitives would do whatever they had to. His men gave a good account of themselves, but, hampered by the cramped conditions and milling horses and the bodies of the slain, their situation was precarious indeed. From the corner of his eye he saw Ironfist swing his war axe and take off a man's head before slicing for another. He heard the foe scream and fall as the blade severed an arm. Wulfrum fought on, a cold anger burning in his gut and a fierce determination not to meet his end here on this forest trail. He accounted for three more of the attackers before their leader, seeing the tide of battle turn against them, shouted the command to retreat. The outlaws fought their way free and began to back off before turning and scrambling up the banking towards the safety of the trees. There was no order about their going, just a desire to escape. Soon the last of them vanished among the trees.

'Shall we give chase?' demanded Ironfist.

'No. Let them go.'

Wulfrum leaned on his sword, breathing hard. He turned and

looked around at the scene of carnage. Apart from several casualties among Halfdan's men, of the dozen who had originally set out with Wulfrum, only five were standing alongside himself and Ironfist. Three more were injured, the rest were slain. His anger grew.

Then Ironfist noticed the blood dripping over Wulfrum's wrist and hand. 'You are hurt.'

'A gash, no more.'

'Best let me bind it.'

Wulfrum stood while the big Viking took a cloth from his saddlebag and bound it expertly round the wound. Having done so, he looked around, surveying the bodies of the attackers.

'Saxons,' he said, 'but why would they risk attacking such a large group?'

Wulfrum shook his head. 'I don't know.' Then he remembered Elgiva's words: *Be vigilant on this journey.* Had she known more about this than she confessed to? Was she implicated? As he beheld the bodies of the slain, all his former doubts resurfaced and with them his anger.

'It seems the rebels grow bolder,' said Sweyn, looking around him with casual interest. 'You will have quite a task on your hands, Wulfrum.' He wiped the blood from his blade before sheathing it again. 'But at least we can look forward to a good fight.'

'No doubt.' Wulfrum turned to Ironfist. 'Have the men mount up. I want to get back to Ravenswood.'

As Ironfist moved away, Sweyn grinned and his expression grew mocking.

'Missing the lovely Elgiva, Wulfrum?' Then, seeing the other's expression, he feigned contrition. 'Not that I blame you, of course.'

'You take a deal too much interest in my wife. I should resent it if the time were right.'

'Let it be a quarrel between us then, if you live.'

'I'll live.' Wulfrum's voice was cold. Retrieving his horse's reins, he remounted, pausing a moment to survey his rival. 'Whether you will do the same is another matter.'

'Trust me…' Sweyn bared his teeth in a vulpine smile '…I'll have Elgiva yet.'

'Over my dead body.'

'Why, so I hope.'

Refusing to be drawn further, Wulfrum touched Firedrake with his spur and the big horse cantered away.

Elgiva breathed a sigh of relief when eventually the pace slowed for a while to let the horses breathe. Already they were many miles from Ravenswood and all hope of aid. Her heart sank to think that she would likely not be missed for some time. Even then, no one would have any idea where she was. Aylwin had laid his plans well, baiting the trap with expert care. All sympathy for him had evaporated now. In following his own desires he had completely ignored hers, thinking to take by force what she could not give. She shivered. If once he and his men reached Wessex, she would be beyond all help. Even Wulfrum could not pursue her there. Wulfrum! If only he might be spared the ambush laid for him. If only he might live. Nothing else mattered.

She was so preoccupied that she failed to notice Aylwin beside her until he spoke.

'Why so sad, Elgiva?'

She turned to look at him, hoping to find some trace of remorse in his expression, some small expression of pity that she might exploit.

'You know why,' she replied.

'Have I not rescued you from the Viking's clutches? Do I not deserve your thanks?'

'Wulfrum is my husband.'

'Not for much longer.'

'He is not so easy to kill.'

'It matters not.'

'What do you mean?'

'A marriage made under duress to a pirate raider is no marriage at all. When we reach Wessex I shall appeal to Alfred. He will be exceeding grateful for the reinforcements I bring and he is withal a most pious king. I anticipate no difficulty in having your marriage to the Viking set aside.'

'And say you do. What then?'

'Then you will wed me as is my legal right as your betrothed.'

'I will not marry you, Aylwin.'

'You will have no choice, my dear, when it is a matter of royal decree.'

Elgiva closed her eyes for a moment, striving against the knowledge that he was right. If the king ordered it, she would be forced to submit to his will. Aylwin could then marry her within the hour. In desperation she made a last appeal to his better self.

'What point, my lord? Would you have an unwilling wife?'

'I would rather have you willing, Elgiva, but if not I'll have you anyway.' His gaze hardened. 'Forget your Viking earl. You belong to me now.'

She drew in a deep breath, fighting down panic. He would not see her weep and plead. In any event it would be useless for all appeals would be denied. She would not give him that satisfaction. Aylwin saw her chin come up and nodded.

'That's better. Do you know, I've always admired your spirit and your good sense. You fight well, Elgiva, but you know when you cannot win.'

'It isn't over yet.' Even as she said it, she was not at all sure it was true. He was strong and resourceful and now he had her in his power.

'Shall we have a wager on that?'

'I would wager only that you will die on the point of Wulfrum's sword.'

'Then you will lose. I am your lord now.'

* * *

Wulfrum urged the stallion to a gallop, a mile-eating pace that closed the distance between him and Ravenswood. As he rode, a lot of things became clearer in his mind and he knew for a certainty that he was supposed to have died in that ambush along with his men. It had been no random incident. The attackers had been Saxons and only one man hereabouts had the necessary knowledge to order it—the knowledge *and* the motive. Aylwin. He had not bowed to the Viking yoke, nor had he forgiven the loss of his lands or his betrothed. He would take Elgiva if he could. His wife's face floated before him in memory and with it fresh suspicion. On her own admission Elgiva had been in contact with the rebel leader. It begged the question—had she aided him in this business? Had the two of them planned his death? The thought was chilling but he could no longer suppress it. It must be faced. She had deceived him before and might have again. However it might be, he would learn the truth soon enough.

He and his companions covered the last miles in a short time and at length saw Ravenswood in the distance. On seeing their approach, the look-outs gave word and serfs came running from all directions. Wulfrum rode through the gateway at the head of his escort and drew rein outside the hall. Ida and several of his men came out to greet the new arrivals. Of Elgiva there was no sign. The feeling of foreboding grew stronger with every passing moment. Dismounting, he flung the reins at a serf and strode into the hall.

'Elgiva!'

His voice echoed round the building, but brought forth no reply. Setting his jaw, he took the stairs three at a time, coming at length to their bedchamber. One glance revealed it to be empty. Wulfrum searched the other room, then went down again to the hall. In the women's bower he accosted Osgifu, but she professed no knowledge of Elgiva's whereabouts. His anger rising fast, Wulfrum grabbed hold of her and shook her.

'Don't lie to me, old woman. Where is she?'

Osgifu went pale. 'My lord, I'm not sure.'

'What do you mean, you're not sure?'

'She said she was going to the burial ground earlier this afternoon. I have not seen her since.'

'The burial ground?' Mentally Wulfrum saw the place. It was but a stone's throw from the forest. He glared at Osgifu. 'What more?'

'My lord, I know nothing more, I swear it.'

'If you're lying to me, this day will be your last.' He let go his hold. 'Now fetch me one of your mistress's gowns and be quick about it.'

Much disturbed, Osgifu scuttled off. Wulfrum turned to Ida.

'Tell the kennel men to bring out the hounds and have someone saddle me a fresh horse.'

'At once, my lord.'

As Ida disappeared, Wulfrum drew in a deep breath, trying to collect his thoughts, to force his anger down. Ironfist's voice broke the silence.

'You think she's run away.'

'I don't know yet, but I will find out.'

'It's possible she was taken by force.'

Wulfrum's fists clenched. 'It's possible.'

'Perhaps you should give her the benefit of the doubt.' The giant met the basilisk glare unflinching. 'I do not think her treacherous.'

Had it been anyone else, there would have been bloodshed. Wulfrum closed his eyes a moment, striving for control.

'Tell the men to mount up.'

Ironfist walked away and for a moment Wulfrum followed his retreating figure. Then Osgifu returned with one of Elgiva's gowns, hastily snatched from the coffer. It was the gold one she had worn for their wedding. The memory cut like a blade. Without a word, he seized the dress and strode out to the courtyard in the other's wake. If they were to find his wife, the hounds needed a scent.

From the burying ground the trail was clear enough and they followed at a cracking pace, coming soon to the clearing and the now abandoned woodsmen's huts. At that point the scent grew confused and there was no clear trace of Elgiva anywhere in evidence. Then, after some casting about, Ida called out, 'A lot of horses were here, my lord. Fifteen or twenty, I'd say.'

For a moment Wulfrum was silent, his face deathly pale. Elgiva had chosen her moment well. By now she and her Saxon lord were well away. His fingers clenched round the fabric of the gown and he bit back the cry of rage and despair welling in his heart. Forcing his voice to a level tone, he turned to Ida.

'We follow.'

The trail wasn't hard to find and the fugitives had made no effort to conceal their passage. Moreover, they were travelling fast. Wulfrum pushed his horse hard, determined to narrow the gap. The party was riding west by south. That could only mean one thing. He gritted his teeth. If they once reached Wessex, Elgiva was as good as lost to him. Her face intruded on to his thoughts once more. How cleverly she had deceived him, using her beauty and her wit to lull him into believing she really cared, only to betray him so thoroughly in the end. Except it wasn't the end, he vowed. Not yet. Not till he caught the fugitives. He would slay Aylwin with his own hand and then... Heartsick, he suppressed a groan for grief had taken on all the sharpness of physical pain, one deeper than any sword thrust. Yet even now, with all the evidence in front of him, he could not bring himself to believe her capable of such treachery. Could Ironfist be right? Could she have been taken by force? How much he wanted to believe that, to believe her innocent for he knew now that the alternative meant her death.

* * *

The Saxon fugitives rode until the sun was low on the horizon before stopping to rest the horses a while. Aylwin dismounted, lifting Elgiva from the saddle. Bone weary and sick with dread, she made no resistance now, knowing she was lost. Wulfrum was in York, would be for another day at least. He would return to find her gone. Worse, he would think she had gone of her own volition. His pain and his anger would be great indeed, but not as great as the desolation in her heart.

Throughout the long ride she had sought the means to escape, but none presented itself. She was kept in the midst of the riders and her horse was led. Besides, with her wrists bound, it would have been impossible to try anything. Even now they had halted, Aylwin was still taking no chances. On his orders, Elgiva was led aside and tied fast to a tree. The bonds were not cruelly tight, but they were secure enough when tested to preclude all hope of escape. Aylwin surveyed the proceedings with a rueful eye.

'I'm sorry, Elgiva. I do this only for your own good.'

'No,' she replied. 'You do it for yours.'

'I wish it had not been necessary.'

After he left her to speak with his men, Elgiva struggled again against the rope, but it yielded not a whit. Hot tears scalded her eyelids and she slumped into despair. She knew now that she would never see Wulfrum again.

Chapter Seventeen

Seeing a telltale cloud of dust some way ahead, Wulfrum experienced a sense of savage satisfaction. When the cloud dissipated, the feeling intensified. The Saxons had stopped. They weren't expecting pursuit yet. Wulfrum reined in and raised a hand to halt his men. Then he gave the order to dismount.

'We'll move up as close as we can. Then we go in fast and we go in for the kill. Take no prisoners save one.' He paused, drawing Dragon Tooth from the scabbard. 'My wife is to be brought to me—alive and unhurt.'

In obedience to the command, the Viking host moved forwards with stealthy stride until they were within fifty yards of their prey. Then they surged forwards in open attack upon the startled Saxons. Wulfrum launched himself forward, Dragon Tooth in his fist, hacking and slashing at the hapless foe. Several fell before they had time to draw a blade. All around him he could hear shouts and curses and cries of pain in the ensuing mêlée. Though surprised and outnumbered, the remaining Saxons fought with desperate courage, determined to sell their lives dear. Surrounded on all sides by the battling throng, Wulfrum had but one immediate aim: to find Aylwin and carve the Saxon cur into small slivers. Seeking his man, he cut down three others on the way, his sword running with their blood. A moment later exultation became impotent rage to see his quarry locked in mortal combat some twenty yards off and half-a-dozen other fighting pairs between. Wulfrum's wrath became incandescent when he saw who it was in that fatal conflict.

'Sweyn!'

If the man heard that furious yell, he gave no sign. Even from his present position Wulfrum could see the fearsome light of battle joy on the berserker's face, the savage delight with which he pressed the attack, forcing his opponent back step by step. Even in the midst of frustration and rage, Wulfrum had to admire the sheer gall of this man who dared steal his earl's rightful opponent thus. Gritting his teeth, he carved his way forwards, determined not to lose this enemy to Sweyn. However, even as he slew one man, it seemed another rose up to take his place. Cursing, he fought on.

Elgiva struggled in desperation against the rope that held her, her terrified gaze following the conflict even as her heart leapt. They were Wulfrum's men. He had come for her. Frantic, she looked for him among the heaving throng, but failed to spot him. She swallowed hard. Dear God, let him win. Let him come through unhurt. Her anxious eyes found Aylwin locked in deadly confrontation with a tall fair-haired Viking warrior. Anxiety became fear as she recognised his opponent: Sweyn! Appalled and fascinated together, she watched as the swords clashed, sparks leaping from their edges with each savage blow. Aylwin fought well, but he was twice the other man's age and no match now for Sweyn in speed or stamina. Already his tunic was stained with the blood from half-a-dozen gashes. Beads of sweat stood on his forehead as he was pushed relentlessly back. Unable to see where he put his feet, he caught his heel on a rock and stumbled. He was off balance for no more than a second, but it was enough. Elgiva stifled a cry as Sweyn's blade thrust deep into his opponent's unprotected body. For a moment or two Aylwin hung impaled on its point before the blade was withdrawn and he buckled at the knees, sinking to the earth. The Viking paused a moment to look down at the fallen foe. Then he laughed, exultant. A moment later he was challenged anew by three furious Saxons who, having seen their leader fall, were bound on revenge. Sweyn fought like a madman, killing one and wounding another before the odds swung against him and the third sword thrust past his guard and through the ribs behind. Checked mid-stroke, he staggered and fell, dead before he hit the earth, the sword still in his hand and the ghost of a smile on his face. Elgiva shuddered and turned her head away.

Wulfrum saw Sweyn go down, but by the time he reached the place, the fighting had moved on and the berserker was dead. Darting fierce glances about him, he found Aylwin hard by. The man lived yet, but his lifeblood was flowing fast from the great wound in his side. For a moment Wulfrum was still, glaring down upon his fallen enemy, knowing he had been cheated of the revenge he had so ardently desired. With dimming eyes, the Saxon registered his presence and spoke through ragged, gasping breaths.

'So it ends, Viking.'

'Aye, it ends.' Wulfrum bent and he seized the front of the other's tunic. 'Where is my wife? What have you done with her?'

'She is unharmed.' The Saxon coughed and blood trickled from his mouth. Every word was an effort now. 'I forced her to come…thought to take her from you but…it is you she loves.' He paused, fighting for breath. 'You must…take care of her.'

There followed a slow exhalation of breath and nothing more. Meeting the Saxon's sightless gaze, Wulfrum bestowed on him a grim smile, his fist tightening round the hilt of the sword.

'I shall take care of her. I swear it to you.'

He straightened, his gaze scanning the scene for the one he sought. Above the din of fight he heard a woman scream and then he located her at last, not twenty yards away from him. Anger blazed anew, but he controlled it now, letting it fuel his strength as he cut a path towards her, relentless, determined, his opponents falling like corn beneath the scythe.

Ashen faced, Elgiva watched him come and, as he reached her, joy was drowned by flooding terror for he was suddenly a stranger to her—not Wulfrum any longer, but a warrior bent on vengeance and fearsome in battle rage, all dark with gore, his sword reeking and bloody, a sword whose naked point was levelled at her. For a moment he stood quite still, the icy gaze taking in every detail of the scene before it met and locked with hers. Then ice became fire. Like one transfixed, she watched him lift the sword, saw it descend. With a solid thunk the blade bit wood, severing the rope that bound her to the tree. Elgiva slumped, barely aware of the powerful arm that caught her just before she fell into a dead faint.

She had no idea how long she lay there. Perhaps no more than a few moments, though the sounds of fighting seemed muted and distant now. Someone was with her, cradling her in strong arms and a man was speaking her name.

'Elgiva, my love. My heart. Speak to me, for the love of Odin.'

Her eyelids fluttered open. What had he just called her? 'Wulfrum?'

'Oh, my love. Thank all the gods. I thought I'd lost you.'

'You came for me.' Unable to help herself, Elgiva began to cry, her body shaken by great racking sobs even as she clung to him.

'Shh. Hush now. It's all right. It's all right.' He rocked her in his arms until she quieted a little. As he did so, he noticed her bruised wrists and his gaze hardened. 'He has hurt you.'

She shook her head. 'Rope burns, nothing more.'

'No one shall ever hurt you again. I swear it.'

'Oh, Wulfrum, he told me you were dead.' Elgiva began to

sob again. 'He said he was going to keep me…that he would take me by force to Wessex. I thought I'd never see you again…'

Wulfrum, feeling her body shake in terror and revulsion, dropped a soothing kiss on the top of her head. 'Surely you did not think I would let another man steal you away?'

As the sobs racked her, his jaw tightened as he bore witness to her anguish. Then, as if that were not bad enough, another thought occurred to him.

'Elgiva, the child. It is not harmed?'

'No. I think it is well.'

Even as he knew relief, it chilled Wulfrum to think of what he might have lost that day. In a moment of blinding clarity he understood then that love was stronger than hate. Love made a man vulnerable, but it empowered him too. It gave his life reason and purpose. Aylwin might have died this day, but his battle had been lost long ago. Anger evaporated on the heel of that realisation and he knew the Saxon had done only what any man worthy of the name would have done—he had fought for his land and his kin and for the woman he loved. The knowledge that his love had not been returned must have been bitter indeed and yet he had acknowledged it at the end. That too required a kind of courage. His heart full, Wulfrum bent his gaze on his wife's face.

'How I have missed you, lady.'

Looked up at him through her tears, Elgiva drew in a shuddering breath. 'Wulfrum, can you ever forgive me for—'

His finger on her lips silenced her. 'There is nothing to forgive. The fault is mine for allowing jealousy to blind me.'

'You had cause enough to be angry but I never meant to betray you. I swear it.'

'I know. As I know there could be no future for me without you. You are my life, Elgiva. My life and my love.'

Then he crushed her to him in a close embrace that needed no further explanation.

Epilogue

Spring—868 A.D.

Wulfrum stood by the casement, watching the first grey light of dawn stealing over the quiet earth. He let his gaze travel over the roofs of the outbuildings to the fields beyond, surveying it all with a sense of pride. The first time he had set eyes on Ravenswood he little thought it would be his or that it would become the place he called home. Yet in the last year he had come to know it intimately, every field and farm, every hedge and ditch. It was good land, rich and fertile, his land. And yet it was more than that—the land had a power of its own that spoke to the heart of a man. Sometimes he thought it had claimed him rather than the other way round. And always there was the great forest, at this season decked again in the fresh green of new growth, new life. He felt its peace steal into his soul as he breathed its scent on the cool air. With a faint smile he glanced at the sword lying on the chest nearby. Let others follow the winds of war or launch the sea dragons to go a-viking. They would do it without him.

A faint sound from the bed drew his attention from the view outside and he smiled to see Elgiva stir. Beside her, in the crib, their son lay sleeping: Wulfgar. Born in the teeth of a March gale, he was a fine lusty babe with a thatch of dark hair and eyes as blue as harebells. Watching them both, Wulfrum felt his heart swell with love and pride, touched alike by their vulnerability and the beauty of the simple scene. Once fate had snatched away everything he held dear, but it had been restored in full measure.

Elgiva stirred and, feeling the empty space beside her, opened her eyes. 'Wulfrum?' Seeing him across the room, she smiled and reached out a hand.

'Come back to bed. It's early yet.'

Nothing loath, he left his station by the window and returned to her, sliding beneath the pelts and drawing her close, sharing her warmth. Feeling his arms about her, Elgiva smiled and closed her eyes and slept again. For a while he lay there, listening to her soft breathing, and then he too began to drowse and sank at last into peaceful slumber. Outside, the first rays of sunlight touched the canopy of the sheltering forest.

* * * * *

Harlequin is 60 years old, and Harlequin Blaze
is celebrating!
After all, a lot can happen in 60 years,
or 60 minutes...or 60 seconds!
Find out what's going down in Blaze's
heart-stopping new mini-series,
FROM 0 TO 60!
Getting from "Hello" to "How was it?" can happen fast....

Here's a sneak peek of the first book,
A LONG, HARD RIDE
by Alison Kent
Available March 2009

"IS THAT FOR ME?" Trey asked.

Cardin Worth cocked her head to the side and considered how much better the day already seemed. "Good morning to you too."

When she didn't hold out the second cup of coffee for him to take, he came closer. She sipped from her heavy white mug, hiding her grin and her giddy rush of nerves behind it.

But when he stopped in front of her, she made the mistake of lowering her gaze from his face to the exposed strip of his chest. It was either give him his cup of coffee or bury her nose against him and breathe in. She remembered so clearly how he smelled. How he tasted.

She gave him his coffee.

After taking a quick gulp, he smiled and said, "Good morning, Cardin. I hope the floor wasn't too hard for you."

The hardness of the floor hadn't been the problem. She shook her head. "Are you kidding? I slept like a baby, swaddled in my sleeping bag."

"In my sleeping bag, you mean."

If he wanted to get technical, yeah. "Thanks for the loaner. It made sleeping on the floor almost bearable." As had the warmth of his spooned body, she thought, then quickly changed the subject. "I saw you have a loaf of bread and some eggs. Would you like me to cook breakfast?"

He lowered his coffee mug slowly, his gaze as warm as the

sun on her shoulders, as the ceramic heating her hands. "I didn't bring you out here to wait on me."

"You didn't bring me out here at all. I volunteered to come."

"To help me get ready for the race. Not to serve me."

"It's just breakfast, Trey. And coffee." Even if last night it had been more. Even if the way he was looking at her made her want to climb back into that sleeping bag. "I work much better when my stomach's not growling. I thought it might be the same for you."

"It is, but I'll cook. You made the coffee."

"That's because I can't work at all without caffeine."

"If I'd known that, I would've put on a pot as soon I got up."

"What time *did* you get up?" Judging by the sun's position, she swore it couldn't be any later than seven now. And, yeah, they'd agreed to start working at six.

"Maybe four?" he guessed, giving her a lazy smile.

"But it was almost two…" She let the sentence dangle, finishing the thought privately. She was quite sure he knew exactly what time they'd finally fallen asleep after he'd made love to her.

The question facing her now was where did this relationship—if you could even call it *that*—go from here?

* * * * *

Cardin and Trey are about to find out that
great sex is only the beginning….
Don't miss the fireworks!
Get ready for
A LONG, HARD RIDE
by Alison Kent
Available March 2009,
wherever Blaze books are sold.

CELEBRATE
60 YEARS
OF PURE READING PLEASURE
WITH HARLEQUIN®!

**We'll be spotlighting a different series
every month throughout 2009
to celebrate our 60th anniversary.**

Look for Harlequin® Blaze™ in March!

0-60

*After all, a lot can happen in 60 years,
or 60 minutes...or 60 seconds!*

Find out what's going down in Blaze's
heart-stopping new miniseries *0-60!*
Getting from "Hello" to "How was it?"
can happen fast....

Look for the brand-new 0-60 miniseries in March 2009!

www.eHarlequin.com   HBRIDE09

New York Times **Bestselling Author**

JENNIFER BLAKE

Kerr Wallace has spent years studying swordplay, preparing to challenge his sworn enemy. The scoundrel Rouillard, now living in Mexico as a profiteer, has decided to take a wife and the lady requires an escort. Kerr seizes his chance—he will deliver the bride…and dispatch the groom.

If only it were so easy. Headstrong Sonia Bonneval will do anything to escape this doomed marriage, and the voyage with Kerr becomes an exhilarating battle of wills. But a very real declaration of war forces them into closer quarters—and greater temptation—in a fight for survival. Before the end, both must choose between duty and freedom, vengeance and passion.

GALLANT MATCH

"Beguiling, sexy heroes…
Well done, Ms. Blake!"

—*The Romance Reader's
Connection* on
the Masters at Arms series

*Available the first week
of February 2009 wherever
paperbacks are sold!*

MJB2619

HARLEQUIN® *Romance*®

This February the Harlequin® Romance series
will feature six Diamond Brides stories featuring
diamond proposals and gorgeous grooms.

Share your dream wedding proposal and you could WIN!

The most romantic entry will win a diamond
necklace and will inspire a proposal in one of
our upcoming Diamond Grooms books in 2010.

In 100 words or less, tell us the most romantic
way that you dream of being proposed to.

For more information, and to enter
the Diamond Brides Proposal contest, please visit
www.DiamondBridesProposal.com

Or mail your entry to us at:
IN THE U.S.: 3010 Walden Ave., P.O. Box 9069, Buffalo, NY 14269-9069
IN CANADA: 225 Duncan Mill Road, Don Mills, ON M3B 3K9

You're invited to join our Tell Harlequin Reader Panel!

By joining our new reader panel you will:

- Receive Harlequin® books—they are FREE and yours to keep with no obligation to purchase anything!
- Participate in fun online surveys
- Exchange opinions and ideas with women just like you
- Have a say in our new book ideas and help us publish the best in women's fiction

In addition, you will have a chance to win great prizes and receive special gifts!
See Web site for details. Some conditions apply.
Space is limited.

To join, visit us at

www.TellHarlequin.com.

REQUEST YOUR FREE BOOKS!

Harlequin® Historical
Historical Romantic Adventure!
™

2 FREE NOVELS PLUS 2 FREE GIFTS!

YES! Please send me 2 FREE Harlequin® Historical novels and my 2 FREE gifts (gifts are worth about $10). After receiving them, if I don't wish to receive any more books, I can return the shipping statement marked "cancel". If I don't cancel, I will receive 6 brand-new novels every month and be billed just $4.94 per book in the U.S. or $5.49 per book in Canada, plus 25¢ shipping and handling per book and applicable taxes, if any*. That's a savings of 20% off the cover price! I understand that accepting the 2 free books and gifts places me under no obligation to buy anything. I can always return a shipment and cancel at any time. Even if I never buy another book, the two free books and gifts are mine to keep forever.

246 HDN ERUM   349 HDN ERUA

Name	(PLEASE PRINT)	
Address		Apt. #
City	State/Prov.	Zip/Postal Code

Signature (if under 18, a parent or guardian must sign)

Mail to the Harlequin Reader Service:
IN U.S.A.: P.O. Box 1867, Buffalo, NY 14240-1867
IN CANADA: P.O. Box 609, Fort Erie, Ontario L2A 5X3

Not valid to current subscribers of Harlequin Historical books.

Want to try two free books from another line?
Call 1-800-873-8635 or visit www.morefreebooks.com.

* Terms and prices subject to change without notice. N.Y. residents add applicable sales tax. Canadian residents will be charged applicable provincial taxes and GST. Offer not valid in Quebec. This offer is limited to one order per household. All orders subject to approval. Credit or debit balances in a customer's account(s) may be offset by any other outstanding balance owed by or to the customer. Please allow 4 to 6 weeks for delivery. Offer available while quantities last.

Your Privacy: Harlequin Books is committed to protecting your privacy. Our Privacy Policy is available online at www.eHarlequin.com or upon request from the Reader Service. From time to time we make our lists of customers available to reputable third parties who may have a product or service of interest to you. If you would prefer we not share your name and address, please check here. ☐

HH08R

COMING NEXT MONTH FROM

HARLEQUIN®
HISTORICAL

Available February 24, 2009

- **KIDNAPPED: HIS INNOCENT MISTRESS**
  by **Nicola Cornick**
  (Regency)
  Plain-Jane orphan Catriona Balfour has never met anyone as
  infuriating—or handsome—as devilish rake Neil Sinclair! Soon
  her facade at resisting his flirtation crumbles and, stranded on a
  deserted island together, the inevitable happens....

- **HIS CAVALRY LADY**
  by **Joanna Maitland**
  (Regency)
  The Aikenhead Honours
  Alex instantly fell for Dominic Aikenhead, Duke of Calder,
  certain he would never notice her. To him, she was brave hussar
  Captain Alexei Alexandrov! Alex longed to be with her English
  Duke as the passionate woman she truly was. But what if
  Dominic ever found out the truth...?
  First in *The Aikenhead Honours* trilogy—Three gentlemen spies;
  bound by duty, undone by women!

- **QUESTIONS OF HONOR**
  by **Kate Welsh**
  (Western)
  When Abby Kane Sullivan became pregnant with Josh Wheaton's
  son, circumstances intervened, tearing apart her dreams for their
  blissful future together.... But years later, though Abby and Josh
  have changed, the spark of attraction between them still burns—
  and there is *nobody* in town that will stop Josh claiming his woman.

- **CONQUERING KNIGHT, CAPTIVE LADY**
  by **Anne O'Brien**
  (Medieval)
  There is no way Lady Rosamund de Longspey escaped an
  arranged marriage only to be conquered by a rogue. But Lord
  Gervase Fitz Osbern will fight for what rightfully belongs to him.
  A warrior to his fingertips, he'll claim his castle—and just maybe
  a bride!

HHCNMBPA0209